Outside the Wire

By

William Leet

Paperback ISBN: 978-1-61929-559-9
Hardback ISBN: 978-1-61929-561-2

Flashpoint Publications First Edition: June, 2024

Printed in the United States of America.

Cover design by TreeHouse Studio

www.flashpointpublications.com

Part One

Yet there be certain times in a young man's life, when, through great sorrow or sin, all the boy in him is burnt and seared away so that he passes at one step to the more sorrowful state of manhood.
— Rudyard Kipling

Chapter One

Larry MacDuff was running. The past nine weeks of his life had been one long run. He ran from the barracks to the rifle range, to the mess hall, to classrooms, back to the rifle range and back to his barracks. This time it was another five miles over the hills and gullies of the two hundred thousand acres inside the boundaries of Fort Polk—one of the easier runs, no rifle or backpack, just boots and fatigues. The August sun had turned him nut brown and the workouts had added ten pounds of muscle. Even Buddy might not recognize the sweat-drenched, bristle-headed young man jogging up the steep hill in Vernon Parish, Louisiana.

Julian Bentley, a skinny kid from Mandeville, ran beside him, his ragged breathing belying his tenacity. Despite his one-hundred-sixty pounds, he could run rough ass over anyone in the field. Only the fools misjudged Juli as a gangly lightweight with jug ears.

Once again, Juli was talking about Prudy, his girl back home, about his difficulty trying to convince her to let the hair grow under her arms since he liked a little fluff up under there.

"What it is, MacDuff, I like the natural smell of a woman. And it smells even better after she's been at work, when I can't wait to get my face right up in it."

"Like a well-seasoned pigeon," Larry panted.

"You got it."

Their run ended at the bottom of the next hill where thirty-four other conscripts in two rows pumped out push-ups under the scowl of a never-satisfied drill sergeant. Because they were not moving fast enough, he screamed at Larry and Juli.

"You pussies move your asses!"

Larry fell into the push-ups with the background grumble of Juli still talking about Prudy, punctuated by his curses at the sergeant.

"Dog-faced motherfucker thinks he's a hardass," Juli

half-whispered, snapping off his usual machine-like push-ups.

Larry remembered the scorching afternoon their first week in when Juli said something the sergeant didn't like. The marching had stopped while they all did push-ups for twenty minutes, the sergeant's boots in Juli's face. At the word to get on his feet, Juli had bounced up, shouting out.

"Yes, sir, Sergeant, sir! Thank you, sir!"

"You're a tough little pissant, ain't you?" the sergeant growled, squinting up close in Juli's face.

He had known the right answer to that, bellowing a response. "No, sir, Sergeant, sir!"

It was five weeks into basic training. One night before lights out, Larry sat on his bunk writing a letter. The page was full, with none of it expressing the thoughts he held tightly inside. Words he wanted to say were forced into hiding, and spilling his feelings was impossible in circumstances that denied privacy.

Every hour of the day, the Army drilled him to suppress the person he was for the sake of creating a disciplined and violent team member. The effort of endless training and exhaustion held Larry in the present. The sweat, stress and forced endurance numbed him completely.

Under that weight, he worried about how the Army treated the private letters of recruits. Did they open and read them looking for something to expose him? Were his bland words, his yearnings, being interpreted by a censor's eye? He was certain his letters lacked any open expression of the heart. They were all dull accounts of training, the plentiful chow, and the lonely sleep he fell into each night between nine and four-thirty. He only hinted at anything personal, in a bland mention of great fun or good times in the Woody. There was only that and the flavorless reports of life in boot camp.

But in a private corner of his mind, other words swirled and pushed against the fear of saying what he longed to write in his letters—*Even here I can feel the beat of your heart against my hand, I close my eyes and breathe again the scent of your skin. I hear your voice in my head.*

Right before lights out, Juli and Larry sat smoking, as

Juli told a story about his crazy Uncle Lemmy coming to his school one day and roughing up the basketball coach for benching his nephew. "He plain scared the bejesus outta that man. The game after that, I played four quarters."

"You win?"

"Hell, no. Playing Eden Isle. Nobody could beat those boys. Uncle Lemmy was in jail and didn't see it."

The talk dwindled, the two sleepy recruits sitting quietly on Larry's bunk, Juli at the foot wearing only a pair of snow-white skivvies. Larry studied his friend, his hair little more than a crop of red bristles, his big ears, bright blue eyes, and clear skin.

"That a scar on your shoulder?" Larry ventured.

Juli's mouth twisted as he turned his head and looked down at the scar, touching it. "Dad shoved me once, fell against a window, glass broke. Cut my shoulder." He looked up half-smiling at Larry. "Simple."

"Sorry."

"Naw, he was drunk. Said some shit, can't remember now what it was."

Larry reached out quickly and put a finger against the scar.

With a quick glance over his shoulder, Juli shrugged off the hand. "Dad works crew on a boat out of Lake Pontchartrain. Shrimp and crabs. Some nights he comes home drunk, spoiling for a fight. But he's all right. Won't lay a hand on mom." He drew squiggles on the bedsheet with a finger. Looking up, he said, "I love the old guy, despite everything."

"Yeah?"

Eyes down, half-smile at the corner of his mouth, Juli nodded a couple of times. As each bank of lights clicked off, he slowly moved to the next bunk. "Good night, buddy."

Larry lay there in the dark. Juli's *good night, buddy*, sent his thoughts back to Buddy Hebert, back to when they were ten years old and in the fourth grade at Audubon Elementary. Their teacher was a woman quick to apply the flat of her ruler to the exposed legs of rowdy students. Larry's turn came on several occasions, but the boy who always got the worst of it was Buddy Hebert. Bad behavior was rarely the cause of Buddy's punishment, it was more a case of sleepiness or boredom.

He sat across the aisle one desk ahead of Larry, and on those days when Mrs. Starling rushed to snatch up Buddy's pants leg and give him a couple of whacks with her ruler, it secretly thrilled Larry every time. Not that he enjoyed Buddy's punishment, which Larry knew from experience was a small sting here and gone. He couldn't say what it was that made him look forward to Buddy's smacks from the teacher's ruler, but that brief glimpse of Larry's exposed calf held Larry's eyes. Each time he saw it, he wanted to put his hand against the reddened skin.

Buddy wasn't tall or stocky, but neither was he short and slight like the runt of their class, Petey McMorris. He always wore blue jeans and a freshly ironed shirt, and his light brown hair was always trimmed neatly above his ears. Larry spent part of each day staring at the back of his head, fascinated by how his hair grew into a point down his neck, fascinated, too, by Buddy's gray eyes the color of cigarette smoke. One day on the playground standing in line, Billy Martin shoved Larry from behind and he tumbled into Buddy, both of them falling to the ground with Larry on top, his face pressed into Buddy's hair. It smelled like baby powder and he remembered not wanting to get up from where they were sprawled on the ground.

It wasn't long before Buddy's was the first face his eyes sought walking into the classroom every morning. Beyond his understanding, he didn't know the why of always looking for Buddy. But that year in Mrs. Starling's class was the first time Larry ever felt an attraction toward another person.

****

At six-thirty the next morning, divided into groups of thirty-six, the recruits started a physical combat proficiency test. They crawled under barbed wire, ran an obstacle course, climbed up ropes and over ten-foot walls, and ended with a one-mile run, a piddling distance for most recruits by then. As battle buddies, Juli and Larry were paired up for the man-carry. The first half would be Larry carrying Juli over his shoulder for a hundred and fifty meters before they switched roles for the return trip. A red-faced drill sergeant stood at the halfway mark shouting for them to hurry the fuck up.

"How you wanna do this?" Juli asked, at the starting line.

"You over my left shoulder, head in back, legs in front."

He got his shoulder under Juli's belt and hoisted him up, left arm wrapped around his legs. The whistle blew and he lurched forward for the finish line, Juli bouncing on his shoulder. Halfway down the course, he heard Juli yell out.

"Awwgh, you're crushing my nuts, fucker!"

He laughed, chugging for the finish line. "Suck it up, Bentley."

When Larry put him down, Juli grabbed his balls and gave Larry a few hard pats on the cheek. After a sixty-second rest, Juli hoisted Larry over his bony shoulder and launched himself onto the rocky and uneven course, hauling Larry over the distance double time. Juli might pretend otherwise, but he was always dead serious about getting the best time.

"What was your time last time we did this?" he asked Larry, as they were loosening up for the one-mile run.

"A little over seven minutes."

"Let's go for six this time."

"You must be drunk."

"Just hang with me, MacDuff."

The last fifty yards, Larry was a stumbling fool but he finished a few steps behind Juli, in a little over six minutes, screaming in his head to give up smoking.

They double-timed it in formation to the chow hall for lunch. Larry was always hungry and loaded a tray with three pork chops, a heap of rice, corn on the cob, and chocolate cream pie. Juli finished his hamburger and said he'd be outside. When Larry came out, Juli offered him one of his mangled Luckies and, remembering his vow to quit, Larry lit up anyway and took a deep satisfying drag.

While most recruits were in the showers or waiting to get in, Larry managed to grab an empty washing machine.

"Give me your stuff to wash, I'll put it in with mine," he told Juli.

Stretched out on his bunk staring at the ceiling, Juli jumped up and pulled an armload of T-shirts, socks, and underwear out of a laundry bag, dropping the pile on Larry's bed. "Thanks, dude. I'll do it next time."

Waiting for the wash to finish, Larry polished his boots and put his locker in order. When the drying was done, he separated everything and dumped Juli's on his bunk, putting away his own folded stacks. By then the showers were empty except for Juli and as he was walking past, Larry backhanded his butt gently, turning on the shower next to him and reveling in the hot water pounding down on his head and shoulders. Juli looked at him, the light reflecting off his wet chest and stomach. Larry turned his back, scrubbing the bar of soap against his neck and face.

Juli was still looking at him.

"What?" Larry said, his voice muffled by the pounding water.

Again, there was that familiar half-smile. Larry's eyes moved down Juli's chest and stomach, pausing before dropping lower. Tickled by the spray of water from the shower, Juli was all pink and boyish, and after he passed a soapy hand over himself it lengthened, lifting. Larry knew he should look away but couldn't. Again, Juli touched himself with a soapy hand, becoming more aroused. Turning with a look to the shower entrance, he worked his soapy hand up and down. That someone could walk into the showers at any second pounded in Larry's head, the sudden excitement intense. He, too, glanced at the shower entrance and, returning his eyes to Juli, masturbated himself. Even in the noise of the water, he could hear Juli's ragged breathing. Legs trembling, Juli exploded with a heavy grunt. Three feet to his left, it happened to Larry a second later, with Juli's eyes on him. The half-smile appeared again, Juli clapped Larry on the shoulder and retrieved his towel.

****

Larry stretched out on his bunk with an old, battered paperback he'd fished from the trash, something called *After Dark, My Sweet,* about a con man and beautiful woman with plans for murder. He had read the same three sentences half a dozen times, while acutely aware of Juli folding his laundry into neat stacks, eyes down with a slight frown. Larry saw that he was red-faced, maybe embarrassed about that thing in the shower. Juli snuck a glance at Larry and their eyes met. Juli quickly looked down at his laundry.

The folding done, Juli stacked everything in his locker with the precision of gold bars in a bank vault and in the next second pulled out a deck of cards. The frown gone, he smiled over at Larry. "Jump over here, buddy. Let's play some poker."

Larry sat on Juli's bunk while Juli shuffled the cards, his eyes hopscotching past Juli's hands to his skivvies that flared open, showing a patch of ginger hair.

"Pair of fours," Larry said.

"Two pair, jacks and sevens," Juli said, fanning out his cards. "I win."

"What do you win?"

"I'll think of something."

Larry dealt the next hand and lost again, Juli laying down three sixes. "You're in the hole, my man." He shuffled the cards and this time dealt Larry a potential winner, one card shy of a straight. "How many cards?"

"One."

"Uh-oh, Larry's got something." He took one card as well, studying his hand carefully. "I bet a hundred."

"Okay, I raise you a hundred. Wha'dya got?" Larry said.

"Twos."

"A pair of twos? Straight," he said, laying down his cards.

"Guess I owe you, buddy."

"Guess you do."

A few hands later, Juli lit one of his Luckies, tossing the pack and his lighter to Larry. He blew a plume of smoke out the side of his mouth and Larry looked at the flush of red across his chest, just under his neck. Juli tilted his head back, scratching his throat. "Got a letter from Prudy today."

"Yeah? Everything cool?"

"I asked her to talk some dirty, sexy shit to me in her next letter. She said it didn't feel right."

"You're fucking weird, Bentley." Larry laughed.

"Weird's good. Ain't it? Kinky's okay, too, right?"

"I guess."

"You got a girl?"

Larry shook his head, lightly touching the end of his cigarette to a callus on his thumb.

"The fuck you doing?" Juli said, gripping Larry's hand and rubbing the callus with his own thumb.

Larry felt a rush of heat, and slipped his hand from Juli's.

"I...I don't feel that way about girls."

"Wha'dya mean?"

"I don't think about girls much."

"Never been with one?"

He shook his head.

"So, no opportunity or...does that mean something else?"

"Yeah. Something else."

"Better keep quiet about that. Guys around here..." Juli's voice trailed off as the barracks went dark. Across from Larry, Juli was a shadowy silhouette, his hand reaching in the dark to grip Larry's for a quick second.

Chapter Two

RWH,

Hey, Buddy. Sitting on my bunk before lights out and thought I'd write to say everything is fine here. I'm tired but that's always the case these days. Today was like most others. Another one of those physical tests, carrying a battle buddy over my shoulder and running an obstacle course. That kind of stuff. I've gained ten pounds since I got here but none of it is fat. My buddy here isn't crazy about the food, but I don't mind it. We get a lot to eat. Lunch today I ate pork chops, rice, and corn on the cob.

I wonder if you ever see Earl. If you do, tell him I said hello. Earl always treated me good, was always there for me. I will be finishing up here in a week and heading off to another place for specialized training. They call it Advanced Individual Training. I'll be doing that for thirteen weeks. After that, who knows? Maybe Vietnam. Whatever, I'll get a chance to come home for a couple of days.

I miss those times we spent driving around in the old Woody. I miss the afternoons poking around Belle Helene. Tell your daddy I miss his garden and think about it often. Your momma, too. I think about how good she always was to me. You already know I value our friendship and hope we'll always be friends. Sometimes I remember the days when we were little kids in Mrs. Starling's class at Audubon Elementary and the fun we had the first time you came to play at my house. Do you ever ask Earl to let you take the Woody out for a drive? It's a beautiful old car and you love it as much as I do. If you want to keep it at your house to use every day, that's okay.

How is your job building the big house out by LSU? Pretty cool building a house designed by a famous architect. You can show it to me when I come home. I would like that. Like I said before, I'm good and I hope you, your momma and your daddy are well, too. Don't let your

daddy work too hard. You guys are in my thoughts.
  LPM

Chapter Three

Sundays were difficult. After the long weeks since Larry had been drafted, Buddy was still momentarily surprised to wake up without the heat and weight of a familiar arm thrown across his chest. The other pillow smelled now of Cheer detergent, and not the grassy scent of Larry he so craved. On those Sunday mornings, staring at Larry's photo he kept in a drawer, he jerked off to memories of Larry, the heat of his body against Buddy's. But that solitary exertion always left him heartsore. He wanted more than anything to walk out to the backyard and find that familiar figure crouched among the strawberry plants, looking over at him with a smile, lighting up the day.

In September, Buddy had gotten his first job on a house, designed by A. Hays Town, that was being built on the lakefront. After working a year at the lumber mill with Uncle Dub, his uncle recommended him to the contractor for the lakefront job. Buddy's mother wasn't sure it was the right thing to do, choosing another job over enrollment at LSU, but Buddy told her college could wait. He was in his element, overflowing with the contentment of work he had come to love, and now he was aided by the cherished Vaughn & Bushnell hammer his uncle had given him on his last day at the mill.

His workday started at seven-thirty when most of the crew gathered loosely around the site foreman, Mr. Hargrove, drinking coffee and shooting the breeze. The days were filled with hard work, the clatter of hammers pounding nails, and each evening Buddy went home tired but at ease, fulfilled by the entity he was helping build. His cousin Tilly was Mr. Town's secretary and she had made copies of the house blueprints, now scattered around Buddy's room, pinned to the walls, and draped over his desk. Evenings after supper, he spent the hours before sleep studying the blueprints, learning the secrets of the wood and stone puzzle that occupied his days. Stacked around his room were books on wood frame construction, house plans, and cabinetmaking. In his time away from the house site, Buddy roamed the stacks of lumber at the mill, memorizing the name and grain of wood samples scavenged from the mill's castoffs, labeling and storing each in a large box he kept in his sister Connie's old room.

Not long after Larry left for basic training, Buddy had traded his old '53 Chevy Club Coupe and two hundred dollars for a beat-up Ford pickup that Larry's old boss, Earl, had found for him. Full of dents and scraped fenders, it ran well and was more practical for Buddy and the new job. He liked the old truck with its torn bench seat and husky rumble and was especially pleased at leaving work in the late afternoon and being able to toss things in the back.

Grabbing his tool belt and thermos out of the truck bed, he slapped the dust off his jeans and shirt and went in the front door. "I'm home!" he called, going straight to the den, dropping the tool belt and thermos on the floor and falling onto the couch.

"Good day on the build, son?" his father asked.

"Pretty good. Started framing the second floor this afternoon."

Buddy's mother came from the kitchen. "You want a glass of iced tea?"

"No, ma'am. I'm good," he said, running a hand through his long hair, sending a scatter of sawdust onto the couch and floor.

"Go get a shower," his mother said, picking up the thermos and retreating to the kitchen.

"Any mail for me today?"

"Waiting on your bed, like usual."

Bolting up from the couch, his face lightened. Picking up the tool belt, he headed to his room, his heart beating a little faster.

From the doorway into the den, Buddy's mother saw her son's reaction to the mention of a letter from Larry. Commenting on the sudden change in demeanor, she said to her husband, "Hearing there was a letter from Larry, the look on Buddy's face was like sunlight breaking free of a cloud."

"I have to say there's sunlight and clouds in my own feelings regarding those boys," Mr. Hebert answered. "I don't need to tell you that I think the world of Larry and look at him as a second son. Like you, I've grown to accept the obvious in their closeness, but I worry about them."

"Lord knows they care for one another, care deeply. All we can do is hope they learn how to deal with the risks they face in a society intolerant of such relationships," his wife said.

Buddy's mother was slicing tomatoes when he came into the kitchen from his shower. "What's for supper?" he asked, standing at her shoulder. He noticed she had two cigarettes going, one in an ashtray on the counter by the cutting board and another over by the stove. "Momma, I'm putting out the cigarette by the stove. It's finished."

"Pot roast tonight. Supper will be on the table in a bit. If you're hungry, there are some leftover shrimp in the ice-box."

He found the shrimp and carried the bowl out to the back porch where he found his father cleaning the cleats on their golf shoes. The crickets were cranking up their twilight chorus of chirrups. Sitting on the top step, he raised his face to the sky, his head full of everything that wasn't in the letter from Larry. He tried to fill in the blanks, the spaces between the lines of a letter that could have been from a neighbor on vacation.

"Everything okay with Larry, son?"

"I guess. He didn't say much in this last letter. Said he misses you and momma."

"Reckon he's got other things on his mind now."

After a silence, barely audible, Buddy spoke. "I'll be honest with you, Daddy. I don't know how to be me without Larry."

Sitting down on the step beside his son, Mr. Hebert replied quietly. "I wish I knew what to tell you Buddy, how to handle this. It probably doesn't help much to say it, but he'll be home one day. Have faith in that."

About to sit down at the supper table, Buddy told his mother he didn't want iced tea, and took the milk from the refrigerator, filling his glass. "Who won the golf game today?" he asked, putting some of the pot roast on his plate.

Buddy's mother laughed at that. "We played with Dr. Stovall and his wife, tied after seventeen holes. I wish you could've seen Harold's face when my ball rolled in for a birdie on eighteen." She laughed again.

"Ten-foot putt. The bottom dropped out of his wallet," his father said.

"I didn't know y'all played for money."

"It's nothing much. What did we win today, Clyde? Five dollars?"

"That's right, but we spent it paying for the beer at The 19th Hole."

"This pot roast is good, Momma. Pass the beans and potatoes, please."

Passing the bowl, his father took a moment to stir his tea, watching his son eat. Finally laughing, his eyes still on Buddy, he spoke to his wife. "Mother, did you ever notice that Buddy closes his eyes every time he puts a forkful of food in his mouth? Just like my brother Thad."

Buddy looked up at his father confused. "Thad?"

"You remember your Aunt Emmy, Buddy. Thad was our little brother." Laying down his fork, he continued. "My mind went off to Emmy and Thad at work yesterday and that picture of us on the bank of Bayou Sara popped into my head."

His supper forgotten, he looked at Buddy. "We never told you much about Thad. He died before you were born. You look a lot like him. Sometimes I see your hands and for a moment it's like I'm looking at brother Thad." He looked at his wife. "Any of that chocolate pie left, Mother?"

"I think there's some left. You want me to make coffee?" She got up and cleared a few dishes before rinsing the coffee pot.

"Daddy, could you show me that picture of your brother?"

"I have an old shoebox full of pictures up on the closet shelf. I'll pull it down tomorrow and we'll look through them together.

****

After supper, Buddy drove over to Billups gas station to sit for a while with Earl. He dropped a paper plate with a piece of chocolate pie on the desk, sitting in the chair beside it.

Earl removed the foil covering the pie. "Your mother's?"

Buddy nodded, caressing the lighter in his hand before lighting a cigarette. He saw a guy he didn't recognize out at the gas pumps. "New guy?"

"Yeah, been here a couple of days. Might work out. Name's Donald. How's the truck running?"

"Like a top."

"Any trouble, bring it in. We'll take care of it."

He nodded, clicking the lighter open and closed. "I appreciate it, Earl."

The minutes passed in quiet companionship, Earl eating his pie, Buddy studying the passing traffic on Florida Street, an unseen presence palpable in the room.

"You hear from him?" Earl finally asked.

"Got something today. He sounded okay."

"How's your job?" Earl said, nodding and reaching for his cigarettes.

"Better than I imagined. Learning a lot."

"One of these days, you got the time, let's drive over there in Larry's Woody. Get a look at what you're doing."

"Next Saturday? That a good day for you?"

"Oh, yeah." Earl stood and stretched his back, watching as Donald came into the office.

"Donald, this is Buddy." They shook hands and Donald said if it was okay, he was going to take a cigarette break.

"Take fifteen minutes."

Donald went toward the men's room and Earl told Buddy, "Nice guy. Not bad under a hood, but nothing like our friend."

Most times that was as close as they got to talking about Larry. "I'll call Saturday, see if we're still on for the build site." He gave Earl a light punch in the arm and headed for his truck parked in the slot behind the station marked *Woody*.

Earl was keeping Larry's rebuilt 1948 Chevy Fleetmaster Woody Wagon—what he lovingly called the Woody—in the garage at his house, driving it once in a while and making sure it stayed tuned and ran just as Larry had left it. On Saturday afternoon, Buddy drove over to Earl's house and they took the Woody to Lakeshore Drive. Earl drove, taking the long way around, first heading downtown and from there south to the LSU campus, winding across to Lakeshore and Buddy's job site.

"Your family from here, Buddy?"

"We been here since I was three, moved from Mississippi. But my father was born on Bayou Sara up by St. Francisville. He went to Mississippi after he came home from the war in France."

"I'll be damned. He fought the Germans in World War II?"

"World War I," Buddy said. "My father's probably a lot older than you'd think."

"Oh, okay," Earl said, shaking his head. "Talk about a war that killed millions."

Opening up about his father's service in the war, Buddy's voice grew softer. "He went over to France, just turned eighteen. He never talks about it but got tired of me asking, I guess. He hadn't been there long, a few weeks, I think he said. He was in a little French town called Nancy. I remember that because of the name. The whole platoon was walking across a field and a sniper got my father. Bullet hit his right arm. 'Bout tore it off. They got him to a field hospital and then on a ship. They wanted to cut his arm off but daddy wasn't having that. He had a few surgeries and finally got back to Louisiana. He has to grip his fork in his fist since that time."

"I'll be damned," Earl said again.

"After the war, he ended up with a job in Dunleith, Mississippi. Met my mother there and they got married." Buddy's attention was momentarily caught by a group of ROTC cadets marching in formation across one of the campus quads. "When we moved here, Daddy started work at the lumber mill."

Looking through the forest of studs framing a bare outline of the house-to-be, and on across the lake, Earl shook his head. "Nice to be rich, huh?" He wove a path through the labyrinth of upright two-by-fours, examining the joints, running a hand along the raw boards. "What is this smaller section here?"

Buddy explained it was a kitchen pantry.

Squeezing himself between two studs and stepping down to the ground, Earl sat on a stack of two-by-fours. "What's the size of the lot?"

"Two-plus acres. The finished house will be big and will have a big yard, front and back. Three-car garage. Property line runs down to the water and at some point, the owner will build a dock. Maybe even a boathouse." He stubbed out his cigarette on the heel of his boot before shredding it.

Earl dusted his hands, walking down the slope toward the lake. "How's your daddy, Buddy?"

"He's a lot better now. It was slow at first after the heart attack but he's doing good. Still complains about no salt or fried food. Misses his pipe, but he's back full-time at the lumber mill, still has his garden. He's gotten back to playing golf once a week with my momma."

"I hear she's the real golfer in the family."

"Women's city champion last year," Buddy said with a laugh. "She plays three, four times a week."

"I'll be damned." Tossing his cigarette in the lake, he looked back at the framed outline of the big house. "How you feel about all this? Work you're doing?"

"Love it. Excited about coming to work every morning."

"This kinda thing, you'll never be out of work. People always gonna be building houses. What do your folks say?"

"My mother thinks I oughta be in school at LSU, but Daddy thinks the carpenter job is a good thing."

"Some experience, a few years on the job, you'll be earning a good wage."

On the way back to Earl's house, they stopped for a beer at the Pastime Lounge. In the late afternoon, the place was jumping, noisy with loud talk and a jukebox at high volume. They found a couple of stools at the end of the bar and Earl ordered. Buddy saw a couple of people he knew from school, one of them Bob Wexler from his chemistry class.

"Back in a second, Earl. Wanna say hello to some-one."

Bob was at a table in back with a girl Buddy didn't know. From behind, putting his hands on Bob's shoulders, he leaned down. "Hey, can you teach me the chemical elements?"

Without turning around, Bob said to the ceiling. "*Mon Dieu*! It's that handsome devil, Buddy Hebert."

Buddy couldn't help but laugh. "How're you doing, man?"

"Buddy, Buddy, what a delight. Carol, this is an old friend."

She extended a hand. "Good to meet you, Buddy."

"You, too," he said. "Bob was my chemistry savior senior year."

"That's right, praise me to the heavens. Can I get you a martini?"

He laughed again. "No, thanks. I'm with a friend at the bar."

Bob's eyes widened. "Do tell."

"Not that kind of friend, Bob. Good to see you, really. Carol." Patting Bob's shoulder once, he turned and found himself face to face with his old high school nemesis, Cullen Mosley.

"Hey, Buddy. How's it going?" Cullen said, smiling and clapping Buddy on the shoulder.

They had become friendly in a casual way since high school, running into each other here and there, their brittle sparring from earlier left behind. Despite that, Buddy still harbored a kernel of resentment about the taunts and bullying he either dodged or endured from Cullen in those younger days. The sight of him now spiraled Buddy back to a time when the two of them had battered one another senseless.

He recalled heading to the locker room in a slow walk, hands on his hips, when someone knocked into his shoulder from behind.

"Outta the way, cocksucker," Cullen Mosley had said. "What d'ya say, faggot? Got any new boyfriends?

"I got nothing to say to you, Cullen."

Cullen had then shoved Buddy hard in the chest with both hands. "Fuck you!"

Buddy could still remember how it felt when his fist slammed into Cullen's face.

The Cullen standing in front of him now looked like a different person. "I'm pretty good, Cullen. How about you? Gotta say, you're looking good."

They talked for a minute about getting together for a beer before Buddy returned to the bar.

After a long swallow of beer, he explained his visit to Earl. "That guy saved my ass in chemistry. Would've failed without his help."

"To the guy who saved your ass," Earl said, clinking his bottle against Buddy's.

Chapter Four

Larry had four days left before leaving Fort Polk for advanced individual training. Orders had come through assigning him to Army Wheeled Vehicle Mechanics, 91B in Fort Lee, Virginia, an assignment coming from his experience in automotive mechanics. He was comfortable with it, though he knew it wouldn't keep him out of Vietnam. That scared the shit out of him, but there was nothing he could do about it.

Juli was headed to Fort Hood, Texas for infantry school. That scared Larry, too. He didn't like imagining Juli in the jungle catching a storm of AK fire from guys in black pajamas.

A lot was in Larry's head during his last days of basic. Even though he'd hated the first weeks, coming up to the end he felt like he had passed through the fire and was truly a soldier. He wanted a ribbon pinned on his chest verifying that fact instead of one for getting shot in the ass while his head was in the guts of a broken-down Jeep.

Larry and Juli were partnered for the last major field exercise, a night bivouac testing their ability to elude enemy capture and maneuver to designated coordinates on the map. They stood smoking and surveying their equipment for the long march to the starting point on the edge of a wooded, jungled area of the base called Tigerland.

"You ready for this, MacDuff?"

"Yeah, we're gonna ace this thing, Juli."

Hoisting their gear, close to a hundred and seventy pounds between them, they set off for the starting point, a place called Culley's Cross.

"You pack your shoe polish and deodorant, Juli?"

"No, my fucking tea set took too much room. You tape your dog tags?"

"No more jungle jingle. How far we have to hump?"

"Total? Maybe a hundred klicks?" Juli scoffed and spit. It was more like a fourteen-mile march, a hard twenty-two kilometers, or klicks.

Platoon Sergeant Gruen yelled for marching formation, and they set off down a dusty road twisting toward a far hill on the horizon, boots stamping up clouds of dust that swirled in the humid air to choke them dry. Thirty pairs of marching soldiers joined the gruff voice of the sergeant bellowing his cadence, all of them joining in on alternating lines.

Up in the morning with the rising sun…Up in the morning with the rising sun. Here we go…Here we go. Down the road…Down the road.

The sergeant called a halt an hour later, but they were on their feet again in fifteen minutes, the sun higher, the dust thicker. It was typical late September weather in southwestern Louisiana and they were drenched with sweat under the load of ammo, rations, water and two dozen other supplies.

"How're your feet, MacDuff?" Juli had checked his ruck before leaving, making sure he had three pairs of socks and baby powder.

"Better than the boil on your ass you been complaining about."

"Hurting like a motherfucker."

The guy in front of Larry stumbled and Larry grabbed his ruck, holding him up until he regained his feet.

"Larry the big brother."

"Fuck you, Bentley."

"Maybe later," he laughed, coughing the words out.

The dust took their voices and they plodded on, silent under the sun and the constant clink of equipment, the rub of canvas against canvas. Larry set his mind on Buddy, his beautiful hands and milky breath. The slight squint when he read a book. That heady mix of sawdust and sweat that said he was near. The taste of him. The thought that his days with Buddy might be numbered always brought a shiver down his arms and neck, the uncertainties of his fate in a far-off war chilling him.

Juli slapped him on the shoulder. "You okay?"

"All good, brother."

Brother. Larry had never said that word to anyone but Buddy.

In late afternoon, they reached the starting point of the

night field exercise, hollow-eyed with fatigue, reactions slowed by fuzzy minds. They had one hour to rest before deploying into the field, a swampy jungle-like expanse off to the north. The task was to navigate a way by compass, map, and stars through a dark tangle of swampy ground to a spot six kilometers to the northwest, evading capture along the way. It would be a long night, and at some point they would need to find a suitable spot to rest and take shelter. No one was expected to complete the exercise before sunrise the next day. During the past two days, Larry and Juli had studied the map and terrain together, plotting a route they thought would bring them to the finish point uncaptured and with a time in the lower range.

Juli took a tube of camouflage paint from his ruck.

"You first," he said, and with a hand on top of Larry's head, began painting two-color stripes of green and brown across his buddy's face. With a finger, he smudged it closer to his eyes and mouth before applying a few swipes to his neck and rubbing it in. "Rub some on the back of your neck."

Larry did the same for Juli, discomfited with the intimacy of his hand on Juli's face. "Put your head down," he said, striping the paint on the back of Juli's neck, his hand slipping from his neck down into the collar of his fatigue green T-shirt, spreading the paint.

"Fucking beautiful," Juli said, taking the tube from him and rubbing more of the paint on the backs of his hands and wrists before passing it back. "Here, do your hands."

Pulling out a can of mosquito repellent next, he sprayed himself and handed the can to Larry.

A fat red sun squatted on the horizon and Sergeant Gruen ordered his men into a line of battle buddies. Larry and Juli were second in line and ordered to double-time it to the tree line, entering the cover with three hundred yards between pairs. The first pair made a straight line for the trees, Larry and Juli fanned right as the third team behind them went left. They had ten minutes to get lost in the dense cover before the next three teams started.

"Move your ass, Larry. Keep up. From the tree line, go to hand signals."

Jumping across a shallow creek just behind Juli, Larry focused on the war game underway. Basic had always been hard but this exercise had elements of fun, and Larry threw himself into the sneaky cat and mouse strategy of it.

They hunkered down behind a huge moss-covered fallen tree while Juli scouted the forest across their line of vision. He felt a tickle on his hand, and Larry looked down at a half-inch long ant crawling across his fingers.

Larry took the night goggles from his ruck and clipped them to his jacket within easy reach. Juli did the same and signaled him to move forward over the fallen tree. As his feet hit the ground, Larry saw in the shadowy half-light a snake slither off into the brush, the snake bite kit in his ruck suddenly a comfort.

An hour of stealthy advance to the northwest brought them to a thick copse of elephant ears, a spot where they could study the map and their compass bearings out of sight. At the snap of a breaking branch, Juli pulled Larry flat against the ground, placing gritty fingers over his mouth. He slowly edged the big leaves apart and had a look, signaling Larry to scan the other direction through his goggles. Satisfied they were safe, they inched their way out of the elephant ears in a low crawl, moving fifteen feet and waiting again, their night vision playing over the terrain in every direction.

"I think we fucked up," Juli said, his lips tickling Larry's ear. "We should have crossed the dry creek bed by now." They were crouched beneath a thick spray of giant ferns. "Think we have to—" He went silent, again pressing a hand against Larry's mouth. A voice threaded the darkness, moving closer to their position. They squirmed deeper beneath the fern, unsure how complete their cover was.

Two men emerged out of the dark in Larry's night vision goggles, stopping eight feet out from where they hid. The two idiots were standing in the open talking like they were the only people in Tigerland. They were looking at a map, one pointing to the northeast. Larry felt a sudden tickle in his throat, sliding a hand hard over his mouth but unable to stop the half croak-cough.

Both men turned in the direction of Larry and Juli,

staring hard into the dark.

One of the two mumbled. "Animal?"

The other continued to study the cover in their direction, eyes passing right over the clump of ferns where they crouched tight against one another. Giving up, the two soldiers moved off into the dark, heading northeast. Larry laid still, waiting until Juli's hand slid up his leg, patting his ass as a signal to move.

They backtracked and found the creek bed but in the next second disturbed a large bird roosting in the undergrowth. It flew up in an excited clatter of wings and sent them diving face down in case the noise had alerted others nearby. Through the night goggles, face an inch off the ground, Larry saw a world of insect life around him. Two inches from his nose, a dark hairy caterpillar clung to a twig, swiveling its body searching for its next move. A tiny beetle crawled up Juli's collar, an inch from his ear until Larry knocked it away. He rubbed a finger across the back of his hand, smearing a mosquito into nothing. They low-crawled the next twenty-five feet before climbing out of the creek bed and turning to the northwest.

At 0200 hours they sheltered for two hours in a shallow cave-like opening. It was under a high bank, hung with vines growing out over the edge of the bank and dropping down to form a thick curtain, hiding them from view. It was large enough for them to comfortably rest and eat, the ground flat and covered in a bed of dead leaves. They spread Larry's poncho liner on the ground, giving them a soft, dry surface. Larry passed one of his canteens to Juli, hearing his swallows as he gulped the water. They ate C-rats— ham and lima beans for Larry, turkey loaf for Juli. They moved about as little as possible and, when necessary, spoke only mouth to ear.

The boil on Juli's ass forced him to rest on his side or stomach, and he whispered that his ass was on fire. His mouth against Juli's ear, Larry said his mother did something when he was kid that eased the pain of a bad boil.

"Anything short of a bayonet."

With Juli on his stomach, Larry leaned into his ear, telling him to undo his pants.

"What the fuck, MacDuff?"

"Trust me."

Barely touching the angry swelling with his finger, Larry traced a circle around the outer edges of the boil in a slow featherlight movement. Juli gasped. "Aaahh shit…that works." His forehead rested against the ground, as he moaned softly at the relief Larry's circling finger brought to his sore ass. "Fucking hell, buddy."

In the dark of their cave-like hideout, the intimacy of his finger on Juli's ass had quickly given Larry a hard-on, and Juli's soft moans of relief only made it worse. He struggled to keep his breathing normal and his hand from straying, pushing from his mind the images of him and Juli jerking off in the shower.

He continued circling the boil lightly with his finger, and not much later Juli fell asleep and Larry gently tugged his fatigues up as far as he could.

Juli slept until Larry roused him, saying they needed to move out. It was time to be something else, soldiers again, their tenderness disguised with male bravura. While Juli buttoned himself up, Larry packed gear. They studied the map once more and decided on a route before working their way up the creek bank.

They weren't home yet. Half a klick into the last leg, they stepped around a big longleaf pine and immediately spotted two enemy soldiers whose job it was to capture them. Facing away, they hadn't seen Larry and Juli approach. Slipping behind the tree again, they crawled into a thicket of brambles, hunkering down low to the ground. From their position they couldn't see the two hunters, their only option to wait until they felt safe in crawling from cover.

But then the hunters made their way toward the dense cover of brambles Juli and Larry were under. A twig cracked underfoot, and the next step brought a boot down on Larry's hand, six inches in front of his face. Juli's fingers tightened on his shoulder with the pressure of a vice. Then, the two hunters were gone, turning and walking away to the east. Another minute passed before Juli sighed. "Let's get the fuck outta here."

They broke through the tree line two hundred yards from their goal, safe from capture and the fourth team to reach home. With a combination of relief and pride, they drank the coffee set out in a mess tent, punching and slapping each other. Two hours later, all the teams were accounted for, all but twelve of them having avoided capture. A cheer went up for Sergeant Gruen when a bus appeared on the road to carry them back to the barracks. Juli and Larry sat in the last row, Larry asleep with his head against the window. Juli's quiet snore was a snuffle against his shoulder, his hand curled against Larry's leg.

Chapter Five

The long bus ride from New Orleans to Fort Lee, Virginia was a fitful stretch of restless sleep for Larry. He had anxious thoughts of the weeks to come, and a drift of faces unrolled like the ribbon of highway ahead—his mother, Earl, Buddy and his parents. There was Juli, still the glowing ember of recent memories, the look on his face that last day at Polk. Not wanting to separate, they dragged out their goodbye while smoking one more cigarette, and with one last slap on the arm. On top of it was the fear he might never see Juli again, one more grunt to be swallowed by the bloody maw of Vietnam. Pushing that image away, he called up from the collection in his head a picture of Buddy, the two of them wrestling over the spraying hose, soaked and muddy, Larry's mom scolding them from the back porch steps. He thought of Buddy's steadfast care and devotion to the Woody, as they polished the wood and chrome luggage space, their private space, their clubhouse.

He watched the red clay hills of Mississippi flashing past, with the surprise of an old and flaking Burma Shave sign. He eventually slept for a while until a knee from the person behind jarred his seat. He noticed the woman across the aisle was wearing a pair of shoes like those his mom sometimes wore and he wondered what had become of those shoes. The day after the accident, Earl had taken him to live in the garage apartment behind his house and later took care of emptying the house on North Street. Larry guessed the shoes and all his mother's clothes ended up in a Goodwill store.

With Earl's help, Larry had packed up what he would need, not wanting to linger. The sight of so many things, especially those associated with his mom, all hit him with the force of an emotional hurricane. They piled his stuff in the back of the Woody and he followed Earl back to the house in Hundred Oaks. Behind the house, stairs led up the side of the garage to a small apartment, which would be Larry's for as long as he needed it.

"You take a few days. I'll make the arrangements for your mom," Earl had told him then.

He watched the trees blurring past the window of the bus, the abandoned clapboard house sitting farther back from the highway remained in focus a moment before slipping out of sight.

He took out a letter he was planning to post at the first opportunity he got.

RWH,

Hey, Buddy. Sorry I haven't written earlier to tell you where I am. I arrived in Fort Lee, Virginia for my advanced individual training. It's thirteen weeks, and if I pass the test at the end, I will become a mechanic in the Army's Wheeled Vehicle Mechanic Unit. Mostly it's what I did with Earl at Billups and on the Woody, a grease monkey job. I like that kind of work so at least I'll be doing something I like. The problem is, in three months I might be facing a duty assignment in Vietnam for twelve months. Scary, but I can't do anything about it. I go where they tell me.

Private Second Class LPM

Larry addressed the envelope and dropped it in the mailbox on the way to a class on the M113, a big twelve-ton armored personnel carrier, a bruiser that could carry eleven soldiers and a crew of two. It was a powerful and impressive vehicle used in Vietnam to break through heavy thickets in the jungle and attack enemy positions. The lesson was on the M113's electrical system, and after forty-five minutes, Larry's head was spinning. The classes were hard, but he was learning a lot about mechanics way beyond the Woody and other street cars he was used to.

The afternoon was spent in a hands-on class taking apart the engine on a Willys CJ-5 Jeep. The British-made Perkins engine was a 192-cubic-inch diesel that produced sixty-two horsepower. Larry could take apart a Chevy or Ford engine easy enough, but the first time working on the

Perkins was a challenge. He got some help from Sergeant Kline, and it felt good going back to the barracks with hands black from grease. After a hands-on class two days earlier, Larry had only halfway washed his hands and later got chewed out when an officer caught him in the PX with grease under his fingernails. He had to double-time it back to the barracks and spent ten minutes with a bar of Lava and a nailbrush.

After washing his hands this time, he changed into shorts and packed a fifteen-pound backpack for a two-mile run. The focus at Fort Lee was not on physical training, but classroom and garage work. Without regular hard exercise, Larry was afraid he'd lose the strength he had gained in basic and he didn't want that to happen.

He had several running trails to choose from, some hilly, some flat. He opted for Pig's Run, in the mood for trees and hills. The running was easier since he'd cut down on smoking, but he wasn't ready to give up his Luckies completely.

The trail was deserted, and the late afternoon sun slanting through the trees and branches had a gloomy look. A half-mile in, he came up on a big wild sow and her four youngsters, snuffling in the grass at the side of the trail. He was relieved when the sow hustled her babes into the trees. Wild pigs sometimes charged a lone runner out on the trail.

At the mile and a half marker, he upped his pace, confident he wouldn't struggle on the one small hill between him and the finish. Back at the main road, he slowed to a walk, and as his breathing eased, he bent over, hands on his knees. He jogged back to barracks, had a shower and dressed in clean fatigues for chow.

The food was better at Fort Lee and they weren't stingy with it. Here, too, he had to be careful, because the big servings were tempting but made staying in shape all the harder. He got a plate of lasagna and chocolate pudding, sitting at a table with a guy named Baker from the barracks. He was in a couple of the same classes, but his name was all Larry knew about him. They talked about the Willys CJ-5 engine, Baker calling it a temperamental bitch. A big guy with sandy hair and freckles, Baker asked if Larry wanted to see a movie, they were showing *Birdman of Alcatraz*.

"Not much in the mood tonight. Maybe next time," Larry told him.

Back in the barracks, he polished his boots and detailed his locker, the habits of basic still intact, then decided to hit the gym and work the weights for an hour. He fished another pair of shorts and gym shoes out of his locker and, after changing, walked across the quad and around the medical unit to the gym.

Larry did push-ups, sit-ups, pull-ups, and some lifting, helped out by a guy from a different barracks Larry didn't know. He was doing bench presses, grunting under a hundred and fifty pounds when someone stepped over and offered to spot for him.

"Thanks," Larry said. After ten reps he sat up. "Appreciate it," he added, extending a hand, "MacDuff."

"Anytime. Name's Lurbil. You just get here?" the man said, shaking Larry's hand.

"Few days ago, yeah. From Fort Polk."

"My guess is, you'll like it here. Everybody's pretty cool, laidback. None of that basic training hardnose shit."

"Good to hear. How often you work out?"

Lurbil was a big brawny guy and made Larry think of those Charles Atlas magazine ads in the back of comic books he read when he was a kid.

"Four, five workouts a week. You need some help or direction, I'm your guy."

After his workout, sweat-soaked, Larry took another shower and sat for an hour with a textbook, having another look at the Perkins diesel engine diagrams. He was determined to have the right answers ready for his next class.

He had trouble falling asleep, a head full of conflicting thoughts about Buddy and Juli, thoughts that made him feel like a sneak. Buddy Hebert was his heartbeat, there was never any question. He had as strong a feeling in that moment as the day he'd left for basic training. A separation Larry wasn't sure he could manage. But he did and was thrown together with the paprika-haired boy from Mandeville who unaccountably wormed his way into Larry's heart.

He didn't feel about Juli the same way he did about Buddy, but Juli was in his head every day. He woke each morning thinking about the clear blue of his eyes, the image of him clear and distinct, the red stubble of hair on his head and chin, him laughing at something Larry said, whomping him in the chest.

And then he remembered the feel of Buddy's hands in his hair, Buddy's palm against his heart. And that nutty time they had been studying chemistry together, Buddy unzipping him and ending with Larry splashing on Buddy's desk and chemistry book. He recalled the look on Buddy's face when he'd smiled and said *oops*.

Now Juli was glowing in his memory. It was Buddy's gentle nature playing against Juli's rougher demeanor. Fuck up and Buddy would hold him, saying it's okay. Juli was more likely to knock Larry on his ass, saying *get it right, numbnuts*, and extending a hand to pull him up. He was a sucker for both.

The last letter from Buddy before leaving Polk was a tentative stutter of things Larry sensed Buddy wanted to say but couldn't. Larry understood his diffidence. His letters to Buddy were written in the same cautious reserve. Still, they had to value the letters as something handmade, which itself had meaning.

As for Juli, there were no letters, his writing only a memory of scribbles, marks on a map, or a quickly jotted note saying, "*Meet me at chow*," a barely legible scratch of letters. But he missed Juli in ways he didn't want to admit, the days and nights at Fort Hood having cemented something with Juli. And now times came when he thought of Buddy leaning against his right shoulder, Juli against the other, his feelings for both confused with no easy way of untangling them.

* * * *

On Wednesday, with a pass into town, Larry found a local bar called Clapper's Bar & Grill, and went in for a few beers. It was loud, filled with soldiers, most of them drunk or halfway there. The jukebox blasted "Sweet Thang" while a couple of locals danced in the middle of the floor, mostly holding one another up. Larry squeezed in next to a loud-talking soldier at the bar and ordered a draft beer. After being bumped or jostled, twice sloshing the beer out of his mug, he opened his mouth to say something when someone tapped him on the shoulder.

"A stool just opened up at the end of the bar," the waitress said. "I'm holding it for you."

He followed her to the end of the bar and as he sat, she reached over him, wiping up a beer spill before going off to serve people at a table in the far corner.

Larry slammed a few beers down, exactly what he needed, each mug emptied under soft-colored lights winking on bottles behind the bar, with animated talk all around him. The waitress passed by his stool, saying he should eat something.

"Maybe later," Larry said to her disappearing back.

Back a minute later, she leaned over his shoulder. "Five mugs of beer? I think you need something in your stomach."

Was she counting? Ten minutes later she was back, placing a ham and swiss sandwich in front of him. "Eat up, soldier."

When she walked away, Larry took a couple of bites of the sandwich and asked the bartender to make the rest disappear.

"Mindy's a good woman. She doesn't like some of the guys coming in here getting too fucked up and into trouble. Protective or some such shit."

"I just don't feel like eating right now."

"No problem."

Larry climbed off his stool and wobbled down the hall to the men's room. Finished and fumbling with his zipper, he ran headfirst into a big guy coming in the door and got shoved face-first into the wall. "Heads up, kid."

Once back on his barstool, Mindy looked at him with a frown. "What happened to your face?"

Larry didn't know what she meant.

"There's a red spot on your forehead. Did you fall?"

"Maybe ran into a wall."

She picked up his beer, cigarettes and lighter and carried them to a table near the jukebox, then she came back and took his arm. "More comfortable over here."

The bartender looked at Larry and, shaking his head, threw him a knowing smile.

He sat at the table and Mindy was back with a bar rag wrapped around ice. She put it against his forehead. "Hold it there."

She left to wait on a table of three soldiers and Larry made his way to the bar for another beer. "What's your name?"

"Lester."

"I think Mindy's looking out for me. Would you do something with this?" he said, handing over the rag and ice.

"Think you're right," the bartender said, passing over the mug of beer and taking the ice pack.

"Thanks."

All the beer made Larry soppy drunk, a little maudlin, and he wondered where Mindy had disappeared to. She was calling him Larry by then and occasionally holding his hand. A first for him, he was looking at her and thinking she was sweet and pretty. She was busy with a table full of drunk soldiers. Larry watched the way she went about serving the five men, keeping them happy and every now and then slapping away a hand groping at her ass.

"You okay, Larry?"

"I am per-fect-ly fine. You want, I can go over and beat the crap out of that guy grabbing at your butt." He had difficulty focusing on the table of rowdy soldiers. "Is that big fucker the one who slammed me into the wall?"

She smiled and lit the cigarette hanging from Larry's mouth. "You feel like getting your ass stomped? For your information, Lester has a bat under the bar in case it's needed. The groping is an occupational hazard. But you're sweet for wanting to protect me," she said, leaning in to straighten his collar. "You a little homesick, soldier?"

"Miss a couple of people mostly."

"And who are they?"

Larry looked at her. What the hell? "Buddy and another guy, Juli."

Her face showed no surprise. "They back home?"

"Buddy is. Juli is in Texas doing his AIT like me." He

pushed back his chair. "Sorry, I have to pee."

When he came out of the men's room he took three unsteady steps toward Mindy, who was waiting outside the door. She reached out an arm to catch him, Larry's face brushing against her hair.

She put a hand on his cheek. "You forgot to zip," she said.

He struggled with the zipper, finally looking down to see what the problem was. He staggered. "Can you see if the fucker's caught?"

"Are you making a pass at me, Larry?"

"I wouldn't know how. Promise."

She slid a hand down his leg and gently tugged the zipper up. Tilting her face up to Larry's, she kissed him, her lips warm against his. After the initial surprise, he liked it. He had never once kissed a girl and had nothing to compare it to. The feel of Mindy was different, smelling like strawberries, with a girlish softness. Buddy was something different altogether. Mindy's mouth lingered on Larry's, and when she bit his lip he pulled back, confused and not sure what was happening.

"Sorry. I've never done this before. My head is a little mixed up right now."

She put a finger against the lip she had just bitten. "You liked it, didn't you?"

He was unable to look at Mindy. "I've never been with a girl before," he said.

She kissed him again. "Do you want to?"

"Not too sure I can."

She pressed her hand against his stiffening dick. "I'm pretty sure you can."

"Sorry, I have to go." He kissed her once more, zigzagged to the bar and paid his tab. He walked two blocks in the direction of the base before turning around and returning to Clapper's, waiting across the street and pacing back and forth in front of a hardware store until he saw Mindy come out. She walked east for a block before turning onto a dark street. Larry followed, closing the distance between them. Just as she reached the steps leading to an upstairs apartment, he touched her arm from behind and she spun around, frightened.

"Sorry, Mindy. It's me, Larry. Sorry I scared you."

"Well, you scared the shit out of me, Larry."

"Can I come up?"

She looked closely at him in the dark. "You sure that's what you want?"

"I think so."

Larry was drunk and a little worried about embarrassing himself with a limp noodle when it came time to do the deed. He was clumsy and unsure of what he was doing, or supposed to do, but Mindy was making noises that hinted he was doing something right. Inexperienced in foreplay with a girl, Larry didn't know what was expected, but he liked kissing her. When she drew a wet finger from her mouth and slipped it inside him, he trembled with a spasm of pleasure, his mind flying to Buddy, who had done the same their first night together.

Mindy had his dick standing at attention. He was surprised at how vocal she was, at one point sure the neighbors could hear her cries. But he went at it himself with unexpected enthusiasm, lasting longer than he ever had with Buddy. The truth was, he was amazed he had been able to last as long as he did.

Afterward, they lay on Mindy's bed, her fingers toying with the sparse hair under Larry's raised arm, until she sat up on an elbow. "Larry, were you being truthful when you said you had never done this before?"

"Huh?"

Mindy didn't say anything else, instead kissing him again. Eventually, her fingers drifted below his waist. Nothing was going on down there and when she moved to put her mouth on him, Larry escaped. "I need the bathroom."

She pointed to the door. "Out the bedroom to the left."

He stood naked at the toilet, looking around him at the bottles and jars, a hairdryer, and a pair of shoes in the corner. Everything was all pink and feminine and smelling of perfume. He flushed the toilet just as Mindy's arm reached around pressing a cold bottle of beer against his stomach, her face against his hair.

"Your hair smells good."

"Buddy says it smells like cut grass. I think that's

weird."

Her head cocked to one side. "Do you sleep with Buddy?"

"Yeah, I do."

"And Juli?"

"That's my problem. I want to."

"Anyone else?"

"Just you."

"So," she said, drawing it out. "If you're ever in the mood..." She kissed him again, this time long and wet, a hand cupping his balls. Easing away and glancing down at Larry's lack of response, she gave a soft laugh. "In the light of day..."

Larry dressed, going to the door. "Maybe see you at Clapper's."

She blew him a kiss. "Hope so."

He was now naked again, this time in the shower at the barracks and glad to be alone. He turned the water as hot as he could stand it, letting it pummel him for a long time before scrubbing himself top to bottom.

In his bunk, Larry thought long about Mindy, replaying in his head the whole sex thing from beginning to end and was happy he had done it. It was a big first time for him, and good in a different way. But he soon fell asleep to the image of Juli in snowy-white boxers cranking out sit-ups on the floor between their bunks.

Chapter Six

One Thursday night after supper, Buddy told his mother he was spending the night at Larry's apartment and going to work from there in the morning.

"That's okay with Earl?"

"I'll clear it with him first, but I can't think why not. Won't be putting them out. My truck is over at the station now. They're replacing a headlight."

His mother held him close for a moment and touched his cheek. Tossing a few things in a backpack, he grabbed his tool belt and thermos and went off to the Billups station, leaving his mother on the front steps.

Ruth Hebert stood watching her son disappear down the street, her thoughts heavy with worry. She was proud of Buddy in so many ways and glad for the loving son he had always been. Like his father, she, too often, thought he resembled Clyde's brother, Thaddeus. The first words his Aunt Emmy said when she saw baby Buddy were that he was the spitting image of Thad. They had named him Robert William, but it was Emmy who called him Buddy. She couldn't have loved that boy more if he'd come from her own womb. What, Ruth wondered, would she have thought about Buddy and his best friend, Larry?

What was it that made Buddy so different from his sisters? He was a happy child, but clear from the start there was something in him unlike the girls. She hadn't worried, just thought, as many mothers do, that this one is different. A rambunctious boy, he loved sports and at one time was obsessed with football. In junior high he began showing an interest in girls, and then in high school had taken a series of girls on dates. The odd thing was, he never once talked about them at home or invited them to the house. It had occurred to her that he was only pretending to have an interest in girls, copying what other boys did with the idea it was something he was supposed to do, expected to do. But the friendship with Larry put an end to dates with girls, and it wasn't long before the two boys were rarely apart. Ruth pondered how the complexity of such feelings had first developed in her son.

She recalled again the picture of her son and Larry entwined in sleep. Passing Buddy's room one morning with a stack of towels for his bathroom, she had glimpsed through his half-open door the two sleeping boys cuddled against one another like a pair of puppies. She wouldn't allow herself to imagine what they did alone together in the night. Couldn't. Such things were beyond her experience. She knew, of course, that some men, and women too, slept together for sexual purposes. Growing up in a small Mississippi town, she had been insulated from the more worldly habits and ways of people in cities. But even in Dunleith, there had been a few, one nameless boy in particular that she remembered seeing several times downtown. She wasn't proud of it, in fact, it was a shameless act, but she harbored the faded memory of an afternoon at the drugstore when she and three friends had laughed, and in loud whispers mocked the effeminate boy reading a ladies' fashion magazine at the soda fountain.

****

Buddy found Earl at his battered old desk fiddling with what looked like a water pump.

"Hey, Earl. What do I owe you for the new headlight?"

"You can bring me a slice of your momma's pie sometime."

"Maybe she'll make you a whole one. You mind if I sleep up in the garage apartment tonight? Easy drive to work from there."

"Hell no, Buddy. I don't mind. You can stay there anytime you want, far as I'm concerned. Nothing in the refrigerator, but there's a bed and a shower you're welcome to. Helen might give you a cup of coffee in the morning."

Up in the apartment later, he brushed his teeth, had a shower, and put on a pair of shorts and a T-shirt Larry had left in the dresser. He found a clean pair of jeans in the closet and decided he would wear those to work instead of the ones he'd brought.

For the first time in weeks, he felt a sense of peace in the dark of Larry's little apartment, in Larry's bed. He relished the feel of Larry, Larry's things around him, and eventually fell into the deepest sleep he'd had in a long time.

He woke early, pale light seeping in through the window, and didn't remember right off that he was in Larry's bed. It was quiet outside, though he figured Earl's family was up in the house out front. He thought about Earl and his family, how they had taken Larry in after his mother died, Earl going down to the state foster care offices and signing papers making him and his wife Larry's legal guardians until his eighteenth birthday. He'd even arranged the funeral, Larry being too young to know anything about that. It had taken a while for Larry to get used to the old woman, Earl's mother-in-law, a nosy and prickly busybody short on patience, at least where teenage boys were concerned. But Larry had eventually found a way around her peevishness.

He was on the edge of falling asleep again but roused himself, pushing a hand down in his shorts to satisfy the urge brought on by being in Larry's bed. At the last second, he grabbed a sock from the floor and clamped it over himself, avoiding making a mess in the bed. He dressed and made the bed, stuffing his dirty clothes in the backpack and putting on clean socks from Larry's drawer.

He was coming down the outside stairs when Earl called from the back door for him to come in and have some breakfast. Buddy was a little reluctant to be under the stare of the old woman but thought it might sound ungrateful to say no. He joined the family around the kitchen table, and a minute later Mrs. Clemens put a plate of eggs and sausage in front of him.

"Thank you, ma'am."

"Help yourself to the biscuits," she said, turning back to the stove. "Your father holding up, Buddy? I been meaning to get over there and visit with him."

"Yeah, doing really good. You'd never know he had a heart attack."

"Well, hello, Buddy. It's good to see you," Earl's wife

said, coming into the kitchen. "How're your folks?"

"They're good, ma'am. I wanna thank y'all for letting me stay the night in the apartment. And for this delicious breakfast, as well."

He must have said something right because Mrs. Clemens told him to pass her his thermos, she would fill it with coffee. "Have y'all heard anything from Larry?" he asked.

"He's written a couple of times telling us a little about his training, how hard some of it has been," Earl said.

His wife agreed. "We know that he's fine for now but still worry where he will be a few months on. I know a thousand mothers are fretting over a son being readied for a crazy war on the other side of the world. I see the president talking on TV about stopping communist aggression, helping the poor people in Vietnam and I want to ask him what the hell he's talking about. What does that have to do with us? Why are American boys expected to go over there, thrown into a horrible war for reasons that don't make sense to anybody but a bunch of politicians in Washington?"

Earl put a hand on her shoulder. "Don't upset yourself, hon."

Buddy couldn't tell Earl or his wife how scared he was.

Reaching around her to put his coffee cup in the sink, Earl spoke to his wife. "You ready for me to drive you to work?"

As Buddy was thanking Mrs. Clemens and going out the back door with his thermos, Earl came up behind him. "Stay up in the apartment anytime, Buddy. It's no trouble to us."

Chapter Seven

Downtown Baton Rouge was often a mixed bouquet of smells from the river and the life around it. Depending on the variables, the air changed with the seasons, the chemicals from two oil refineries and the cargo of passing ships bringing their own particular exotic smells. Often a salty tanginess floated on the air, and if the breeze was just right, the community coffee plant across the river in Port Allen sent the fragrance of roasting coffee wafting across Third Street. Sometimes, a sensitive nose might catch the smell of river catfish swimming the murky water of the Mississippi. The bellow of a tugboat pushing a barge upstream was a familiar sound, and on some Sundays, Dixieland jazz came floating across the water from a modern paddle-wheeler playing "Old Man River."

As he leaned against a wall outside the bus station on North Boulevard, the familiar musky, oily smell of the Mississippi was strong in Buddy's nose. Working on his third cigarette, he glanced again down the street for an approaching Greyhound bus. Larry had said three twenty. He knew he was early and he was down to his last cigarette, still pacing the sidewalk when he spotted the distinctive hulk of a bus coming toward the bus station. The tension of waiting was suddenly replaced by excitement. The bus turned into the terminal entrance and disappeared around the back where the passengers would disembark. Buddy jogged to where it stopped, his heart beating in his throat.

The bus door opened, and for what felt like five minutes no one got off. Finally, an old Black woman with cherries on her hat emerged, descending the steps carefully while managing a big purse, a cloth bag, and a large parcel wrapped with string. An agitated mother and young daughter were next, followed by one slow passenger after another. Impatient, Buddy was tempted to push his way onto the bus. Larry was the last one off and spotted Buddy a short distance away.

Walking toward him was a Larry that Buddy had never seen. He was taller and bigger, tan and fit with crew-cut hair under a gray-green Army cap. His uniform of brown pants and gray-green coat with insignia and stripes on his sleeve identified him as a U.S. Army Private Second Class. Buddy could only gape at the new Larry.

"Hey."

Buddy's responding greeting was choked off, and despite the people milling around them, they threw their arms around one another in a bear hug. Larry's bulk, hard against Buddy, was a relief like none he'd ever known.

Larry hoisted his duffle bag over a shoulder as Buddy guided him. "The Woody's this way," he said, his hand clasping the shoulder without the duffle bag.

They were without words walking to the car, looking at one another and smiling, and Buddy even gave Larry a playful shove. Tossing the duffle in back, Buddy spoke against Larry's ear. "That uniform is giving me a stiffy."

He passed the keys to Larry. "Your apartment at Earl's. No one's there. Eileen and the old woman took the kids to Baker to see their aunts and Earl is at the station. He'll go straight to my house from there."

"What's up at your house?"

"A welcome home supper. My mother's idea."

"With nobody around, what do you have in mind?" Larry asked with a knowing smile.

When they were finally in the garage apartment, Buddy sat on the bed, Larry standing in front of him, clothes at his feet. He stepped closer and Buddy reached to run his hand over Larry's muscular chest and hard stomach. He tore off his own clothes, and Larry was on him in the next second.

Neither could hold back and it was over quickly. The next part started slowly, lingering, finding again those remembered sensations, holding tight to one another. Aroused again, Buddy hinted at what he wanted and they slipped into the familiar position of Larry spooned against Buddy's back, pushing into him.

In another moment Buddy's breath caught, as he felt an overwhelming oneness like nothing ever imagined before, something different, something far beyond fucking. For him—and he knew it was for Larry, too—an inner humming locking them so completely together they couldn't have been more in sync had they been one body, one mind. There was the ultimate feeling that they were for that time one conjoined consciousness, two hearts beating in tandem, bodies humming in what he thought must be rapture.

Slick with sweat, Buddy mumbled into Larry's hair. "I was lost without you." The Army haircut brushed against Buddy's cheek, he rubbed his face in it, gulping at the grassy fragrance of it.

Later they dozed in a tangle of arms and legs, spent from a marathon of urgent, reverent intimacy. Sitting up, wanting a cigarette, Buddy scrabbled around on the floor for his shirt before remembering he was out. "No cigarettes."

"Check my coat pocket."

Buddy dug out a pack of Luckies and the lighter, lighting two and putting one in Larry's mouth, again staring down at the boy he worshipped. But Larry was a boy no longer. Buddy rolled over, lying against Larry while they smoked in silence.

"What time are we supposed to be at your house?"

"Whenever we get there. Earl will probably be there a little after five."

They slept, and later they talked about Buddy's parents and Earl, Buddy telling Larry that he and Earl had become buddies since he'd gone off to training. He told Larry about his work at the building site, that he had managed to get ten days off.

"Tell me about you, your training, all that soldier stuff."

"Not much to tell. It's hard, but good in some ways. The discipline works for me. Not much time to think when a drill sergeant is down your neck all day long. I made a friend, a guy I told you about in a letter, Juli Bentley. We were battle buddies for the ten weeks of basic. But then he went to Fort Hood in Texas. Haven't seen him since. He'll be off to Vietnam in a couple of weeks. Infantry."

"How was Virginia?"

"A little like Fort Polk, but different, too. Went to a bar in town a few times. Got to know a waitress there,

Mindy. She kinda watched out for me. I went home with her a couple of times." He turned to Buddy, eyebrows raised. "It didn't mean anything, didn't even like it very much."

Buddy smiled at him. "That's kinda sexy," he said, squeezing Larry's dick. "So, my friend here has been fishing in foreign waters."

"Not much to it. Sweet girl though."

Buddy glanced at the clock. "They'll be waiting for us."

They showered and Buddy washed Larry's crew cut, him leaning against Buddy's chest.

"Did what's her name do this to you?"

"She could never do what you do to me," Larry answered.

Larry put on his uniform and Buddy took clean clothes from the closet and dresser. Leaving the apartment, Buddy stopped to straighten the knot in Larry's tie, patting his cheek. "You're fucking beautiful."

****

They were all waiting in the den. Buddy's mother jumped up and ran to hug Larry, kissing his cheek and stepping back. "My goodness, look at you!" Her eyes took him in, absorbing the sight of a grown-up Larry. Buddy's father climbed out of his recliner and embraced Larry, slapping him on the back several times. "Mighty good to see you, son. Welcome home."

Larry spotted Earl leaning against the door jamb and walked over to him. Earl took his extended hand and pulled Larry into a one-armed hug. "You're looking good, grease monkey."

"It's damn good to see y'all," Larry said, his eyes moving from face to face. He pulled off his cap. "I love you all."

"You're different, son, I'll give you that. You may even be able to kick my behind now," Earl said, shaking his head.

"You're so handsome in your uniform, Larry," Mrs. Hebert said.

"Waiting to get out of it for a while," he replied.

"Well, go on back to Buddy's room and find something else to put on," she said.

Buddy gave him a push. "Go on."

"Let me get the food on the table," Buddy's mother said with a big smile on her face.

She bustled into the kitchen and began carrying bowls and platters to the dining room. Mr. Hebert guided Earl out to the backyard for a quick look around the yard, giving Earl a chance to have a smoke. Buddy went along with them.

"Supper's almost ready," his mother called as they went out the back door.

Though it hadn't needed it, Buddy ran the lawnmower over the yard earlier and it was fresh and trim. His father's winter garden was green with broccoli, collards, and scallions. Looking down at the collards, Earl said there was nothing more delicious than a pot of greens.

From the screen door, Mrs. Hebert called them inside.

"Larry, you sit at the end opposite Daddy. Earl, you sit on this side, and Buddy and I will sit on the other."

Bowls and platters passed from hand to hand, sparking low-voiced supper table compliments.

"Just one more spoonful of these mashed potatoes."

"Have some of the squash, Earl. Homegrown."

"Can't beat a backyard garden."

"Buddy, pass Larry the cornbread."

Half the bowls had yet to reach Earl, but his plate was brimming. Larry had three pieces of fried chicken on his plate, a drumstick already down to the bone, and was saying he'd get some of the other food after the chicken. Earl asked if the squash had a pinch of sugar in it. Buddy's father kept mostly to vegetables, a single chicken wing on his plate. Buddy was nose down in the barbecued ribs, cornbread on the side. His mother got up and refilled glasses of iced tea.

"Miz Hebert, I wanna know what voodoo you did to these butterbeans. Larry, you eat like this in basic?" Earl said, as he watched his glass being refilled.

"Nothing tops this, that's a fact. But the food wasn't too bad. Even better at AIT," Larry answered.

"What's AIT?" Mrs. Hebert wanted to know.

"Advanced Individual Training," Earl explained. "Tell 'em about it, Larry."

"For me, it was training for the maintenance of Army vehicles. A lot of it I knew from working with Earl at the gas station."

Earl quickly spoke up. "That's not all true. No way I could deal with a tank or troop carrier."

"I think I speak for all of us, son, in hoping you never have to get near a tank on the battlefield," Mr. Hebert said.

The words settled over the quieted table until Larry timidly asked if there was any more cornbread.

"There's plenty, Larry," Buddy's mother said.

"You have your orders yet, Larry?" Mr. Hebert asked quietly.

"Yes, sir, I do," he said, prodding the chicken bones on his plate. "In two weeks I report to Travis Air Force Base in California. From there, Vietnam."

At the turn in their conversation, the taste melted away from the food in Buddy's mouth. He read the resignation on Larry's face and struggled to suppress his fear.

****

Since learning that Larry was two weeks from deployment, his helplessness had made Buddy queasy and out of sorts. He and Larry had driven out in Buddy's truck to Belle Helene, the old antebellum manor house on River Road built in the 1840s. It had once been a sugar plantation with slave cabins, an overseer's house, and a blacksmith's shop. Posted trespassing signs hung at the broken gate, but they knew from experience that people sometimes went onto the property and were generally ignored.

Parked in their old spot under the big oak tree and cramped on the truck's ragged seat, Buddy's legs stuck out the passenger window, his head in Larry's lap. Larry looked off toward the decaying mansion, a finger tracing Buddy's lips. His eyes gritty with a lack of sleep, Buddy fought off another image of hollow-eyed soldiers on a muddy footpath in the jungle. He had been tormented all night by the recurring picture of wounded soldiers being loaded onto a helicopter, a soundless loop playing in his head. Larry had woken, grumbling that Buddy was squeezing him too tightly.

It came as an unexpected relief when the pictures in Buddy's head were interrupted by a growl from Larry's stomach. Buddy lifted his T-shirt, pressing his ear closer, craving the intimate sounds of Larry's healthy, strong body rumbling with the noise of a life-affirming process. He had never loved Larry more than at that moment and wished he could be swallowed up by the body pressed against his ear.

Looking down at Buddy in his lap, Larry studied his face. With his finger he wiped a wet spot from Buddy's lips and, plucking a piece of foam from the torn seat, tickled the end of his nose. "Elegant seat cover you have in this truck."

"Fits my job. I like it."

"Ask Earl, he'll send you to the right place for a new bench seat."

"I know."

Larry looked once more out the window, his gaze carrying beyond the old house and across the road to the distant levee. His head still cradled in Larry's lap, Buddy saw the squint of his eyes as he seemed to turn something over in his mind. Buddy knew that like himself, Larry was stuck on something about his immediate future, anticipation of a violent shift barreling toward him.

With a deep breath, Larry spoke. "I wrote a letter to give Earl when I leave. If something happens—"

"No! Shut the fuck up!"

"Buddy, listen. If anything happens, I told Earl that the Woody belongs to you. And any of the stuff up in the apartment."

He was making Buddy furious. Pulling his legs inside the truck, he lurched upright, pushed the door open and jumped out. "Not a conversation we're having, brother." He jogged to the ruined house, dodging inside a doorless frame.

Larry found him on the second-story balcony looking down into the littered yard below. He put his hands on Buddy's shoulders from behind, but Buddy shrugged them off.

"Buddy…stop, please. I'm going to a bad place for a while. Nothing I want more than to come back home. I love you like crazy but that can't change my going. I won't be out on patrols in the bush but something could happen. Nothing we can do about that." He closed the distance between them. "Can I please hold you?"

Buddy nodded and felt Larry's warmth against him. "We don't have to talk about that again, okay?" Larry said, his mouth pressed against Buddy's neck.

They drove back, detouring through the LSU campus and over to the lake. Larry wanted a look at the house Buddy was working on, though there was not a lot to see other than a bare framework of studs surrounded by stacks of lumber. They didn't bother getting out of the truck, instead driving a half mile to the first house Buddy had worked on. The family was living there now, preventing them from wandering around the house and land for a closer look.

"Beautiful house. Got your handprints all over it," Larry said, looking out the truck window.

Backtracking across the campus and over to Highland, Buddy told Larry to cut over to the Pastime on Nicholson. "Let's grab a beer."

As they were about to sit at the bar, someone called Buddy's name and looking over, he saw Bob Wexler waving an arm at him.

"This is getting to be a habit. How's it going, Bob?"

"Marvelous. You're looking hunky as always. Who's the friend?"

"That's Larry." Buddy waved him over. "Larry, this is Bob. I told you about him. Helped me with chemistry back in high school."

Larry nodded and shook Bob's hand.

"Well, sit down, sit down," Bob said while gesturing to his friend. "This is Damien." He signaled to the waitress, asking what they wanted to drink.

"Beer, draft." Buddy said.

Larry nodded. "Same."

Bob looked at his friend Damien and spoke conversationally. "So butch. I love it. I'll have another vodka martini.

Damien?"

He held up two fingers.

Half a beer in, Larry was talking to Damien, while Bob was looking at Buddy with raised eyebrows, an implied question.

Buddy nodded his head once, prompting a broad smile from Bob.

Bob leaned in. "Gorgeous," he whispered.

"So, what are you doing now, Bob?"

"Oh, gawd. Pre-law at LSU. More boring than an episode of *Queen for a Day*." Larry and Buddy laughed. "I wish I had as much passion for the law as Damien does for music. Wanna find him? Check the university's music library and listen for any strains of jazz winding through the stacks."

With Damien and Larry deep in conversation, Bob explained to Buddy that Damien had been a close friend for several years. They were introduced by a mutual friend and quickly discovered they shared a wry sense of humor and a love of reading. Damien was four years older, and for the past two years had been working on his dissertation for a doctorate in music history. "Damien is one of those fortunate few, not forced to juggle his studies with a night job to pay off student loans. He teaches a survey course to freshmen once a week, and assists one of his professors in another, but otherwise lives comfortably on a trust fund. Most of his time he spends in the library researching obscure movements in the history of jazz music," Bob explained. "Damien's father was one of those science nerd inventors who held ever-flowing patents for parts in airplane engines."

From the look of it, jazz was the last thing on Damien's mind. He had the appearance of being rendered dopey by Larry's company.

"And Buddy now has arm muscles. Working out?" Bob said, touching Buddy's bicep and giving a sizzling hot shake of his fingers.

"No, I guess it's the work I do with a contractor building houses."

"Building houses...and you're happy doing that?'" Bob said, with some surprise.

"Yep. That and being with him." He turned to see a smiling Larry.

****

Sunday was warm for February. Buddy was out front doing some maintenance on his truck while Larry was in the backyard with Mr. Hebert. Leaning over the sun hot hood and replacing the worn-out wiper blades, Buddy had a feeling his father was talking about him to Larry.

At that moment, Larry was actually pointing out an idea to Mr. Hebert. "I been hassling Buddy about that ratty seat in his truck. All the rips and padding coming out doesn't bother him."

"I expect his mind is elsewhere. His mother and I worry about him. He's not himself."

"I don't know what I can do or say. He got pissed off at me saying the Woody was his if something happened," Larry said, his voice low.

"Mm. He jumped on his mother for mentioning the danger you would be in over there." He squeezed Larry's shoulder. "He's terrified of the possibilities."

Larry hugged his knees, picking a flake of tobacco off his lip and clicking his lighter open and closed several times.

Just then, Buddy came around the side of the house and sat on the ground in front of Larry and his father. He picked up the cold cup of coffee at Larry's side. "Y'all talking about me?"

"Yeah, talking about your truck." Larry passed his cigarettes over to Buddy. "Let's drive out to the junkyard in Denham Springs, see if they have a bench seat better than what you got."

Buddy shrugged. "You can't wait to get a new seat in that truck."

"Son, your boss okay with you taking so much time off from work?" his father asked.

"Mr. Hargrove didn't hesitate when I asked. Never took a day off before. I woulda quit if he'd said no."

"What's he paying you now if you don't mind me asking?"

"Four seventy-five an hour."

"Damn good wage, Buddy. Don't quit on that."

"I'd work seven days a week if he asked me. Just not now," he said, finishing the last of Larry's coffee.

****

On the way to the junkyard in Denham Springs, wind blew through the open windows of the truck, whipping hair around Buddy's face. He'd been quiet since leaving the house. He noticed a smear of dirt on Larry's neck and licking his thumb, reached across and wiped it clean.

"Bob Wexler invited us to a party Friday night," Buddy said. "At his house over by the golf course."

"Damien gonna be there?"

"Should I be jealous?"

Larry frowned, shaking his head. "Someone I can talk to."

The junkyard was huge, acres of cars crammed together that went over a slight rise in the land. A young guy missing two front teeth slouched on a broken-down sofa breathing heavily over a ragged copy of *Heels & Hose*. His shirt identified him as *Toby*, stitched in blue. He looked up and laid aside the magazine, tugging at the bulge in his jeans. He said there were a bunch of trucks in the back left corner of the lot. They thanked him and started off, accompanied by a tattered old white pit bull with a long pink tongue hanging out of huge jaws.

"Don't pay no mind to Curly. He don't bite," Toby called from the office door.

Buddy knew it was an adventure for Larry, getting a look inside some of the cars all around them. "Brother, stop scoping out every car we pass. Come on."

Larry had been snooping under the hood of an old Packard. Jogging to where Buddy waited, he hung on his back. "This is like presents under a Christmas tree."

Larry found what they were looking for wedged among a dozen wrecks. They squeezed between fenders and bumpers, their hands brushing against jagged and rusty edges.

"Careful. Watch the nasty corner on that fender,"

Buddy said.

Larry had gotten through to the truck. It was close against another truck and they couldn't get the passenger door open more than about eighteen inches, but it was enough to get a look at the front seat and see what condition it was in.

"What do you think?" Larry said.

Buddy pressed up against him, trying to see inside. The closeness and smell of Larry distracted him, and he was unaware he was pressing his hips against Larry.

"What are you doing?" Larry said, Buddy's mouth against his sweaty neck.

"Sorry...nothing.'

"This is better than the seat you've got and it's a perfect match. Should we pull it?"

Buddy's chin rested on Larry's shoulder for a better view. "Yeah, if you say so. Can we get it out?"

"Easy-peasy. Make your way around to the other side but hand me my tools first."

Larry had thrown a few tools in a bag before leaving the house. He loosened the front floor bolt on his side and, passing the wrench to Buddy, told him to do the same on the driver's side. Sliding the seat forward as much as possible, Larry nosed around in back looking for the rear bolt. The space was limited, but he managed to reach the bolt with a socket wrench.

"Same thing in back." He passed the socket wrench to Buddy. "Feel around back there with your hand. You'll find it."

When Buddy had loosened the second one, Larry asked him to pass over the two nuts he'd removed.

He dropped them in his pocket with the other two. "Slide the seat back as far as it'll go. Grab the front edge with me and fold it up to meet the back."

With more room on the driver's side, they lifted Buddy's end up as high as the door opening and slid the whole sandwiched seat out of the truck.

Back at the ratty old office, the dog was splayed out, head on a paw like he was a part of the junk to each side of the door. Debris rose to the bottom of two dirt-fogged windows. There were empty oil cans, tire rims, cardboard boxes collapsed by repeated rains, and slick tires holding rainwater and a multitude of wriggling mosquito larvae. Buddy and Larry stood in the sun squinting to see inside, while waiting for Toby to notice them with the front seat they had pulled out of the truck.

"You think he's in the bathroom with his magazine?"

Larry laughed, his mirth building until he couldn't hold his end of the seat.

"What's so funny?"

"I don't know, Buddy. Us being part of this country junkyard snapshot," he said, still sniggering.

"You boys find what you need?" Toby stood at the door finally, straddling the pit bull.

"What do we owe you?" Larry asked.

Toby scratched his chin, looking out at them in the glare of sun. "Gimme fifteen dollars and I'll throw in a couple of Co-Colas for the road."

"Done," Larry said, pulling a ten and a five out of his pocket.

Toby brought two bottles of pop out and stood at the driver's window with his forearms resting on the door, hands dangling inside the truck. "Got some deer pups that'll be ready in two weeks. Y'all want one, give me a call. Mother's a worker, sweeter 'n pussy."

Pulling out of the junkyard, Larry leaned, sniffing at Buddy's neck. "You smell like a pussy hound."

"Fuck you," Buddy said, laughing.

Chapter Eight

Two steps down at the back of a rambling house, the den at Bob's was a room of dark paneling and a long wall of books. Soft pools of light spilled from a pair of table lamps, picking out the red and blue arabesques of a Turkish carpet beneath a leather sofa and matching armchairs. A spotlight washed a dark painting over the fireplace with light. It captured a snowy-haired woman in blue with a Labrador retriever at her side, its muzzle resting in her lap. The wraparound windows were shadowed with the silhouette of night-dark banana leaves close against the house.

In one of the oversized armchairs, legs in a V-shaped tuck, sat a slim young blonde in a black pencil skirt and scarlet blouse. One hand held a pinkish cocktail, the other a swizzle stick resting against her bottom lip. Carol was smiling at something Damien was saying from the sofa to her right. Debonair in off-white chinos and a brown linen jacket, he fondled a large pineapple-shaped Ronson table lighter in one hand, the other smoothing his perfectly cut head of reddish-brown hair. Carol and Damien weren't alone. Leaning against the bookcase were two college boys and on a matching sofa opposite Damien sat another couple in their mid-twenties. Beneath the portrait on the fireplace wall, with one arm resting on the mantle, Cullen Mosley stood talking with his artist friend. Damien leaned toward Carol about to resume his story when he noticed Bob standing with Larry and Buddy in the doorway.

Clapping his hands twice, Bob raised his voice. "Attention, you heathens. Another delightful couple for your amusement. Damien? Introductions, *s'il vous plaît*. Pardon me everyone. Denise is screaming like a harridan in the kitchen."

"Good to see you both," Damien said, rising from the sofa. He turned to the others in the room. "Everyone, Larry MacDuff and his friend Buddy Hebert." He introduced the others in the room, before turning back to Larry and Buddy. "What can I get you to drink?"

"Beer, please," Larry answered. "Any kind is fine."

"Yeah, beer for me if you have it," Buddy said.

They followed Damien to a bar in the back corner where he took two bottles of Heineken from a small refrigerator near the floor.

"Come join Carol and me," he said, aiming them back to the others.

Buddy was about to sit down when he hesitated. "Back in a second," he said to Larry, and went over to the fireplace where Cullen Mosley and his friend stood.

"Hey, man. How's it going?" he said, shaking Cullen's hand.

"Good to see you, Buddy. You remember Freddy."

He shook Freddy's hand. "Small world, huh? Didn't know you knew Bob."

"We got to know each other in senior year, had a couple of classes together." Cullen looked around Buddy toward Larry. "Guess you're glad your friend is back. He looks different."

"Larry, yeah. The Army beefed him up some. Unfortunately, he'll be shipping out soon."

"Vietnam?"

Buddy nodded.

"You still building houses?"

"Still at it. What about you?"

"Gulf States Utilities. Been there a little over a year now."

"Freddy, you're an artist, right?"

"When the work is there. Excuse me, anybody want another drink? Cullen?"

"I'm good." Cullen said. When Freddy stepped away, he leaned in to Buddy, "I'm glad we're friends now."

"We worked things out, didn't we?" He clapped Cullen on the shoulder. "We'll talk later." Before stepping away, he added more quietly. "You're looking damn good, Cullen."

Carol was between Larry and Damien, all three of them laughing at something. His eyes fastened on Larry, Damien's attraction would have been clear to a blind man. Larry was wearing a red polo shirt that was once not so tight across his chest, and a pair of khakis with beat up brown desert boots he'd had forever. He tipped a cigarette from his pack and before it reached his mouth, Damien was there with the Ronson. Carol laid a hand on Larry's wrist and asked if she could have one of his cigarettes. He shook one out for her and seeing Buddy, handed the pack to him. Buddy settled on the arm of the sofa next to Larry.

"What's this record playing?" Larry asked about the music in the background.

"Chet Baker," Damien answered. "From his 1954 album, *Chet Baker Sings*. You like it?"

"I do. Love the trumpet."

"Same. Chet Baker started out with Charlie Parker playing West Coast Jazz."

"Cool."

Bob came into the room with Denise, a long-necked woman in her twenties with a coiffed helmet of black hair and bright red fingernails. She was balancing a large serving platter, setting it in the center of the coffee table.

Damien caught Larry's suspicious look, eyeing the tray of canapés. "Denise calls it fish, though I suspect it's more in the line of a mystery paste on raw spinach," he said, too quietly for Denise to hear.

Looking sharp in a tailored black suit, Bob rapped on the table. "Help yourselves to the canapés, everyone. The fish roe and fresh tuna is Denise's recipe *extraordinaire*."

"I could kill for a martini," he muttered, heading to the bar.

Wanting another beer, Buddy got up to follow Bob, and leaning over, putting his face in Larry's hair, asked if he wanted a beer.

Bob was shaking a silver canister at the bar. "Martini?"

Buddy held up the empty beer bottle. "You have another couple of these?"

"In the refrigerator below the bar."

"To you and Larry," Bob said, clinking his glass gently against Buddy's beer bottle. After a sip, he reached a hand to Buddy's shoulder-length hair, running his fingers through it. "Gorgeous hair. Prince Valiant with a better barber."

"Did you lock your parents in their bedroom?"

"They're off to Dallas for some business thing."

Damien was talking to Freddy and Carol had inched closer to Larry, their heads huddled in conversation. Buddy slipped the bottle of beer into his hand and went to find the bathroom, the woman named Patrice pointing him to a door at the end of the hall. When he returned to the den, Larry was still in close conversation with Carol and he wandered over to the bookcase. Running his finger over the titles at eye level, he overheard the two guys he remembered as Stanley and Kurt in a quiet argument. "Get over it, will you?" one of them whispered.

Buddy edged away along the bookcase.

"See something you like?" Freddy said from nearby.

"I'm not a big reader. Think the last book I read from beginning to end was the one called *City of Night*, a couple of years ago."

"Yeah, I read that one."

"This is going to sound crazy, but I feel like I owe you."

"How's that?"

"Cullen used to beat up on me in high school. A lot of teasing, always calling me a fag. But then he stopped all that and from what he told me later, you had something to do with making him see things in a different light."

"He did the same with me. Just one more mixed-up kid scared of what he was feeling. Carol over there is about to eat your friend up." Freddy added, looking over Buddy's shoulder.

Buddy glanced at Carol and smiled. "Yeah, I noticed. I think he likes a bit of that once in a while."

"Another drink? Something stronger?"

"Sure. Why not?"

Buddy sat in one of the armchairs, a box on the coffee table catching his attention. He recognized it was teakwood, beautifully made, and he turned it over in his hands studying it. Lifting the top, he saw it was filled with cigarettes. He lit one and leaned back, attention turned to the music. "Bob, what's this record?"

"Maybe Charlie Parker? Damien can tell you the album. He's our permanent music director for all gatherings, he brought the LPs from home. Something makes me think his roommates are Nelson Riddle and Max Steiner."

Freddy passed a drink over Buddy's shoulder. "Thanks," Buddy said.

Bob leaned down to Buddy. "If you're starving, Cullen and Damien are in the kitchen making peanut butter and jelly sandwiches. Damien claims he's allergic to Denise's food inventions."

The words barely out of Bob's mouth, Damien and Cullen came in carrying a platter stacked with peanut butter and grape jelly triangles. Damien sat on the arm of the sofa beside Larry. "Go powder your nose, girl," he told Carol and extended the platter to Larry.

"Watch this," Buddy told Bob.

Larry ate one of the small sandwiches, nodded thanks to Damien and before the platter could be moved away, ate two more. When Damien moved to put the platter down, Larry grabbed another triangle. Damien looked over at Bob and Buddy and deadpanned. "I love a man with an appetite for fine dining."

Buddy got up, moving to sit beside Larry. "Hey. You good?"

"Yeah. What's that?" he said, taking Buddy's glass for a sip. "Vodka? I'll have one of those."

Larry started to get up but Damien put a hand on his shoulder. "I'll get it."

From the sofa opposite, Bob spoke in Carol's ear. "Damien is in lust."

She looked at Bob blankly. "You think?"

Damien passed a vodka on the rocks to Larry but before he stepped away, Larry grabbed his hand. "Sit down and tell me about this album that's playing."

Sitting on the sofa arm and turning an ear to the music, he shared what he knew about what was playing. "It's tenor saxophonist Coleman Hawkins on a 1957 album titled *The Hawk Flies High*. This track, the fourth, I think, is a number called "Laura" from a Gene Tierney movie of the same name. It's been recorded by dozens of different artists, the best known probably Frank Sinatra. Would you like to see the liner notes?"

"They couldn't tell me much more, I don't think." Larry said, amazed at the scope of Damien's answer. He leaned his head against Buddy's. "Crazy about this music and crazy about you, RWH."

"Mm."

"So, Damien," Larry said turning back to him. "What do you do in real life?"

Picking a speck of imaginary lint off Larry's shoulder, brushing his hand down Larry's arm, he answered. "I slave the hours away in the archives at LSU's music library. Graduate work in music history with the occasional article in *High Fidelity* or one of the jazz monthlies. I had a piece in *Downbeat* last month on the moldy fig jazz musicians of 1945."

"Our jazz savant," Bob moaned.

"Moldy fig?"

"Odd name, yes, but a handful of swing musicians reluctant to accept bebop as the new jazz."

"What's your last name?"

"Marsleigh."

"I'll keep my eye out for your name in the magazines."

"I'm honored," Damian said.

Stanley and Kurt had settled their argument and appeared to be back in love. Bob looked over at them. "Stanley, you and Kurt come and join the party."

They came over, Stanley sitting in the big armchair, Kurt perching on the arm.

"Did you try Denise's canapés, Stanley?" Bob asked. "Cullen and Damien made some peanut butter and jelly if you prefer that."

Stanley fed one of the PB&J sandwiches to Kurt, taking a canapé for himself.

"Stanley is in med school, specializing in gynecology. How's that for a mad choice?" Bob tittered.

"Oh, Bob if you only knew." Looking around at everyone, Stanley went on. "My boorish father insisted. I guess he thought it might cure me, but to be perfectly honest if I have to study the anatomy of one more snatch, I might lose my mind. Sorry Carol, but I know you understand."

"Oh, I study mine all the time," she countered.

Larry got up, saying he was going to find the bathroom and Damien busied himself with the uneaten PB&J

sandwiches. He moved them to the tray with the canapés and, taking the empty plate and three beer bottles, headed to the kitchen. He quickly left the plate and bottles on a kitchen counter and glancing back toward the den, continued to the end of the hall and knocked softly on the bathroom door, turning the knob and opening the door a couple of inches. Larry was washing his hands at the sink.

"Larry, can I come in for a second?"

"Sure," Larry said, drying his hands.

The two looked at one another through a short silence before Damien leaned in, kissing Larry, holding it for several seconds with Larry making no motion to stop it. Damien tilted his eyes to Larry's, his mouth still close.

"Is there a chance I could see you again?" His breath fanned across Larry's lips.

For several beats Larry was silent, studying Damien's face. "I like you, Damien, but I've always been with Buddy." He reached a hand up, brushing his fingers against Damien's face. The disappointment he saw there was clear and trying to find a way through the difficult situation, he opted for a half-lie. "It's always been just Buddy for me. I'm sorry. Anyway, I'll be shipping out in two days."

Eyes widening, Damien nodded once.

"Come on, let's go back to the party," Larry said, pulling Damien to him and kissing him briefly. "Go on. You first."

Back in the den, Larry found Buddy sleeping, head resting on the sofa back while the others talked quietly around him. He tugged on a lock of Buddy's long hair. "Let's go home, Buddy."

Bob and Damien walked out to the Woody with them. Just before Larry got in the car, Damien spoke quietly. "Take care of yourself, Larry. You come home."

Chapter Nine

The Central Highlands of Vietnam in March was a season of hot temperatures and mostly dry days. Ordinarily, in a place where he wouldn't step on a bouncing betty or get his head shot off, Larry would be enjoying the weather in nothing heavier than a T-shirt and fatigues. But now, driving on Route 19, two and a half klicks outside the base camp perimeter, he was hot, sweaty, and scared shitless in a flak vest and helmet. A team of four from the maintenance hangar was delivering a new ride to a squad of men stranded in a busted troop truck. It was a hundred yards ahead of them.

He was driving a tow truck rigged with a .50 caliber machine gun, manned by Perk, a twenty-one-year-old PV2 from Lime Sink, Georgia. Behind them in the replacement truck were two more Big Red One infantrymen protecting Larry's cherry ass outside the wire. The stalled truck was transporting a squad of men to a small artillery base on a hill ten klicks farther up the road. Larry pulled up behind the busted truck, walking around to the driver's side, and motioned the other truck to pull up beside him.

Larry was less than a week in-country, this was his first time outside the wire as a target in Charlie's hunting ground. Even with a squad of Big Red One infantry at his elbow, Perk in back with the .50, and the Colt .45 1911 on his belt, he was close to squirting in his pants from the fear of men in black pajamas with AKs suddenly appearing out of nowhere. The whole area was hardcore Viet Cong territory. The mountains around An Khê were blanketed by thick jungle, an ideal sanctuary for the VC's constantly mobile guerrilla warfare.

He had arrived at Camp Radcliff the Sunday before. Located in the Central Highlands smack in the middle of Vietnam, it was a huge green and brown cluster of men and equipment and the largest helicopter base in the world with the 1st Cavalry's four hundred-plus helicopters. A bowl-shaped depression inside a twenty-six-kilometer perimeter, they called the airfield the Golf Course for its grass landing field. It was protected by seven rows of concertina wire and watchtowers every fifty meters. Larry had been given a pamphlet at charm school his first day in Vietnam, one called, "Soldier's Guide to Vietnam." He learned quickly what was and wasn't dangerous at Camp Radcliff and shit outside the wire was definitely the dangerous part.

He looked up at the driver of the busted truck, half-hidden behind a cloud of cigarette smoke. "I'm from mechanics, brought you a new truck. Quick as you and the men transfer over, you're ready to roll."

"What are you, about sixteen? You got somebody watching your ass, cherry?"

"Yes, sir," Larry said, nervously adding, "Perk on the .50 just behind me, and two more set up in the bush on either side."

"Can the chatter soldier and get on with it," the driver said, getting out of the truck.

The squad was in the new truck in under a minute and the driver goosed the engine, leaving Larry in a cloud of acrid exhaust.

"Ain't that a motherfucker?" Perk said, looking down from his perch on the .50, smiling at Larry and fanning the smoke from his face.

"Let's get this truck hooked up," Larry replied, climbing in the tow truck.

Back on base at the maintenance hangar, Larry initiated a delivery form for the truck and his sergeant, the shop foreman, told them they were done for the day.

"You two back here at 0700 tomorrow. Got that?"

"Yes, sir."

Perk and Larry walked half a klick before making a right and going another ninety meters. Walking beside him, Larry noticed for the first time Perk's distinctive smell. Nothing disagreeable, just an individual scent more male than anything else. For all he knew, part of it was the smell of Vietnam, a lush mixture of jungle and diesel and sweat and cigarette smoke. Perk had been at Camp Radcliff for six months and was a big fan of Vietnamese food, especially the fishy noodles Larry had seen him eating at lunch.

Larry had been assigned the empty bunk in Perk's hooch when he got to Radcliff. Two other guys shared the hooch, a white guy, Rolly, and a second Black guy, Dwayne, both of them mechanics. Larry hardly ever saw them at the hangar. They worked on the big, armored vehicles. Perk wasn't a mechanic, but a grunt with Big Red One whose job was to guard dog mechanics outside the wire.

Larry felt better after a shower and change of fatigues, though it was still more than ninety degrees, humidity over the top. One of Perk's tapes was blasting Martha and the Vandellas' "Dancing in the Streets" while Perk dug around under Larry's bunk.

"What are you looking for?" he asked, climbing over Perk.

He was the new guy and didn't have much, nothing to take up space, and Perk had filled some of the space under Larry's bunk with his overflow. Rolly had a couple of pictures of country singers over his bunk and a portable radio that played AFVN when Perk didn't have Motown punching out the decibels. The radio usually woke everyone up with Cronauer's *Dawn Busters* show and his shouted drawl, "Goooooood morning, Vietnam!" Perk hated it, his first words every morning were "Turn that shit off, Rolly."

Dwayne was a quiet man, up before the others, sitting in the doorway where the light was good, reading his Bible. He was the oldest at twenty-two and what people call a gentle giant. He kept a big stack of car magazines no one was allowed to touch.

After he got another tape going, Perk tossed Larry a can of warm beer and turned his attention to rolling a joint.

Growing up in the deep South, before basic training, Larry had never had much contact with Black people. In basic he slept among seventeen Black guys, eating together, showering together, and training side by side. Close proximity never bothered him like it did some. Claude Burrell and Malcolm Calder were Black soldiers he became friends with during those weeks, and he was sorry they went in separate directions after basic.

In his few days at Camp Radcliff, Perk was always

around. Perk liked a good time, liked to joke around in the maintenance hangar, always smiling about something, willing to pass Larry tools when he was working on an engine. He became something else outside the wire when riding that .50 in the back. Quiet, focused on the terrain, unsmiling, with a dangerous glint in his eyes, he was in guard dog mode and ready to unleash hell.

"Try this, my man," Perk said, offering Larry a joint for the first time.

"I've never smoked marijuana before."

"Damn, boy. You really are a cherry. Go on an' fire it up, take a hit. Ain't gon' kill you."

The smell was strong, and Larry took a drag like he would off one of his Luckies. The second it hit his lungs he started coughing. He grabbed the warm beer out of instinct, the other three laughing and Perk slapping him on the back. "Ease up, Mac. Hit it a little easier first time around."

When Larry got his breath back, Perk passed the joint to him. "Little bit now."

Halfway through the joint Larry noticed the music had a softness he could feel and everything around him was brighter, more colorful. Perk said something he didn't hear all of, but it made him giggle. He was across a cable spool table from Larry wearing nothing but a pair of white jockeys and his dog tags. Larry had seen that a dozen times in basic but the lighter skin of the shirtless Perk was newly fascinating, the color of coffee with cream, his wiry frame made of lean, hard muscle with a tattoo just below his throat that said *Hired Gun*. He had perfect white teeth and his hair was a neat black cap of tight wiry curls. Larry hadn't noticed it before but sitting across from him in a haze of smoke, he saw Perk's left eye twitched at times.

"You ain't saying nothing over there, Mac. You cool?" Perk's voice came to him from what he thought was a long way off, but he was right there, leaning across the table and looking at Larry.

"Everything is cool. Never better," he said in a voice he didn't recognize.

"You're just high, boot. Lay back and dig it." Perk went on with the business of cleaning his .44.

Maybe an hour later, maybe ten minutes, someone yelled above the Marvin Gaye music. "Yo, Perk! You and the cherry want something to eat?"

"Mac, you hungry?" Perk asked, shaking Larry's foot.

"Fuck, yeah. I'm starving."

Rolly was standing over him. "What do you want? We got beans and dicks or beans and motherfuckers."

"What'd he say?" Larry asked, leaning toward Perk.

"Wha'dya wanna eat? Hot dogs and beans or lima beans and ham?"

"Sorry, Rolly. Can I have some lima beans and... whatever?"

Walking away, Rolly tossed back a comment. "He's stoned out his mind, Perk."

Climbing over the table and sitting beside Larry, Perk reassured him. "Don't worry about Rolly. He don't smoke weed." He slipped a joint in Larry's mouth. "Sip on this."

He smoked the joint, ate the lima beans and ham and asked Perk what was for dessert. Perk dug around under his bunk and passed Larry a can of sliced peaches.

"Best damn peaches I ever had," Larry said, swallowing the last one.

"The weed got something to do with that."

"You got any cigarettes?"

He rummaged on the spool table and uncovered a pack of Kools, passing it to Larry. He was still working on his .44, gently rubbing it with a soft cloth that smelled of gun oil.

"Where'd you get that pistol?" Larry asked.

"Bought it off one of them Green Beret motherfuckas."

"Can I shoot it? Next time we're outside the wire?"

"Yeah, but ain't no need to go outside the wire. Got a range just up the road." Perk looked at him, turning Larry's head with a big hand and looking at his eyes. "About ten minutes you gon' shut down. You want another beer?"

"I'm good. You got any Pat Boone tapes?"

Perk looked at him closely, Larry watching the slow build of a smile before he cracked up.

****

At Radcliff, Larry worked with a team of officers and mechanics maintaining combat and administrative vehicles that numbered around one hundred and twenty. The job description was simple. Keep the Army rolling. All the vehicles at An Khê ran hard and fast over rugged ground and there were always too many needing repair or maintenance to stay ahead of demand. It was hard, dirty work that kept Larry in the rear for the most part, but there were always days when a recovery operation put his ass in Charlie's sights. Maybe once or twice a week in the beginning, but that increased the longer he was there. Most days he worked in the maintenance hangar with a dozen other grease monkeys doing fuel system maintenance or repair, replacing brakes, rewiring electrical systems, and a lot of times knocking dents out of trucks and Jeeps.

At the moment he was under what they called a Gama Goat, replacing the worn wheel bearings that were making it shake on the road bad enough to rattle teeth. A one-and-a-quarter ton six-wheel drive, semi-amphibious off-road vehicle, the Goat could bull through any kind of terrain. It looked like a huge beast with a mashed in face that could hit ninety kph on smooth ground but was hard to handle, and in amphibious situations it required a trained driver. A test drive around the hangar that morning was like riding a bucking horse. Loose and worn wheel bearings were making the steering even harder than usual. There was also the problem of low oil in the gear box, plus a broken hood hinge. Goats were prone to these problems from the pounding they took on the rough and wet terrain.

Done with the wheel bearings and the oil for the gear box, Larry was replacing the hinge on the hood when Sergeant Rodriguez came out. "MacDuff, how long you going to diddle with that Goat? I need you to run out to the perimeter and rescue some asshole who drove his Jeep onto a pile of cinder block. Take Perk with you." He shoved a camp map at Larry that was marked with the location of the Jeep. "Take one of the tow trucks."

Walking out to the truck, Larry gave Perk the map who studied it and told Larry to go left out of the hangar gate. He might have been lost without Perk, the camp roads still not solid in his head.

"Go straight out to the wire until you see the watchtower. Make a right there. After you make the right, count four watchtowers and the Jeep should be maybe a hundred feet past that." he said, tracing a finger along the perimeter line on the map,

"Got it." Larry lit a cigarette, passing the pack to Perk.

"You supposed to fix the Jeep or haul it back to the hangar?"

"Have to see what condition it's in."

The crippled Jeep was canted up off the ground on a big stack of cinder blocks. Nearby was a structure of half-built walls, a team of grunts at work, and a red-faced sergeant fuming at Larry and Perk to get that goddamn Jeep off his fucking cinder blocks. Larry backed the truck up to the Jeep and hooked it up, pulling it off the blocks and watching it bounce a couple of times coming down but rolling away smoothly from the pissed off sergeant. No sign of the Jeep's driver. Wherever he was, he'd be in the shithouse for wrecking the Jeep.

"You ever ate any eel, Mac?" Perk asked when they were underway.

"No, man. Why?"

"I got a hankering for a bowl of eels. That mama-san, the one that makes those noodles I like, she cooks them eels up real good. I'm gon' get some of that for you." Perk was pulling on the almost goatee just under his chin, staring out the window at the helicopters buzzing like bees over the landing field. Larry's stomach turned over at the thought of those mama-san eels. No matter, Perk had a way. At some point, he would force Larry into eating one of those things.

When he pulled into the hangar with the Jeep, Sergeant Rodriguez had him stow it in back with the dozen or so other vehicles waiting for repair. He slapped a sticker on the driver's seat identifying where and who it belonged to.

Larry finished replacing the hood hinge on the Goat and the sergeant told him to drop off the just serviced M718 ambulance at the hospital. "You and Perk take off after delivering the 718," he said, turning back to his office. "Get on that Jeep you brought in at 0700 tomorrow."

After dropping off the meat wagon, he and Perk walked past an area where they were changing out the shit-cans in a latrine, the air foul with the smell of diesel gas, jet fuel, and burning shit. A pall of black smoke partially obscured a shirtless grunt stirring one of the fifty-five-gallon drums. Larry pulled the collar of his T-shirt over his mouth and nose, disgusted by the smell.

"You ain't been on shit detail yet, but I guaran-fuck-ing-tee it's in your future, my man," Perk said, lighting one of his Kools. "Nasty piece of business."

"How do you get singled out for that?"

"Fuck up," Perk said. "Maybe not this week or the next. But it's gon' happen."

They got past the bad air and were about to turn right toward the hooch when looking down the road to the left, Perk spoke up, pointing. "Hold up, man. Look yonder. That's my mama-san and her Howard Johnsons pushcart."

He started off toward the old woman, Larry reluctantly following.

"Come on, let's see what she's got."

"God help me," Larry mumbled to himself.

Perk got his face right down in the different pots of whatever the mama-san was hawking, talking to himself about the look or delicious smell of something. He found what he was hoping for and asked the woman for one bowl of eels and another of the fish noodles. On a plank shelf rigged to the front of her pushcart were some bottles filled with sauce or seasoning. Perk motioned to the old woman to open a bottle. She pulled a cork out of a one bottle and held it up to Larry's nose. He reeled backward, almost knocking over a tiny Vietnamese man who scampered away, laughing at him. Perk was doubled over laughing while the mama-san looked at him with a toothless grin.

"You want some of that armpit sauce on your noodles, Mac?"

They walked back to the hooch with the two bowls of food, Larry thinking he could 'accidentally' drop his bowl of eels. Perk told him the nasty sauce was called *nuoc nam* and made from fermented raw fish. It was an acquired taste, he said, once you got over it smelling like a garbage truck that ran over a skunk at the fish cannery.

It was Larry's favorite time of the day. A little past seven, work was done and he was fresh from a cold shower that felt good and did a fine job of washing the mud off. He was naked on his bunk. Smoking and sipping on another of Perk's warm beers and picturing Buddy shirtless on a ladder hammering nails into the studs of a half-built house. He would have stayed another year in Vietnam for one hour with Buddy in the back of the Woody at the drive-in. It had only been ten days since leaving home and saying goodbye for the second time.

That day at the junkyard in Denham Springs came back to him. He smiled at the memory of Toby, the boner he had from his girly magazine and the old white pit bull called Curly. Buddy, sweaty in the truck driving home. That sawdusty smell of him. Pulling his thoughts back to the present, head propped on an elbow, Larry watched Perk set out the Vietnamese food he'd bought, wiping and arranging the always messy spool table like a girlfriend was coming for supper.

"Mac, you ready for some of mama-san's special chow?" He lit a pinch of C-4 under one bowl, and then the other. From the heat of the pea-sized pieces, tendrils of steam rose off the noodles and the eels, coaxing from the bowls what Larry admitted was a tantalizing aroma.

"Put some shorts on, man. I don't wanna look at your junk while I'm eating." he said, glancing at Larry in his bunk,

"Still can't get over the smell of that sauce," Larry said, staring down into the bowl of eels.

"None here, man. I love this food, but I won't touch that sauce."

"I've never seen you in the mess hall."

"I go a couple times a week. They got some good food over there. We can go there for breakfast in the morning, if you wanna. Thing I don't like is, eating over there too much and not out humping in the bush makes a man fat."

"You spent much time in the bush, Perk?"

"Done my share of it. No fucking picnic." In a quieter

voice, he continued. "Had the blood of buddies all on me." He reached over and dipped into a spoonful of Larry's untouched eels. "Be glad you're here, Mac," he said,

Larry tried a couple of bites of the eel but couldn't get past the thought of eating water snakes. He finally pushed the bowl over to Perk.

"Ain't you hungry? What are you gon' eat?"

"I'll have a can of beans and dicks," he said, smiling at the wacky soldier slang.

"I got a can of chocolate cake I been holding back. Maybe even a can of chocolate pudding. Little bit later we'll fire up a reefer and build up a hankering for all that chocolate."

"Sounds like a banquet to me," Larry said, falling back against the beanbag chair.

Later, he was near sleep when an explosion less than forty meters away shook the hooch. Larry's eyes flew open and the heavy patter of debris peppered the roof of the hooch, pieces of it falling in his hair.

"Mortar! Get your ass up!" Perk screamed. He dragged Larry outside and around the back of the hooch, sirens going off in every direction as they sprinted in a crouch to a shipping container a short distance away. They dove through the open door and landed against a dozen other men huddled with arms over their heads, as another dozen crowded into the container behind them. The explosions continued pummeling the camp, the giant metal box shaking with the force of each mortar shell. Larry lay trembling in the darkness, pulled against Perk's chest in a fetal curl.

Two dozen or more grunts hunkered inside the container-bunker until the all clear. From the look of his sheltering compadres, Larry wasn't the only one with a bad case of the shakes. He held onto Perk's arm until he found his legs. After the sirens, it was eerily quiet until an answering barrage from camp artillery lit up the distant tree line where the mortar fire had come from. Larry stood in the road in front of the hooch with hands over his ears, watching the distant barrage.

"I need a cigarette," he mumbled to Perk, when the earth settled.

"I got something better than that," Perk answered.

Victor Charles had lobbed a hundred and nineteen mortar rounds into the base camp. Seven soldiers were dead and eighty-three injured. Sixty-seven of the Air Cav's helicopters were damaged. In those thirty minutes of bombardment, Larry had learned what helplessness was like, and the noise of exploding mortars would be forever embedded in his brain.

Chapter Ten

It was raining, and he was outside the wire again, Perk riding the .50 in back. After six weeks in-country, Larry knew not to distract him with talk, just to let him do his thing. The Jeep's storage well was packed with oil and his bag of tools. Sergeant Rodriquez had gotten a radio call asking for help with a troop truck out on Route 19 carrying a squad of grunts in from a small firebase eight klicks out. The M715 had a bad oil leak and was burning up its engine. The driver had used up his stock of reserve oil and the truck's engine was close to seizing up, stalled in Indian country. In his few weeks at An Khê, Larry had already learned that the Kaiser Jeep truck had its problems, and guzzling oil was at the top of the list. Smart drivers didn't go far in the M715 without a case of oil in the back.

Coming around a curve in the road, they sighted the truck up ahead. Perk told him to slow it to a crawl, he didn't like the stretch of road they were on. "This a bad spot, partner. Take us in real slow unless I tell you to stomp on it. And put that fucking helmet on."

"Big Red is set up just inside the bush on our left, twenty feet this side of the truck," Perk said quietly. "Put us past them, same side, ten feet off the rear of the truck."

Larry stopped where Perk had indicated.

"Tell me you're wearing that vest, Mac." Perk growled.

"Yep." He lifted the case of oil out of the Jeep and carried it to the truck, putting it down beside the right front tire and going back for his tools. Through the window he signaled the driver to pop the hood.

A hand came down on his shoulder and someone was speaking in his ear. "Stay this side of the truck as much as you can, but get to pouring that oil, soldier."

He put eight quarts in and lifted the box with the remaining oil into the passenger side of the truck. "Don't go anywhere. I'll be under your truck for a little bit," Larry said to the driver. Dragging his tool bag under with him, he fished out a piece of Bazooka bubble gum and popped it in his mouth. It was easy to see where the oil was leaking from and Larry wiped it as clean as he could, holding the rag tightly over the leak until the bubble gum was soft in his mouth. Tearing off a six-inch strip of green tape and sticking it to his chest, he took the rag from the leak and pressed the bubble gum hard against it, quickly wrapping the strip of tape around it.

"Once we're inside the wire follow me to the maintenance hangar," he called out to the driver and jumped back in the Jeep, shaking his burned fingers and making a three-point turn.

Three guys from the Big Red squad were hustling out of the bush and running for the truck. Two of them jumped in but the third said something to his squad leader and turning, ran for the Jeep and made a leap into the seat beside Larry.

Larry looked over into the face of Julian Bentley.

"Get this Jeep moving, Mac!" Perk yelled.

Juli punched him on the arm and, looking back at Perk, shouted at him. "Hey, gunner. Thanks for the cover."

Juli and Larry looked at one another, slapping, smiling and laughing. Finally Juli yelled into the wind. "You got a smoke?"

He never took his eyes off Larry until they pulled into the hangar, the truck limping in behind them. "Gimme a second," Juli said. He hopped out and went to talk with his squad leader.

Larry was still in the Jeep staring at Juli and Perk stepped up beside him. "Long lost buddy?"

"Yeah, it's my friend from boot camp. Juli. Julian Bentley." He was still staring when Juli came back to the Jeep. "Juli, this is my sidekick, Perk. Perk watches my flank."

They bumped fists, both saying *Big Red* at the same time.

"Can you hang here for a while? I gotta work but the sarge won't mind you being here," Larry said to Juli.

The rest of Juli's squad, along with the driver, had already gone and Sergeant Rodriquez came out, yelling at him. "MacDuff, get that fucking truck outta the way. Take it in back."

They walked back to the hooch in the drizzle, slowly with little talk, mostly just Juli and him looking back and forth at one another. Larry studied his dirty face with its scant unshaven red bristles, hair longer than he'd ever seen it, and those big ears now crusted with dirt.

"That's a funky smell you got going, Bentley," Larry said.

Juli gave Larry a playful shove. "Fuck you, MacDuff."

"What do you hear from Prudy? She writing nasty letters to you?"

"No, man. She wrote me one time and bailed. Said bye, couldn't handle the distance."

"That's cold. Sorry."

"It's cool." He reached over and clamped Larry's neck with his left hand, shaking him gently.

That hand was the first touch since Fort Polk five months ago and the warmth of it ran down Larry's back and legs like a trickle of hot oil. It was killing him to keep his hands off Juli, fantasizing about something that couldn't happen now. The paradox was still there, tormenting him one minute with yearnings for Buddy and Juli the next. Now Juli was beside him again and Buddy nine thousand miles away. Less than an hour with Juli, and already he was overcome by feelings of guilt.

The hooch was empty. Juli found the shower out back and stripped down, standing for a moment in front of Larry, his arms, chest, and stomach sunburned, ending at a line just below his navel. Larry's eyes wandered over him and unable to stop himself, he ran his hand across Juli's chest and down his stomach, stopping at his navel. Stepping back, he dug out a pair of shorts, fatigues, a T-shirt and a towel, passing them over. "Go wash the bush off."

Juli came back toweling his head, and Perk, rolling a joint at the spool table, looked up. "Damn, brother. You look like you come through the car wash."

"Yeah, feels good, too. Any Q-tips around?"

Larry fished a box from his locker and tossed it to Juli. Looking down and seeing his beat-up feet, he passed him some foot powder and a clean pair of socks. While he was in the shower Larry had cleaned his boots and put some polish on them, soaking the laces in a mess pan full of soapy water.

Perk handed him a can of beer, passing over the lit joint and Juli fell back onto the beanbag chair, sighing like a man pulled from the fire. He took a hit on the joint and passed it to Larry.

"You hungry? Wanna walk over to the mess hall?"

"Later. Lemme chill for a while."

"How long's your stand-down?" Perk asked.

Juli shrugged. "Don't know. Two weeks maybe. How'd you get this cushy job in camp, man?" He was rubbing powder into his feet, picking at the blisters and calluses.

"Did my time humpin' the boonies," Perk said. "They pulled my ass out, afraid I might frag that lame ass FNG lieutenant. He was the third one. I don't know how Charlie never got that dumb motherfucka."

Juli was asleep, the can of beer tipping over in his hand. Larry reached over and stood it on the table. Perk stared at Juli sleeping. "I know the feeling. He might not wake up 'til tomorrow."

"You mind if he bunks on the floor? He can use my sleeping bag."

"That's cool, Mac. Let the man sleep."

"What about Rolly and Dwayne?"

"What about 'em? Fuck 'em if they don't like it," Perk said, passing Larry the joint. He pulled a T-shirt on over his head and said he was going to buy cigarettes. "You want anything?"

Larry pulled some MPCs from under his mattress and passed them over. "Get me two cartons of Luckies. Use the rest for beer."

He picked up Juli's bush clothes and stuffed them in his laundry bag, along with the other clothes from his ruck. The hooch girl would be by the next day for laundry. With a clean wet rag he wiped the inside of Juli's boots before rinsing the laces in clean water, wringing them out and restringing them in the boots. He sprinkled foot powder in each boot, working it in with his hand.

Larry looked down at Juli sleeping against the beanbag chair, ears now shiny clean, his face freshly shaved and smooth. He traced a finger down Juli's cheek and stopping at his mouth, pushed a finger gently between his lips and wiped a drop of drool from the corner of his mouth. The memory of the night they'd spent on bivouac in Tigerland lived inside him, as fresh as if it had happened only an hour ago. He knew the feel of Juli's hands and the warmth of his breath against his face, knew the sounds he made when tired, hurting or sleepy. Larry left him to sleep and climbed onto his bunk forcing down the hardness in his fatigues.

Rolly and Dwayne were back, raising a clamor ducking down into the hooch. Seeing Juli asleep on the floor they went silent before seeing Larry. "Who's this guy?" Rolly asked.

Larry sat up on an elbow. "Buddy of mine from basic. Juli, he's Big Red. In from six weeks in the boonies."

Rolly looked down at Juli with a blank face and big Dwayne took a step closer.

"Welcome, brother," Dwayne said to the sleeping Juli.

"So he's bunking here?" Rolly said.

"If he feels like it," Perk said, appearing behind Rolly in the doorway. He stepped past them, handing two cartons of Luckies to Larry. He looked down at Juli. "Come on, Mac. Let's you and me wrestle his skinny ass up on your rack so we can do our thang here at the table."

He grabbed Juli's ankles, Larry hooked his hands under his arms, and they lifted him easily onto Larry's bunk. Juli never stirred.

"Ain't no way we coulda done that in the bush without him snapping awake, swiping a Ka-Bar at the nearest throat," Perk said, as the three of them sat around the table. He blew a smoke ring, spearing it with his finger. "Head's in a good place now, sleeping it off."

"Y'all been to the mess hall?" Larry asked Dwayne.

"Yeah, same old thing. Roast beef, mashed 'taters, chocolate milk and chocolate pie."

"I'm gonna go get me some of that." He stood up looking over his shoulder at Juli. "He's down for the count."

Larry sat with a couple of guys he knew from the hangar and ate his fill of roast beef and mashed potatoes. Later he walked over to the officer's club and went around to the window in back and bought three burgers for Juli. It was twilight, everything was mostly in silhouette when he spotted Perk's Vietnamese weed man coming his way, making for the gate before dark. When he got close, Larry signaled him over to a less visible spot off the road and pantomimed smoking. He pulled a twist of newspaper out of a pocket and held up two fingers. Larry passed him the money and tucked the weed in his pocket.

Sam Cooke's "A Change Is Gonna Come" was playing at low volume when he sat down across from Perk and dropped the twist of paper on the table. Juli was still asleep on Larry's bunk.

"What? You run into my man on the way?"

"Yeah, but he don't know me. Might have sold me some crap."

"Pass me them rolling papers," Perk said, untwisting the paper.

He lit a joint, took a hit. "Naw, it's his usual good stuff." He passed the joint across. Cocking an ear to the music, he mouthed the words Cooke was singing. "Sam made this record only a few months before a woman shot him dead. Thirty-three years old."

"You ever heard any of Chet Baker? Plays the trumpet, sings. Not anything like this. Jazz. My friend back home calls it cool jazz. Says Baker played with Charlie Parker in the 50s."

"If he played with Bird, he can't be no slouch."

****

It wasn't long past sunrise when Larry woke in his sleeping bag, eyes going straight to his bunk and seeing it was empty. The loneliness hit him like a punch to the gut, Juli was gone again. Sitting up, he saw that Rolly and Dwayne had already left for the maintenance hangar. Perk's bunk was empty as well. He rolled the sleeping bag up and stuffed it under his bunk and went out back to brush his teeth and splash water on his face. As he was about to leave for the hangar, Juli stepped inside the hooch and kickstarted Larry's heart.

Juli nudged him back inside, standing close against

him. "I stole your bunk." His face was inches from Larry's. "And you cleaned my boots, gave me clean clothes."

"Yeah, it's cool." He didn't say *I'd give you anything*, which was the thought running through his head.

"Talked to my squad leader. I have three weeks minimum stand-down time. Do what I fucking want." He pressed closer against Larry. "Know what I want?"

Larry shook his head.

"I wanna hang out with a Louisiana boy. If your hooch buddies wouldn't mind me crashing on your floor."

"Fuck 'em. I'll beat all three of them down if I have to."

"Missed you, buddy." Juli whispered, just an inch away. He quickly stepped back. "Get your gear, let's go."

Juli said he was going to ask Sergeant Rodriguez if he could hang out at maintenance and ride shotgun when needed. "It's okay on my end. Like me, your buddy Perk is Big Red, so I'm thinking the sergeant won't mind one more." He leaned in closer. "Nobody's gonna guard your ass like me."

Larry nodded, smiling inside. "So much for standing down."

"How come we never connected before yesterday, both of us here at An Khê?" he said, as they passed through the gate to the hangar.

Juli shrugged. "Big place, a lot of soldiers here. Like a small city. Plus, I been out in the bush a lot of the time. Us meeting up yesterday was meant to be."

Juli went to Sergeant Rodriguez's office and Larry looked at the posted worksheet, finding his name next to a two-and-a-half-ton cargo truck, an M35A2. A deuce and a half. He'd seen them, studied them, ridden in them, but had never worked on one. This one was in the house for transmission trouble. It was going to be a long day if he was rebuilding a 5-speed manual transmission with a divorced 2-speed transfer case, a ball-breaking job.

Out back, the truck's transmission was bad, noisy, and popping out of gear, but Larry got it back to the hangar, pulling into an open bay at the opposite end from the office. Juli would have to find him.

A quick check of the fluid and the filter, no problems there. Under the truck, he took the ring gear and flywheel out and right off saw the teeth on the flywheel were badly worn. Replacing the flywheel wasn't quick, but it wouldn't take all day. Could have been worse.

Still under the truck, something made Larry think of his dad. He couldn't remember a whole lot about him but knew he too had been a mechanic, had worked at the Buick dealership before walking out of their lives. Sometimes it felt like yesterday, a familiar taste in Larry's mouth.

One day Larry had been playing alone on the front steps. His dad pulled up to the house, leaving a woman crouched low in the front seat. He came up the walk, his face different from usual, but he grabbed Larry up, tossing him in the air and catching him under his skinny arms. "There's my kangaroo!"

Ruffling his hair, his dad looked at him, his forehead wrinkled, then set Larry down on the steps. He took a deep breath before going into the house. Larry returned to his game, eyes on the woman in the car, seeing only the top of her head. Mom shouted something in the house and his dad came banging out the door. Brushing Larry's head with a hand for the last time, he got in the car and said something to the woman. Larry was five years old, standing on the steps watching him drive away, never understanding why his dad always called him kangaroo.

Shaking his head to clear the memory, he rolled out from under the truck and saw Juli leaning against the wall, smoking a cigarette. "Rodriquez would have your ass if he you saw you smoking in here."

"What's he gonna do? Send me to Vietnam?" Juli said, eyes wide and wiggling his hands in the air. He tapped the cigarette against the bottom of his boot and field-stripped it, dropping the remains out the window behind him.

"What'd he say?"

"Said he could use my help when Perk and Troutman were out riding shotgun."

"You tell him you're my designated guard dog?"

"I'll work that out with Perk." He ruffled his T-shirt a few times, fanning air against his stomach and pointed to the creeper. "What's that thing called? I always wondered."

"A creeper."

"You do your thing and I'm gonna go huddle with Perk and Troutman." He gave Larry a whack on the shoulder and walked off but turned back with a sly grin. "I'll collect on your poker debt later."

Larry dropped the ring gear and flywheel on a worktable, recalling their poker nights at Fort Polk and thinking that was a debt he couldn't wait to pay off.

Chapter Eleven

Over the seven months since Buddy had first spent a night at Larry's apartment in Hundred Oaks, he had begun, little by little, spending more nights there. Earl told him not to worry, he was always welcome. It was a place away from home, a constant reminder of Larry, the rooms full of memories where the bulk of Larry's clothes still sat folded in the dresser or hung in the closet. Earl was never the problem, but after his third or fourth night at the apartment, he began catching appraising looks from the old lady, Mrs. Clemens.

At the breakfast table one morning, getting what Larry had once called the gimlet eye, he devised a way to catch her alone, thanking her warmly for breakfast on the several times she had fed him and slipping twenty dollars into her apron pocket. Buddy renewed his bribe every second or third week and that solved the problem. It became their secret, Mrs. Clemens even going as far as asking what Buddy preferred for breakfast after a third twenty had slipped into her hand. Before long, Buddy was a welcome guest at her breakfast table.

That went on until Buddy made the decision to find his own apartment. By then his parents had become used to his nights away from home and were not surprised to hear he was looking for his own place downtown. He was still working for Mr. Hargrove and earning good money, most of it sat growing in a bank account. Driving on St. Louis Street one day, he spotted a for rent sign in front of an old Victorian house and pulled over to check the telephone number on the sign.

Two days later, the owner met Buddy at the house to show him the apartment. The house, he learned, had just been renovated. They had divided the upstairs into two apartments, the downstairs becoming one apartment, the largest with a higher rent. They went around to the back, the owner pointing out the garage before leading Buddy through a back door opening into the kitchen. There was a front room looking out onto the street and two bedrooms, front and back with the bathroom between them. Buddy's eyes widened in excitement, asking what the monthly rent was and when he could move in. He had stumbled onto the perfect place, and for a bargain, and he quickly agreed to return the next day to sign a lease and pay first and last month's rent.

By noon on Friday he had signed the lease, becoming the first tenant at 222 St. Louis Street, a tall house built in 1920, not more than a hundred yards behind the Old State Capitol. That afternoon he made an appointment for the phone company to come out and put a telephone in. He called his boss and asked for Monday off, giving him time to get water and utility accounts set up.

On Sunday morning, a shiny new key in his pocket, he asked his mother and father to follow him downtown, saying he wanted to show them something. At the house, he led them to the front door, slipping the key into the lock.

"Buddy, whose house is this?" his mother asked.

"It belongs to Mr. Laurens," he said. "Mr. Otis Laurens." Opening the door, he ushered them inside. He let them look around for a minute before surprising both. "I rented the downstairs. Signed a lease on Friday."

His mother turned quickly, her mouth open. "Are you pulling my leg, Buddy?"

"No, ma'am. It's mine. At least the first floor and the garage. Hundred a month. You think it's worth that?"

Neither of his parents answered, leaving him standing in the front room while they ventured deeper into the other rooms. A minute later he heard his mother in the front bedroom. "It's all so clean."

Buddy joined his parents, explaining that the whole house had just been renovated, the carpenters not long finished and gone. "Mr. Laurens said it was fine if I wanted to do any additional carpentry in the place. I'm thinking I might replace the kitchen cabinets." Opening the back door and pointing out the garage, he told them his plan to make it his workshop.

He was locking the front door when his father spoke. "Mother and I are happy for you, son. It's a grand apartment. Let's have a bite of lunch at the Piccadilly."

His mother hugged him long and hard before they got back in the car.

****

On Monday, he was at the office of Gulf States Utilities arranging for the power to be turned on at the apartment. Standing at one of the counters while filling out a form, someone bumped him from behind. Looking over his shoulder he was surprised to see Cullen Mosley, this time dressed up in a shirt and tie, no less. Once more Buddy was taken aback by this strikingly handsome Cullen who two years before he'd never looked at twice.

"You just keep on surprising me. What's with the tie?" Buddy said, smiling at him.

"The job requires it. What are you doing here?"

Holding up the half-completed form, Buddy explained. "I rented an apartment downtown and I need to get the power turned on."

"Let me help you with that. Come on, follow me," he said, taking the form from Buddy.

Cullen gestured to a chair. "Have a seat." Sitting at the desk beside the chair, he went through the form quickly, asking Buddy a few questions about himself and the property where he needed service. It was all done in ten minutes. Cullen rubber stamped the form and gave Buddy a receipt showing the day and time the utilities man would be there.

Their business done, Buddy made a move to stand but something in Cullen's eyes held him to the chair. For a few beats, their eyes locked. Buddy told himself, *fuck it.* Glancing about to be sure no one was within earshot, he spoke quietly. "If you're not busy, maybe you could come to the address yourself after work today. Check it out, make sure everything is in order."

"I could do that. Five thirty okay?"

"Perfect. See you then."

Along with no water or power, the St. Louis Street apartment was also empty of furniture, with not so much as a chair or a footstool. It had four bare rooms and a temporarily useless bath, with curtain-less windows open to the street. None of that was enough to quell the hardness in Buddy's jeans as he stood at the front door looking out, thinking it must be close to five thirty, his mind spinning on what Cullen looked like beneath that shirt and tie. And then Cullen was turning into the driveway. Mouth dry, Buddy watched him get out of his car and walk to the front porch. Buddy opened the door as Cullen came up the steps, motioning him inside.

"I forgot my clipboard." Cullen quipped, loosening his tie.

Buddy had no answer to that, instead stepping up and kissing Cullen hard on the mouth. He grabbed Cullen's tie, pulling it off and quickly unbuttoning his shirt. In under a minute their clothes were scattered as two horny, impatient and grasping men wrestled one another to the floor.

Breathing hard, Buddy pulled back from Cullen. "I could show you the bedroom."

"You sure you wanna take it that far?"

They both laughed at that.

"Yeah, pretty sure." Buddy huffed.

"Fuck, Hebert. You've grown," Cullen said, eyes and hands on Buddy's chest.

Sometime later, they were still tangled together, both gasping for breath and slick with sweat."I want a cigarette," Cullen said.

Buddy got up, fished a pack of Newports and his lighter from his jeans, then returned to Cullen's side.

"Thanks." Cullen propped himself against Buddy, smoking.

Reaching for his jeans, Buddy turned up a cuff, telling Cullen to put his ashes there.

"Why now?" Cullen asked.

"Why what?"

He waved an arm to encompass the picture of them bare-assed on the floor among a scatter of clothes. "This. Why did it take so long?"

"I honestly never thought it would happen. Last time we bumped into one another, it was at the Pastime, remember? It hit me then for the first time. Then I saw you today at Gulf States and…it was all I could think about when we were sitting at your desk."

"First time I ever saw you at Alan Shepard High School I got a hard-on."

"Yeah? Then how come you were always such a hard ass? I thought you fucking hated me." He play-slapped Cullen on the chin. "But then you finally told me after that fight you had with Dutch Reinholtz."

"Yeah, I was scared and angry about the feelings I was hiding. It was Freddy who helped me work through all that." His hand trailing down Buddy's stomach, Cullen added. "I fantasized about this for a long time."

On their backs, staring up at the ceiling, their talk dwindled until Cullen asked, studying Buddy's lighter. "Your initials? I get the H—"

"Robert William."

He looked at Buddy for a moment, grabbed a handful of his hair and pulled Buddy's mouth against his. "Where'd Buddy come from?"

"Nickname from when I was a little kid."

Another look and he turned the lighter over. "What about LPM?"

"That's Larry."

Buddy didn't want to talk about Larry, pushing thoughts of him away. When it was happening with Cullen, it hit him like a punch that he was an unfaithful asshole, struggling to hold Larry at bay, a damning thought while he was fucking another guy.

He slipped the lighter from Cullen's hand and dropped it on the floor. He rolled onto Cullen, losing himself, rutting on a bare floor with a beautiful someone not named Larry.

He woke with Cullen's arm across his chest, no idea of the time. It was pitch black inside and out. They had been on the floor who knew how long. A little longer, he thought, reaching over to caress the tempting ass only inches from his hand. Cullen was a first-rate surprise, his lovemaking was at times tense but fun, openminded, gentle and affectionate, and then also a little scary.

He had expanded Buddy's sexual horizons in more ways than one, and in the process made Buddy come like a racehorse. He very definitely wanted more, telling himself to get Cullen's phone number. They might even manage a bed next time. It occurred to him that Cullen may have had his own guilt trip about fucking around, as Buddy was pretty sure Freddy was still out there. Still, he had a feeling he could entice Cullen back to St. Louis Street one of these days or nights.

When the morning sun brought a wave of glare through the windows, Buddy pulled himself to his feet and retrieved the towel he had brought in from the truck, wondering what good it was after the fact. He roused Cullen, passing him the towel and reminding him there was no water. Cullen tossed the towel aside and grabbed for Buddy, his morning hard-on reaching, hungry for more.

Kissing Cullen briefly, Buddy said he had to find some coffee and get to work.

"Shit. What time is it?"

Buddy shrugged, sending Cullen to scramble for his khakis, digging for the watch in his pocket. "Almost seven," he said, climbing back on Buddy and mumbling into his neck. "Two more hours."

"Less for me, I'm afraid. Come on, get up. We can meet again later today."

With a bedraggled Cullen in his car, Buddy asked for his phone number at the Gulf States office and promised he would call later. Buddy locked up and left the apartment minutes later, heading for the Toddle House to fill his thermos and drive to his job site in Jefferson Place, mind dopey, body drained.

Chapter Twelve

It was late September, the tail end of the rainy season in the Central Highlands, but Friday brought another day of hard rain, with dark clouds hovering over a watery muddle of bush and shortened sightlines. A little past 0700, Sergeant Rodriguez called Larry, along with Perk, Troutman, and Juli into his office. Ordnance had called requesting help in red balling an ammo re-up to a small firebase five klicks northwest off Highway 19.

It was not normally a job for the mechanics hangar, but with the hard rain, supply choppers were grounded and supply was in a bind. Soldiers needed ammo. Contact with Charlie was a possibility, but Rodriguez said MacDuff was his wheel man on this one. Access to the drop point was just over six klicks north on the highway, on a trail wide enough for a mule, or M274, a four-wheel drive vehicle weighing under a thousand pounds and able to carry a half-ton. With four men fully armed with M16s and extra clips, the .50 caliber machine gun, and twelve cans of M16 ammo, the package would be just under the mule's weight limit. The ammo was on its way from supply and the sergeant told them to saddle up.

They studied the map showing the route as a basic L-shape, north and west, a few curves on the long leg. Once they entered the access trail, the curves became four klicks of twists and squiggles. Perk was on the .50 positioned to Larry's right. Troutman was behind Perk, watching the rear and Juli was behind Larry. All of them were in camo paint. Visibility on the highway was no more than fifteen meters in any direction, the rain creating a shape-shifting curtain in every direction. Sight would be further reduced by half once they entered the trail heading west.

At the trail access point, Juli said in Larry's ear to make the turn, get them about sixty meters off the highway and stop. "Me and Trout are gonna look around. You lie flat, locked and loaded 'til we come back. Perk will stay with you on the .50."

He and Troutman slipped quietly into the bush, one on either side of the trail. Larry was flat on the bed of the mule, his M16 clutched to his chest, rain pounding his face, mind racing about what basic and teamwork training was all about. But this was a real fucking fire zone, he and his buddies, back-to-back, locked and loaded.

Troutman reappeared, giving the all clear. An anxious wait passed and Juli slipped out of the brush like a camo-painted ghost. Larry moved them forward deeper into the bush, Juli again at his neck.

"Watch the trail for anything not right. Close eye on the margins."

It was wide enough for the mule to pass clear of any brush, but close enough that most of the time, the tires raked against waist-high grass. At the first turn in the trail, Juli signaled Larry to stop, and once more disappeared into the trees to scout the curve ahead. Reappearing on the trail ten meters in front of the mule, he motioned them forward.

It took over an hour to reach a point on the trail where two grunts from the firebase rose from a clump of tall grass signaling the okay. Eight others were hidden in the trees around them. They'd gotten a radio message of the ammo's ETA and had come out to meet them. Their squad leader was a lean sergeant with a saturnine face and sad eyes. The name tape on his jacket said *Ridley*. He checked the boxes of ammo and looked at the four of them. "Any of you spare some smokes, we'd appreciate it."

The four passed over their cigarettes.

From one of the packs Ridley shook out a cigarette and lit up, passing the cigarette packs to a man behind him. "Ninety meters up the trail is a turnaround to get you back out." Eyes scanning the tree line to their right, he signaled three of his men to grab the ammo cans.

"Charlie keeping you busy out in this neck of the woods?" Perk asked the squad leader.

"Had a little bump and run with a handful of 'em three days ago." He raked the ash off his cigarette with a finger, saying, "Radio call earlier saying a company of NVA regulars is poking around nearby. Don't want none of that." One more scan of the far tree line and he waved a hand, moving off into the tall grass. "Thanks for the smokes."

Five steps into the grass, a shitstorm of AK fire took Ridley and the man closest to him down. One round pinged off the safety railing beside Larry's left knee and an instant later Juli pulled him to the ground on the far side of the mule, spinning to help Perk swing the .50 off the mule. Without pause, Perk set up on the ground using the mule for cover, shredding the trees where the fire was coming from. Juli, Trout and Larry poured M16 fire into the trees as well. Trout took a hit from one of the AKs, creasing his thigh two inches below his groin. He struggled out of his jacket, slicing off one of the sleeves and tying it tightly around the bleeding leg.

Larry was sitting with his back against the left front wheel, gulping air through the heavy rain, slamming a fresh clip into his M16. Above the clatter of gunfire and clunk of bullets smacking into the mule, Juli screamed, "Incoming!" and a grenade from the VC's thumper exploded four meters out from the mule. A stab of heat tore at Larry's left hip, knocking him flat, the scream rising from his throat cut off by Perk's big hand clamped over his mouth, words soft in Larry's ear. "Don't let the fuckers know, brother. Suck it up."

It was pure adrenaline that guided his right hand across his body to pull a hot chunk of shrapnel out of his hip. He gave a long low, grinding moan as he pressed his left hand over the wound, staring up into Perk's face.

"Where are you hit?" Juli said, crawling over to Larry.

"Left hip."

"Hold still. Lemme get a look." Juli's fingers scrabbled at Larry hip. "Motherfucker," he mumbled, bringing his face closer and ripping at the tear in Larry's fatigues. Seeing the bloody mess, Juli removed his jacket and vest, tearing his T-shirt off and folding it into a square that he clamped against Larry's hip, pressing hard. "You're bleeding like a stuck pig. Shrapnel?"

Larry nodded, pointing to the triangular piece of metal he had dropped on the ground.

"Aren't you the fucking John Wayne? Keep pressure on that hip." Juli said, juggling the still-hot piece of shrapnel in his hand.

From the trees, Charlie was increasing his fire but getting

a barrage of return fire from the depleted squad of men on the far side of the tall grass. They saw the grass being jostled where the squad leader and his man went down in the first burst of AK fire. Meanwhile, Larry's eyes were roving over the mule looking for damage. From his position, Perk told him the right front tire was blown, and Trout called from his end that the right rear was gone as well.

"Then our ride home is fucked," Larry said to the other three.

"I guarantee you Big Red over yonder has already called for backup. Just a matter of time."

"Meanwhile, we gotta get out of this box we're in. Through that tall grass or straight up this trail," Juli said, studying the map spread on the ground. "Either way, we need to work our way to the highway."

Mortar fire was ripping up the tall grass and trees beyond, an explosion sending a body cartwheeling into the air above the grass. Debris from the last mortar was still falling when a line of figures in khaki emerged from the trees advancing on the trail, the mule, and the squad of Big Red in the grass and trees. Perk counted thirty of them before shouting out. "Move! *Didi mao!*" He sprinted up the trail, the .50 against his chest, Juli, Larry and Trout close on his heels.

Half a klick west on the trail, the four turned south, losing themselves in thick jungle. Trout was managing with the leg wound and Larry was keeping up with a still-bleeding hip, his left leg down to his boot soaked dark with blood. The ongoing rain made progress difficult both underfoot and in the line of vision. Movement was slow and uncertain, each of them navigating the thick growth on a hair trigger.

Juli whispered to Perk. "Trout and Larry need to rest."

Perk nodded, turning one eye to scout for a spot that would hide them from sight. Another half klick and he pointed to a dark culvert-like opening under a ledge of rock. It was not completely hidden but well camouflaged by the branches of a fallen tree. He sent Juli with Trout and Larry to get them situated under the rock and hidden as well as possible. Leaving the .50 with Juli and taking Trout's 12-gauge shotgun, he disappeared in the dense green to scout the area.

Larry was drinking from a canteen, and was startled by Juli, who leapt three feet to the other side of him, falling to the ground and waving a hand at a snake slithering from a spot near where he had been sitting. "That's one of those two-step fuckers. He bites and you're dead in two steps." Larry had never seen Juli scared of anything.

Perk was back, saying he had circled the spot they were in and not seen anything but trees, bush and rain. He tilted the canteen up, but before drinking told his buddies who'd attacked them. "That was NVA back there."

Juli asked him, "You seen any action with them before?"

"Nope. All my run-ins been with the VC 'til now. Can't say I'm anxious to get to know these boys any better."

"When I finish with all this shit, the only time I'm leaving the house is to stock up on more King Bourbon. Fuck it all." Trout said, his voice barely above a whisper.

The rain slackened and they sat listening to the water drip from everything around them. Juli was peeing against a slab of rock when from above they caught the soft sing-song of Vietnamese. In the silence that followed, they aimed an arc of weapons outward from under the ledge of rocks, Juli whispering through gritted teeth. "Come get some, motherfuckers."

They all heard the sound of a footfall, someone scrabbling down to the entrance of their hiding place.

And there they were, two small men in khaki NVA uniforms and pith helmets, AK-47s pointed straight at the four Americans.

In a pure jungle-hardened reaction to threat, without thought, Perk let loose with the .50 from two meters away and Larry watched two men disintegrate before his eyes, blood and flesh spiraling outward. There was a deadened silence before a third man appeared out of the pink mist, shooting Trout in the throat before Juli reacted and put two rounds into the man's head.

Trout's look was of total surprise, eyes wide, the blood gurgling in his throat like beer poured from a bottle, the barrel of his M16 slowly tilting to the ground. Unable to move, Larry saw the green of his friend's eyes replaced by the glassy sheen of death. Perk knelt at Trout's side, hand gripping his arm and shaking with soundless sobs. Juli climbed from under the rocky ledge empty-handed, and stood looking into the jungle around him, his rain wet face wearing a look of being forever lost.

Two hours later, a squad from Radcliff found them. There was little talk. Friend and brother, Private Second Class, Marvin Troutman was going home tits up, and from Staff Sergeant Ridley's squad, three were dead and another going home half what he was the day before. Larry was at the base hospital, the doctor saying he should stay overnight. But Larry insisted he was fine, he just needed some sleep. He left woozy on painkillers, clutching a bag of Darvon with Juli's hand on his shoulder.

The doc had given him a tetanus shot and sewn him up with a dozen stitches in his hip, the painkiller reducing it to little more than a dull ache. A driver from the maintenance hangar came and drove them back to the hooch. Larry's face, like Juli's, was slack with loss and exhaustion.

Digging into the bag of Darvon, Larry swallowed two of the pills on top of the shot, holding out another two to Juli. Juli popped them in his mouth, crunching them up like candy.

Below where the doctor had cleaned and stitched the hip wound, Larry's leg was still half covered in dried blood. Juli wet a towel and cleaned the blood off as Larry sat on his bunk, the two of them silent, unsure of everything.

"Give me a towel," Larry said hoarsely.

Juli held out the towel he had used to clean Larry's leg, but Larry waved it off. "Not that one, another one."

From a locker Juli took another towel, passing it to him. Larry scrubbed his hair roughly with the towel, continuing until Juli held his arm. "What are you doing? What's wrong?"

"I have to get it out."

"What is it, Larry?"

"It's in my hair. Help me get it out." He scrubbed his hair again with the towel.

"Tell me what you have to get out."

"The two men Perk shot. It's in my hair, their blood."

"Okay. We'll get it out. But stop Larry, stop."

"Did you see Trout's face?"

"Yeah, I saw Trout's face. I saw it all. Stop. I can't talk about it. Can't replay that fucking carnage in all its detail. Let it go, Larry. Only way to get through this is to remove yourself, or your head at least from all the goddamn slaughter."

Perk, Rolly and Dwayne had already left for the maintenance hangar when Juli got up early the next morning. He stood gazing for a while out at the road and then woke Larry, asking how he felt. He was groggy and Juli studied the bandage on his hip, peeling back the tape and lifting one edge to see the row of stitches. Satisfied that it looked okay, he resealed the tape and laid a hand on Larry's chest. "You'll get through this, Larry. You have to. It's the 'Nam and we're in the middle of it. It don't mean nothing."

Chapter Thirteen

Larry was late getting to the hangar, and not seeing his name on the day's work schedule, went to Sergeant Rodriquez's office. The sergeant told him to take the day off, rest up. Wandering around the hangar for a while and not wanting to go back to the hooch, Larry got on one of the forklifts and began hauling the stacked crates out by the gate to the warehouse. On his third trip, Rodriguez saw him on the forklift and, shaking his head, handed over a list with the crates and where they should go. Eleven crates of replacement parts needed to be stored according to the sergeant's precise floor plan of what went where.

With Juli hanging off the forklift's overhead bar, Larry was maneuvering a crate into a slot far in a back corner, the rows of stacked crates creating a warren of pathways wide enough for the forklift in and out. For anyone unfamiliar with the floorplan, getting lost among the rows and stacks wasn't hard to do.

Larry lined up the crate on the forklift even with a stack. Juli swung around onto the arms of the lift and slid the new crate into place on top. He jumped to the floor, and looking at the top crate, verified it was in the right place by checking the number on the floor.

He looked up at Larry in the driver's seat. "Come down here and doublecheck if we have it in the right spot."

Larry killed the engine and stepped down, limping over to where Juli stood, looking up at the crate just put in place. "That's cool. It matches the list and the floorplan."

Juli turned his head in a three sixty to see where they were. The quietness around them was total. He nudged Larry against a high stack of crates, bringing his mouth against his. It was the first time they had ever kissed. Biting gently at Larry's lip, a hand gripping his head, he pulled Larry hard against him. Larry's legs trembled with the sudden reality of what he had dreamed about for seven months. "You think we're okay here? I can't hear anyone else in this part of the warehouse," Juli said, still against

Larry's mouth.

"We're good," Larry answered, turning Juli to put his back against the crates. He quickly opened Juli's fatigues, pushing them lower. Careful of his hip, he lowered himself to his knees and took Juli's hardness in his mouth. There was a sudden gasp and Larry thought this was a totally new sensation for Juli. At least the half moan, half growl that rose from his throat made him think so. Through it all, Larry could smell him, the soap, the sweat, the oatmeal he'd eaten at breakfast. Juli pushed harder, more urgently, against Larry and at one point Larry lifted a hand to stifle his loud moans.

When it was over, Juli held Larry's head against his stomach for almost a full minute, his chest heaving, his hands caressing Larry's head and face.

Juli kissed him again before reaching inside Larry's fatigues and doing as best he could, what had just been done to him.

All too soon Larry was warning Juli, trying to lift his head but Juli pushed the hands away and when it was over, tilted his head up to look at Larry, his Adam's apple bobbing twice with his swallows.

Larry scanned his face for answers.

"I've thought about you every day since Tigerland," Juli said, his voice barely audible.

Chapter Fourteen

Perk was a short-timer, eighteen days and a wake up. In two days, he was transferring to a firebase sixteen klicks north of Saigon where he would wait for his final orders to board a freedom bird for the world and home.

Eight guys were crowded into the hooch, Perk, Dwayne, Rolly, Juli, Larry, and three other friends from An Khê. Perk punched up The Supremes' "Baby Love" on his cassette player and lighting up a *bong son* bomber, passed it to his friend Nelson, clapping his hands and rolling his hips. Rolly was opening C-rats and setting them on the cable spool table that was already crowded with beer cans and a box of crumbled crackers from a care package Larry had gotten from Buddy's mother the day before.

Juli was racked up on Larry's bunk, eyes closed and nodding to the music, beer can in one hand, joint in the other. Larry was sitting on Perk's bunk eating a Slim Jim from the same care package. He slipped a Darvon out of his pocket, crunching it up and swallowing it with beer. The day he'd caught the shrapnel in his hip was eight weeks gone, but the hip still ached. That was true, but he also liked the pills, and the doc handed them over like they were candy.

Perk was laughing at something Badger was saying. Larry would miss Perk.

"Clarence Perkins, high yella native son of Lime Sink, Georgia," was how he'd introduced himself the first time Larry met him. Perk had been friend and brother to him since the day Larry had showed up at Radcliff, a dumb fuck shaking in his boots. At least two times he'd saved Larry's ass from being turned into chopped meat, and along with Juli there was no one he'd rather have at his back in a tight spot.

It was never a real thing, only a fantasy, but Larry had thoughts about Perk he knew Perk wouldn't be cool with. Sometimes he wondered what it would be like if one night Perk crawled up in Larry's bunk, snuggling against him.

He banged a fist against his left hip, bringing a flare of pain and jarring his thoughts back from the impossible.

Juli appeared at his side, handing Larry his half-smoked Lucky. "You look lonely over here."

"Thinking about Perk." He touched the tip of the Lucky against a callus on his palm and Juli knocked the cigarette away.

"Why do you do that?"

"A little pain never hurts."

He looked at Larry and said nothing.

"Helps me focus. You stopping me means maybe you care."

The look on Juli's face this time was hurt. "Don't you know that already?"

"I'm fucked up."

Juli looked around at the other people in the hooch, watching Nelson shotgun marijuana into Badger's mouth. Turning back to Larry, he studied his face. "I would step in front of a bullet for you."

"That's heavy," Larry replied.

"Better fuckin' believe it."

He looped an arm around Juli's neck and pulled him closer.

Juli took a piece of folded aluminum foil from his pocket. "Got a little something special from my friend Telvis. Wanna give it a try?"

"Okay. What is it?"

"Heroin."

"Whoa, man. That shit's dangerous, no?"

"This little bit ain't gon' hurt you." He unfolded the foil, showing Larry a small heap of white powder. "We smoke it."

He passed Larry a plastic drinking straw cut in half. Sitting at the spool table, he held his lighter under the foil until smoke rose from the heroin. "Suck up the smoke through the straw."

They took turns until there was only a small amount of powder left, which they snorted off the foil. "Now lean back and enjoy the ride," Juli said with that half-smile.

****

With Perk gone, Sergeant Rodriguez worked it out with Juli's captain for him to get duty assignment to the maintenance hangar as a guard dog. With the duty change came a housing order giving him Perk's old bunk in the hooch. Just like basic, Juli and Larry were together every day and night as Larry had hoped for all along. Nothing changed in their days at the hangar. They were safe and sometimes several days went by without leaving the base. There were no more ambushes or shoot-outs like the one two months back. Though it was dumb to think it couldn't happen again.

Larry was servicing a Jeep one morning, nothing more than a tune-up, rotating the tires, simple stuff. He hadn't seen Juli for a couple of hours. He was probably hanging with the other guard dogs somewhere around the hangar. They had a clubhouse in a corner of the warehouse, with several dented metal chairs and shipping crates as tables. It was the one place smoking inside was allowed and where ashtrays sat heaped with butts. One of the mechanics, a guy from New Jersey called Boomer, came over to tell Larry that Sergeant Rodriguez wanted him and Bentley in the office.

Rodriguez was banging on his typewriter. He raised a hand to say hold on, whipping the paper out of the roller and dropping it in a wire basket on his desk. "You two are flying out to a firebase in K'bang, thirty klicks northwest. Tomorrow morning. Delta Company's Goat got shot to shit, needs a lot of work, new parts. A driver will pick you and a parts pallet up at the hangar gate at 0500. Get your ass over to the warehouse and load a pallet with your tools and what you think you'll need. Here's a list of parts I got from the guy on the radio. Forklift it out to the gate." The sergeant relit his cigar and brushed a spark off his shirt. "Be careful and double up on your Deet. A bird will pick you up in seven days, or sooner if you finish before then."

Juli and Larry looked at one another with expressions of excitement and apprehension. For Larry, it was a little more of the latter.

He studied the Goat manual and went over the list of parts Rodriguez had gotten, poring over diagrams of the engine, looking for the components most susceptible to damage from gunfire. He set aside for packing everything on the list and other parts the engine couldn't run without, working his way down to the less essential parts. With Juli's help he got it all wrapped in canvas, loaded on the pallet, and strapped down. He hauled the pallet out to the hangar gate on a forklift, leaving it there with the pallet still on the lift. Back in the office he reported to the sergeant that the parts pallet was parked at the gate and ready to go. Rodriguez ordered Larry and Juli to get some shut eye before returning at 0500 the next morning.

Back at the hooch and alone with Juli, it would be at least a couple of hours before Dwayne and Rolly got back. Even with the place to themselves, it was still risky to fool around, with anyone able to walk unannounced through what was nothing more than a long piece of soft carpet hanging in the doorway. That didn't stop Juli and Larry from falling onto one another. Juli was an accumulation of smells that Larry inhaled hungrily with his mouth as much as his nose. Juli before a shower was Larry's private brand of catnip. As he had once or twice before, Juli again asked about the smell in Larry's hair, but Larry shrugged it off.

He felt bad thinking of Buddy, that somehow it would hurt him to know another guy was asking that question. Despite his love for Buddy, he couldn't resist the redhead from Mandeville who was like a drug in his system and who by that time he had also come to love. Bent over his bunk, a deep moan poured out of Larry when Juli bit his ear and neck, pushing himself inside Larry. He wanted it to last forever. Pushing back hard against Juli, he felt him tremble, growling at the same time, unable to hold back for long. Catching his breath, Juli flipped Larry over, and it was Larry then who couldn't hold back.

Juli showered first, coming back inside the hooch still damp, his body cool and pink. Larry lay back watching him examine his feet, and as was his habit, dusting them with powder and rubbing it between his toes. From Larry's locker he took a pair of clippers and, still naked, sat on the floor to clip his toenails. Larry went to shower, trailing his fingers through Juli's hair as he passed.

When he returned, Juli was on his bunk and Rolly and

Dwayne were back, one listening to the radio, the other reading another of his *Car and Driver* magazines.

"Juli tell you guys we're gonna be upcountry for the next week?"

"What up, Mac?" Dwayne said, looking up from his magazine.

He explained the repair run to K'bang and told Juli to pack his ruck.

"Yeah, I will," Juli answered, staring at the ceiling, one hand toying with his balls.

The four of them went for chow, Dwayne through the line twice, roast beef the first time, ham steak the second. Juli ate a hamburger. Larry leaned against him. "Better eat more than that. Nothing but C-rats for the next week."

Juli shrugged, taking out his cigarettes and getting up. "Meet y'all out front."

Larry finished his roast beef and mashed potatoes, opening the first of two chocolate pudding cups. "Rolly, that radio of yours ever play any jazz?"

"An hour one or two days a week. AFN's got a bunch of stuff. Why I like it."

****

The Huey set them down in a swirl of dust. A lieutenant with two grunts was standing off to the side of the LZ when the helicopter's crane set the pallet of engine parts and Larry's tools on the ground. Larry and Juli jumped off after the pallet. The bird lifted off and disappeared over a hump of green, the thump-thump of its rotor fading quickly. The LT pointed to the shaded work area and a tent where they would bunk. "You need anything, tell anyone you see. They'll find me." And then he was striding off to some grunts digging holes for piss pipes. Larry and Juli began unloading the pallet and humping everything a hundred feet to where a tarpaulin was stretched over four poles to provide shade. The busted Goat was sitting under the tarp.

"Watch your step out by the wire. The perimeter is rigged with claymores." One of the two grunts told them.

Watching him walk off, Juli spit in the dirt. "Fucker

must think we're a couple of cherries."

"Come on. Let's finish unloading." He slapped at a mosquito.

Juli reached up with a thumb, wiping a smear of blood off Larry's cheek and looking at the mashed mosquito on his thumb. "Big fucker, B-58. You take your orange pill?"

"Yeah, and I have the shits." He wondered why K'bang had so many fucking mosquitos in December.

It took an hour to move everything to the shaded area and get it spread out on two poncho liners off to the side of the Goat. Using the pallet and a couple of long poles he'd scrounged from somewhere, Juli set up a tented cover over the engine parts. The boxes were at least partially protected from rain and dust. Larry carried their rucks and weapons over to the tent, nothing more than a couple of old sleeping bags unrolled inside.

Slinging his M16, Juli wandered off for a look around the firebase. Larry watched him stop to talk to a grunt reassembling his .45 and a minute later, they headed out toward the wire. Larry went to work on the Goat, assessing the damage and noting the order of what he had to do. It didn't take long to get a general idea of the job ahead and see that a week would be plenty of time to overhaul the vehicle. They would have some downtime before the chopper came to take them back to An Khê.

He was under the Goat when Juli kicked his boot. He smiled down at Larry when he came out from under the vehicle. "Bet you wish you had your creeper."

"Wouldn't work on this dirt. Where you been?"

He extended a hand and pulled Larry up. "Checking out the sitrep. Could get hairy if Charlie decides to send out a probe or two while we're here. I talked to the LT. He assigned us a spot up at the wire in case we get hit. Nice little foxhole for two. Cozy."

Larry popped a couple of Darvon in his mouth and noticed Juli looking at him. "Doc said the hip bone might be chipped."

"Gimme one."

He quickly swallowed it and ducked inside the tent.

Larry went back to the Goat's engine.

Later that afternoon, a grunt came over with a box of

C-rats and dropped it in front of their tent. He pulled out a cigarette, saying his name. "Murtall." He and Juli bumped fists, with a nod to Larry. "I hear you guys come from Radcliff at An Khê." He squatted beside Juli. "What's a Big Red One doing in mechanics?"

"Thing is, these sissies need protection when they're out in the boonies juggling nuts and bolts."

Larry laughed at that. "It's true. He saved my ass in an ambush not too long ago."

"Always good to have an elite guard slap at these mosquitos for you," Murtall said and laughed.

"Yep." Juli pulled a Slim Jim out of his pocket, cut it into two with his Ka-Bar, and passed half over to Murtall. "What's the LT like?"

"He's no rookie. Second tour." Murtall looked out into the green on the other side of the LZ. "You boys hang easy." He stood up and walked over to the Goat. "You figure you can fix this thing?"

"Oh, yeah."

"Glad to hear it. This ugly beast is a powerful tool out here." He walked off, back to a group of his buddies.

****

They slept in their fatigues, T-shirts, and boots, all exposed skin slathered with Deet bug juice.

On their third day in K'bang, at 0320 the night was ripped by the explosion of a claymore, followed instantly by the stuttering chatter of AK-47s and answering M16s. Juli and Larry leapt up reaching for vests and helmets, grabbing their M16s and spare clips of ammo, and tumbling out of the tent. Juli sprinted, bent at the waist, zigzagging in the direction of their assigned foxhole, Larry hot on his tail. Juli flung himself into the foxhole, Larry landing half on top of him.

"Short bursts! Up and down. You fire from twelve to three, I'll cover nine to twelve!" Juli yelled in Larry's ear.

Black figures moved through the bush, in and out of Larry's gunsight. He alternated with Juli, popping up when Juli was down, down when he was up. To the left a .60 was splintering the trees ahead, the noise a freight train spitting fire and thunder. Juli was slamming another clip in his M16, Larry was firing left to right, semi-auto bursts, seeing little more than fleeting shapes slipping in and out of the shadows. A bolt of pain tore across his right arm, slowing his fire for several beats.

Out of the exploding night a figure appeared, running straight for their foxhole. There was no thought, only an automatic response accelerated by adrenaline. Larry put four shots center mass in the black shape before the body tumbled into the foxhole, landing on top of him. Juli was focused on the broken perimeter to his left, firing in measured bursts. Unbelievably, he was unaware of the body sprawled on top of Larry. From under the body, Larry reached out a hand, clawing at Juli's arm. "Get him off me!"

The firing lessened and in a reverberation of the hellish noise, the lieutenant shouted a cease fire.

From a bloody darkness Larry heard Juli bark, "Jesus!"

After the body was pulled off Larry, Juli gaped at his friend's red-painted face. "You hit?"

"Not my blood," Larry sputtered, spitting out blood and swiping at his face. Shuddering, he rolled the body out of the foxhole and as far away as possible, staring at the face of a boy no more than sixteen, his chest blown apart by Larry's M16.

He turned away, hunching down in the foxhole, trembling, telling himself in the moment that it was war. The result was a shattered boy dead by his hand, his blood painted across Larry's face. He leaned away from Juli, throwing up in the dirt and onto his boots.

Floodlights illuminated the battleground. Half a dozen grunts moved stealthily through the shattered bush twenty meters beyond the perimeter. They counted three dead Vietcong, heaping the bodies inside the perimeter, one soldier rifling the black pajamas and bodies for intel. Or maybe just souvenirs. No dead on the American side, one wounded–Larry nicked on the right arm. He sat outside the lieutenant's tent sipping from a cup of brandy the LT had put in his hand.

"How you holding up, soldier? You did good back

there." The LT put a hand on Larry's helmet before joining his squad leaders in the operations tent. A medic knelt in front of Larry, cleaned up his arm and wrapped it in gauze before squeezing his shoulder and moving on.

Still shaking, he couldn't banish the shiny vacancy of the boy's eyes. A hand brushed across his face and Larry looked up. It was Juli.

"Mosquitos."

Larry touched his knee and in a cracked voice asked for his pills. Juli nodded, moving toward the tent. Back in front of him again, Juli held out a hand with three Darvon tablets. Larry chewed them up, swallowing them with a mouthful of brandy.

"You need some sleep." Juli leaned toward him, speaking in his ear. "You saved my ass."

Larry downed the last of the brandy, put the dented tin cup down as if it were a fragile porcelain teacup, got to his feet and found their tent. Tossing aside the helmet and laying the M16 down carefully, he pulled off his vest and curled up on the sleeping bag, afraid he would see those eyes for the rest of his life.

Larry woke with Juli smearing bug juice on his arms, face, and neck. "Larry, you awake?"

"Mm...what?"

Mouth close to his ear, Juli asked if his hip was hurting.

"Told you, it hurts like a motherfucker."

"The pills help any?"

"A little."

Shrouded beneath the whine of mosquitos, they lay in the blackout of their tent, unmoving until Juli's finger brushed Larry's lips. "My friend Telvis in An Khê, he can get you something for the pain. Better than the pills. If you want."

"Yeah, okay." His arm pulsed. "Hold me, please."

Juli curled against him, arm over Larry's chest, mouth against his neck. Larry felt safe again.

Six days later a bird flew them out of the K'bang firebase. They left the Goat with a fully rebuilt engine and Larry with dreams he didn't want.

In the days after, Juli rarely took his eyes off Larry.

Chapter Fifteen

At 0500, his usual time of Bible reading, Dwayne found Larry standing at the door of the hooch shivering, despite the warm weather. The just risen sun had laid a diagonal of gold across the dirt road and Larry's unseeing eyes were fastened on a puddle of muddy water, glistening in the sunlight. The horrible dream was still roiling in his head, freezing him in place.

In it, he was trying to find his way from the apartment at Earl's to Buddy's house but all the streets were different. He finally found his way there over a bridge, but once inside the house, the rooms were jumbled. Wandering into a misplaced kitchen, he was blocked by the chaos of pots bubbling on the stove and Mrs. Hebert running from cabinet to cabinet flinging open doors searching for something. His mom sat at the kitchen table in her white nurse's dress, broken glass twinkling in her hair, trying to staunch the flow of blood from Juli's head. The kitchen evaporated and he was in Buddy's room, Mr. Hebert shouting outside the window for Larry to hurry out to the garden, the plants were covered in beetles. Standing in the rows of strawberries, Mr. Hebert slapped at him, screaming for him to rip the plants out of the ground. Another turnaround and three of them sat on the porch steps, Larry and Buddy lower down, his father behind them talking about his secretary, Agnes. Larry leaned, whispering *November 16th* in Buddy's ear. That angered Buddy's father and he scolded Larry, telling him to stop talking gibberish and hurry over to Clegg's Nursery for more strawberry plants before they were sold out. Larry ran around to the front and jumped into the Woody but couldn't get it started. When he looked up, Mr. Hebert was standing beside the driver's window crying.

He came back to himself at the touch of a hand on his shoulder. "You okay, Mac?" Dwayne's voice was soft in his ear, but enough to rouse him.

"I had a bad dream. It was…uh, nothing. Thanks,

Dwayne." He moved toward his bunk, stumbling. Dwayne put out a hand to steady him until he found his feet. Looking over at the sleeping Juli, he shivered again at the disturbing image in the dream. Watching him now, there in the dimness of the hootch, his friend looked child-like.

Larry rummaged for his cigarettes and lighter and returned to the doorway. "Dwayne, you mind if I sit here? I won't interfere with your reading. Just want some company."

"I welcome it, brother."

****

It was February, and their last month in Vietnam. Larry and Juli were short and would be going home in March, going back to Louisiana together. They had a week of R&R coming and after talking about it, they settled on the Philippines. Neither of them wanted the bars, prostitutes, and drunken stupor of a week in Bangkok, so they found a small uncrowded island called Boracay that didn't get many tourists in February. It would be a quiet place where they could pass the time, never more than a few feet apart and unbothered by prying eyes. A small, little-known island in the Philippines sounded like paradise.

Sergeant Rodriguez helped them arrange their R&R for the same week. After filing the paperwork, they whooped with elation when permission came through to fly out of Saigon for Manila on a DC-6 leaving in seven days.

On lunch break a few days later, Juli took Larry to meet one of his Big Red buddies. Telvis Hickey was a slim brother with an afro and a goatee.

"Thinking you might help my friend Larry out with something," Juli told him.

Telvis looked at Larry, checking him out and giving Juli a nod. "Step inside, my man. Juli, you hang here at the door, keep them big blues open."

Inside his hooch, Telvis addressed Larry. "What can I do you for?"

"Something for my hip."

"Your hip?"

"Shrapnel. Fucked up my hip bone."

"So, we're talking pain management here?" He looked Larry straight in the eyes.

Larry nodded.

"All kinds of pain in this place. Fuckin' museum of pain," Telvis said, guiding Larry over to his bunk, telling him to have a seat. He turned his back, taking something from a box. Facing Larry again, Telvis held out a small vial of white powder. "You know what this is?"

He shook his head.

"Smack. Heroin." He looked into Larry's eyes again. "It will sure as shit manage that pain you talking about. Onliest thing is, take too much of this stuff and you ain't gon' wake up. You want, I'll give you a taste. If you like it and can handle it, you come on back and we'll do some business."

"I want it."

"Lose that jacket." Telvis turned to the box behind him and took a long strip of rubber from it, a strip cut from an innertube. He wrapped it around Larry's upper arm, twisting it like a tourniquet until a vein in the crook of his arm stood out.

"Watch what I'm doing. Best you learn good."

Telvis emptied the white power into a spoon, adding a few drops of water. He flicked his lighter, holding the flame under the spoon. When the water bubbled, dissolving the powder, he dropped a small ball of cotton into the liquid, sucking the liquid into a syringe through the cotton.

"You ready to step through the gates of heaven?"

He nodded and Telvis lightly rubbed the vein in his arm with a finger before slipping the needle in. A tiny swirl of blood appeared in the syringe as Telvis slowly depressed the plunger. The needle slid out, the rubber strip released, and Larry was falling back on the bunk with every bad thing in Vietnam, in the whole world, lifting off him and vanishing in the clouds above his head. He couldn't move, couldn't speak, could only ascend to a place he never knew existed. Bliss. Top of the world.

"You cool, man?"

Larry lifted a hand to a voice from far, far away and reached out, saluting a shadowy face in the clouds above him. "Yeah, I'm cool. Never fucking better."

Telvis nudged the hand away. "Whoa, now. You ain't gotta be touching me."

"Trying to salute."

Juli came in. "He okay?"

"Look of it, he's a few klicks past okay."

Larry sat up on the bunk feeling like he never thought possible. "Telvis, can I come back in a few days?"

"That'd be cool."

Sarge was being a good guy and lightened the workload on Larry and Juli. Assignments were all simple, quick repairs or servicing, and no trips outside the wire. Juli spent his days playing poker with Quinn and Peplowski, Perk's and Trout's replacements, or hanging out with Larry in the hangar.

Larry went back to Telvis on Friday, the first time since the day Juli introduced them. The effects of the heroin that first time had lasted most of the day. He wanted more.

"I'm leaving on R&R tomorrow, hoping to get enough to cover me for a week. If that's cool."

"It's cool if you got the bread."

"I got it."

He took the same box from under a towel and brought out a plastic bag of fine, pure white powder, scooping some onto a small scale before tipping the powder into a smaller plastic bag.

"Where can I get a syringe?"

"I can sell you one."

"I don't want to take too much. Can I buy one of those vials to measure it out?"

"You don't need that. Look here." He spooned out a small mound of heroin onto a square of glass, and with a razorblade carved out a smaller heap. "See that? Take a good look now. That's how much you use for one time. Get greedy, you get dead."

Telvis took out a new syringe from the box, still in its wrapper. "You gon' need something to carry your works. Best thing is buy an eyeglass case at the PX, one of those hard cases that snaps closed."

****

They left An Khê on Saturday, hitching a ride on a Chinook to Tan Son Nhut in Saigon. By 1400 hours they were in Manila. From there it was a forty-minute flight on an eight-seater plane to Boracay, the plane setting down on a grass runway. A tuk-tuk ferried them two klicks down the beach to a group of small houses on stilts hidden among trees just off the beach, a place called Green's Hotel.

There was not another person in sight. The driver left them on a palm-lined beach, pointing to the hotel's sign faintly visible through the trees.

"Where the fuck is everybody?" Juli said, turning in a circle.

The blue-green water was empty of swimmers and boats, the long beach of powdery white sand stretching away into the distance. They wondered if they were the only ones on the island other than the tuk-tuk driver. They waited, finally hearing a faint voice.

"Hello! Hello! Welcome to Green's." A girl ran toward them from the trees.

"So sorry I come late. Welcome! Please follow me."

She was a pretty girl, not more than eighteen, no doubt a hotel employee. "My name is Amalia. Nice to meet you."

Larry and Juli followed her through the trees and onto a smooth curving path lined with white stones that led to a white Spanish-style house. She ushered them inside to red tile floors and a check-in desk. A fortyish blonde behind the desk smiled at them and whispered *number eight* to the girl. Taking up their rucks, she disappeared among the trees. Larry signed a register, saying they would stay five nights.

"Welcome to Green's. My name is Lotte and I am the proprietor. Please don't hesitate to ask if there's anything I can do to make your stay more comfortable." She had an accent that Larry thought might be German or Swiss.

The girl Amalia returned, asking Larry and Juli to follow her to their room.

The guesthouse was on stilts six feet off the ground,

with steps leading up to a shaded front porch with two rocking chairs. Inside was a large shadowy room with wide plank flooring and a tented ceiling of woven palm fronds. There were windows on three sides, and in the back. Off the main room was a huge bathroom with a toilet, a sink, and shower. White towels stacked on a shelf near the shower were bathed in a beam of sunlight from the window. Against one wall in the main room was a bed bigger than any that either of them had ever seen, and on top of a dresser was a stack of beach towels. Their rucks leaned against the dresser.

A rustling sound from the ceiling of palm fronds drew Larry's attention, and looking up, he saw an iguana at least two feet long. "We have a roommate."

"They don't bite, do they?" Juli said, following his look.

"Don't worry. It is harmless and will not disturb you. Breakfast is served on the patio between eight and ten, lunch from twelve to two, and dinner from seven to nine. If you need ice, please ask at the desk." The girl bowed and retreated through the door.

Juli and Larry looked at one another with growing smiles.

"Are you fucking kidding me? How did you find this place?" Juli said, eyes scanning the room.

Ignoring his question, Larry started pulling off his clothes. Juli took the hint and a minute later they were in the shower. A few swipes of Larry's hand across his chest and Juli looked down at himself with a mischievous laugh.

It was a long shower and after drying off, Juli dropped his towel on the floor and sprawled across the bed with a satisfied groan. It was as though he released the weight of the months of living with mud, heat, mosquitos and gunfire.

Larry dug a small bag out from the bottom of his ruck and took it into the bathroom. Juli appeared in the doorway a moment later, to find Larry with a belt around his arm, cooking up heroin. He was unsure what Juli would say.

He came over, sitting cross-legged in front of Larry. "Your hip hurting?"

Larry nodded.

Juli placed his hands on Larry's ankles and watched him shoot up.

Sinking back against the bathroom wall, the heroin flooded through Larry, a golden river of warm sunlight. It was even better than the first time and he wondered if Juli being so close was the reason.

Juli leaned in, touching his mouth to Larry's. "The look on your face is…I don't know. Do it to me."

"Huh?"

"Shoot me up. Please," he said, studying the look on Larry's face.

"Okay. You sure?"

Juli nodded.

He tied off Juli's arm and carefully measured out the heroin into the spoon. With a few drops of water, it bubbled over the heat of his lighter and he drew it up through a cotton ball into the syringe. Juli tipped his forehead against Larry's as Larry shot him up.

Within moments Juli's face bloomed in a half-smile as he half-collapsed against Larry. "Holy shit."

On the wide bed of expensive white sheets, they touched one another with dreamy slowness, exploring with previously unimagined freedom. In that bed, in that minute, the feeling of Juli was stronger than the drug pumping through Larry's body and he wanted that closeness, the entirety of Juli against him forever. Juli's fingers traced the scar on his hip, pressing gently to see if Larry would wince or pull back before putting his mouth against it. When he nuzzled Larry's balls and ass, Larry wondered again at his easy acquiescence to intimacy with a man. With him. Juli's physical response, his sexual eagerness, always surprised Larry.

Most of the time he thought of Juli as a heterosexual man caught up in his clutches. Whatever his attraction to Larry was, the idea of his one day walking away was something Larry didn't want to think about. Being honest with himself, he loved Buddy Hebert in a way that would never change, but he loved Julian Bentley as well, neither more nor less than Buddy. The problem was how he could manage to keep both without it turning into a bad Hollywood movie, ending with a suicide or two.

Unsteady on dope and lovemaking, they put on swim trunks bought at the Manila airport and ran like wild boys down to the beach.

Looking around at the complete absence of people, Juli stripped off his trunks and ran for the water. A second later, Larry, naked as well, followed him into the warm water of the Sibuyan Sea.

They clung to one another, splashing and rolling over and over like a pair of porpoises. Juli wrapped his legs around Larry's waist pulling Larry's mouth against his, his stiffness rubbing against Larry's stomach. They floated on their backs, fingers entwined. They kissed underwater and swam far out until the bottom fell away and they dog paddled, faces inches apart. Underwater again, they swam with eyes open until they were able to stand in the water chin deep.

"Wrap your legs around my waist."

Juli hung on him, legs clamped around him. With one hand, Larry positioned himself and slowly pushed upward.

"What are you doing?"

"I'm not going to hurt you. Relax, let yourself go and look in my eyes." He eased upward, slowly pushing into Juli until his mouth opened and his eyes closed as Larry gently pushed deeper.

They stayed as still as possible until Juli opened his eyes and settled himself onto Larry, a growl of pleasure rumbling in his throat. With the water's movement, a soft smile bloomed, tweaked by the feel of Larry moving inside him. Buoyed by the water, they swayed, allowing its gentle movement to guide their joined bodies. On the edge, Juli held tighter to Larry, urged him deeper and moaned hoarsely. "Feels so good. Like shooting stars...Larry Mac-Duff."

Drowsing on the beach, Juli drizzled handfuls of sand on Larry's chest and stomach. Larry answered with sprinkled fistfuls on Juli's cock and balls and soon they were wrestling, at the end two sandmen battered in the white powdery stuff. Rinsing off, they walked back to the guesthouse as naked as a pair of primitives, never seeing a soul. After a shower, in beach shorts and T-shirts, they padded barefoot to the torch-lit patio of the big Spanish house.

They drank beer, studied the menu and shared a huge grilled fish with french fries, corn on the cob, and bowls of vanilla ice cream drizzled with Kahlua. The only ones there, they sat for another hour, smoking and sipping Jack Daniels on the rocks.

Lotte, the owner, drifted across the patio to their table. She was German, it turned out, and had discovered the island fifteen years earlier by mere chance. Using her savings, she decided to open a hotel, hiring workers and building the house and the guesthouses on stilts, hiring a staff and putting advertisements in travel magazines.

"It didn't happen overnight but tourists began to trickle in and eventually it became profitable enough." She signaled for Amalia to bring two more drinks. "We have a much larger clientele in the summer months. You young gentlemen wouldn't be able to swim and caper naked in the high season."

Suddenly embarrassed at the thought of being seen, the faces of both Larry and Juli reddened under the torch light.

"But please, please do not let me stop you from your *au naturel* enjoyment. You are welcome to pursue your pleasure at Green's either dressed or undressed, and not think there is anyone to spy or complain."

The two looked at one another and knew they had accidentally landed in fantasyland.

They stretched out on the cool sheets of the big bed that night as moonlight flooded through the windows and painted leafy shadows across their bodies. Too tired for anything more than a linking of fingers, they slipped into their soundest sleep of the past twelve months.

****

After a big bowl of fresh fruit on the patio the next morning, they were off to the water with beach towels. Once again it was a world of sunlight, empty beach and blue-green water. Juli went straight into the water but Larry chose an after-breakfast nap and stretched out on one of the beach towels. Later—no idea of the time—he opened his eyes to see a boy of about nine or ten looking down at him. Turning his head, he saw Juli asleep on a towel beside him, both of them naked as jaybirds. The boy looked coolly down at them.

"You like Co-cola?" he asked. "Orange juice?" A satchel over his shoulder clinked with the movement of his hand. He continued to stare down from under his battered straw hat.

Larry shook Juli's arm. "You want a cola?"

He opened one eye and squinted first at Larry and then at the boy in the straw hat. "Yeah."

"Two," Larry said, tapping Juli's arm. "You bring any money?"

"Uh-uh."

"Wait here," he said to the boy, getting up and running back to the guesthouse. He dug a couple of dollars from his ruck and jogged back to where the kid was waiting. "Here you go."

The boy made change and opened two colas, pouring them into plastic glasses. He passed them over one at a time and then sat on the sand looking out to the water with his legs folded, waiting to get his glasses back.

"What's your name?"

"Ambrosio."

"Cool name. You live around here?"

He pointed off down the beach. He was quiet for a moment before asking in return. "Why no swim pants?"

Larry shrugged. "Comfortable?"

The boy looked at his dick and giggled, shifting his eyes to look at Juli's. "You biggest," he told Larry.

Finished with the soda, Larry handed back the glass. Juli passed his glass to him and putting both back in his satchel, Ambrosio stood. "Goodbye, G.I. Joe." He went off down the beach without a backward glance.

Squinting after the boy, Juli shook his head. "That was weird."

"Let's go up the beach. Lotte said there's a small village not far that way," Larry said, beginning to feel the sting of the sun.

Putting on beach shorts, T-shirts, and flip flops, they took the path under the trees and followed it for half a klick. They came upon some low buildings and a few people, along with a small grocery store, a pharmacy, and a shop that rented bicycles and motorbikes. Three old women sat talking on a bench under a big tree, staring at them like the Martians had arrived. Even with their surprise, the women smiled and waved, one breaking into a wide grin and raising a hand to cover her mouth.

Larry pulled Juli toward the shop that rented motorbikes. "You know how to ride?"

Juli's silence answered the question and Larry asked the man how much to rent a bike.

"Two dollars, one hour."

Larry passed over four dollars, pointing to the bike he wanted, a Kawasaki Catalina 250.

Straddling the bike, he looked at Juli. "Hop on."

The look on Juli's face told Larry he wasn't sure about it but he gingerly climbed on.

"Hold on."

He drove off down the path, Juli's hands at his waist. "Hope you fucking know what you're doing," Juli muttered.

Larry yelled back at him. "You gonna cry, Big Red?"

Once clear of the village, the road ahead empty of people, Larry goosed the bike and it leapt forward, Juli grabbing him tighter.

"Hold on!" Larry yelled back at him.

Juli leaned in and bit Larry on the ear, growling. "I'm gonna get you for this, MacDuff."

Laughing and accelerating, Larry shifted the bike into a higher gear and seeing a gap in the trees, raced through it down to the hard packed sand at the tide line. This far up, the beach was still deserted and he wondered how few people lived on the island.

When he opened the Kawasaki up and they flew along the water's edge, Juli's arms tightened around his chest, but he was silent. Kicking it into second, downshifting and sliding into a turn, Larry jacked the bike up on its rear wheel for a few meters and raced back in the direction of the hotel, Juli's heart hammering against his back. Three klicks past Green's he killed the engine.

They shed their clothes and dived in the water, Juli wrestling Larry under, needing some revenge for the scare

Larry had given him on the bike. They tumbled once more through the clear water, arm throws and tackles, rolling about until they were both hard and wanting something else. Breath coming in heaves, they sprawled in the sand along the waterline, letting the softly rolling surf wash over them.

"You got plans when you get back to Mandeville?" Larry asked, sometime later, his voice barely carrying above the sound of the rippling water.

"I don't know, Larry." Juli hooked two of Larry's fingers. "Maybe Baton Rouge…hanging out with you."

Hearing those words, Juli's breath tickling his ear, Larry's ongoing dilemma flared. Buddy was tearing at one side of his heart, Juli the other. He saw no solution to being emotionally bonded to both men. With the difficulty and uncertainty clawing at him, he jumped up, saying he was going for swim. Before Juli could say anything, he was in the water and swimming underwater away from the beach.

****

Lifting his head to see Larry disappear into the water, Juli, too, wrestled with a tangle of confusing thoughts. He was confused about what was happening to him with this unexpected buddy from Louisiana. He had never known such feelings, had never, until Larry, imagined the things he was doing now. It was hard getting his head around the idea of sex with another guy but one touch from Larry and what the fuck was happening to him? Maybe it had something to do with all they had been through together, first in basic at Tigerland and then in the 'Nam.

A year ago, if anyone had called him a fag, he would have put a boot up their ass. He couldn't even imagine doing with any other guy what he and Larry did. Before the Army, he'd had some good times with Prudy, loved getting into her pants. She was the only girl he'd ever been with and it was never more than twice. He'd wanted more but Prudy had said no.

When he first got to Fort Polk, he thought about Prudy all the time, imagining the sweet taste of her mouth, that first time out by the lake on a patchwork quilt they had spread in the bed of his dad's pickup, the memory of her like a bowl of cream in moonlight. Once he got to Vietnam, Prudy couldn't handle the separation, sent a dear John and all that shit.

Then there was Larry, the battle buddy and that night on bivouac in Tigerland, another time carved in his memory. He was both surprised and embarrassed when Larry's finger circling the boil on his ass had made his dick hard, he worried that Larry would see. It was after that experience that his thoughts about Larry began edging in another direction.

Reconnecting in 'Nam when Larry showed up to repair the stalled truck was another confusing time. The sight of Larry had excited him in a way he hadn't expected. That day in the warehouse had been the first time for them and it had shifted the ground under Juli's feet. Maybe he really was a fag, but if so, he was Larry's fag and no one else's.

Surprising Juli, Larry was back from his swim and flopping down beside his friend. He reached for Juli, making clear what he wanted. And for the next half hour they lost themselves in one another, all thoughts of confusion or uncertainty banished. Clothes back on, they nuzzled briefly before riding back to the rental store.

It was three more days of the same, swimming, eating, fucking, lying in the sun, and thinking about home. On the fifth day, they paid the bill and Lotte called the tuk-tuk man to pick them up. They sat silent on the beach with their rucks, sunburned and uncomfortable in scratchy jeans and boots, both regretting that the experience in Boracay was unlikely to ever be repeated.

"Juli?" Larry knocked a knee against Juli's. "Back in the world...let's find a place to live, someplace we can share."

Juli squeezed his arm, looking at Larry before turning his eyes to the far horizon of that blue-green sea.

Chapter Sixteen

With their senses calmed by the laziness of five days in a watery Garden of Eden, the first experience of downtown Saigon was pinball crazy. They spent eight klicks and thirty-five minutes in a kamikaze taxi from Tan Son Nhut Airport, then they entered a madhouse teeming with buses, trucks, tiny motorcycles, pedicabs, Renault taxis, and bicycles, all zooming helter-skelter down streets with few traffic rules. A loud, teeming city huddled around twists and turns of the Saigon River hit them like an avalanche of shrieking confusion. Beautiful women wafting by on bicycles. A family of six was stacked on a motorbike, the father under all his familial weight guiding a ragged and multi-limbed pyramid through a madhouse maze of people and cars. Military traffic bullied its way down alleys and wide avenues lined with plane trees, the exhaust from too many cars mixing with the hothouse air of two million people. Passage through this heaving mass was an intimidating welcome for two soldiers more accustomed to a dinky dirt road town in the Central Highlands.

The driver let Larry and Juli out at an intersection near Tu Do Street and they scouted the adjacent alleys for a small hotel, eventually finding a place called *Hoa dá*. The room was narrow and stunk of insecticide, useless against the beetles, geckos, ants and cockroaches that wandered unfazed through the room. The bed was lumpy, and somewhere between single and three-quarter. But it would do for two nights, and they were both aware that wartime Vietnam was the bottom of the barrel compared to a quiet paradise in the Philippines.

"What d'ya wanna do? Look around? Find a cold beer, a girl to fuck?" Juli asked.

"The second one sounds good."

Larry went into the tiny bathroom with the bag he used for his works.

Juli's head appeared around the door. "Want me to sit with you?"

"Always." Wrapping the belt around his arm, he pulled Juli against him. "You want a taste?"

"Sure, why not? You first."

Afterwards, on Boulevard Nguyen Hue, they found a sidewalk café and sat at a table, ordering two beers. With the bottles of *Ba Muoi Ba*, the waitress dropped a menu on the table. "I come back."

The menu had translations in English below each item. They studied it, smiling.

"What do you think this is? *It burns the charcoal fire of chicken*," Juli read.

"Who the fuck knows?" Larry said, laughing. "I'm down with *the noodles of the pork*."

"Think the mixed pizza is safe enough?"

The waitress brought two more beers and they ordered the pizza and noodles of the pork. Juli's eyes followed her as she was walking away from the table.

"You like that?" Larry asked.

Juli raised a hand, palm out. "Between you and me, Vietnamese women don't turn me on."

"You never fucked one?"

He shook his head.

Later, the waitress came to take away the lunch plates and they asked for two more beers.

"Hold the fort, man," Larry said, hand against his stomach. "That noodles of the pork is coming back on me." He went looking for the men's room and finding it, he latched the door and leaned over the toilet, throwing up a clump of oily brown noodles. Not trusting the water, he skipped rinsing his mouth, doing the job later with beer instead.

On the sidewalk, Juli stopped one of the little Renault taxis and told the driver to take them to Ben Thanh Market. A quick ride ended in a swirling mass of people, bicycles, and motorbikes below a tall clock tower entrance to the market. Jostled by the crowd, and awed by the size of the market, Larry and Juli stood inside the entrance gaping at the huge vaulted wooden ceiling. Ahead were jumbled heaps and towers of clothes, cloth, and shoes. On the left was a long aisle crammed with jewelry stalls on either side.

"It would take a week to see everything in this place," Juli said, staring at the stacks and stalls. "Come on, let's find a necklace or bracelet for my mom."

A left turn, a right, another and another and they were lost, wandering up and down and eventually surrounded by a hundred different kinds of fruit and vegetables. "They grow all this stuff in Vietnam?" Juli asked, running a finger over something green and round, covered in warty bumps. A few feet farther along, Juli's nose wrinkled from the smell of a freshly cut durian.

"Smells like dirty socks and rotten onions," Larry said, hand over his nose.

An hour later, they found a way out of the market, each leaving with a bag of souvenirs. In the back seat of the taxi, Larry watched a trickle of sweat run from Juli's hairline down his face. He held a finger just beneath Juli's jaw, catching the drop as it fell. There was a deep sigh from Juli. "All I want now is a nap at our crummy little hotel."

Stripping off their sweaty clothes, they lay on the narrow bed with a small fan blowing across them. Larry threw open the one window hoping it would blow in cooler air but instead heard the raucous squawks of bar girls from a doorway in the alley below. He climbed back onto the clammy sheet against his friend, running a hand down his sweat-slicked chest and studied his damp coppery hair. Sweat dripped from Larry's nose, splashing against Juli's lip, quickly swiped away by his tongue.

It was dark when Larry eventually woke, flush against Juli, a neon sign from the building opposite the hotel flashing, coloring Juli's face in green and pink. The neon flickering across his features was oddly beautiful in how it accentuated the sweaty sheen of his skin. When Larry traced a finger down his nose, Juli batted at his hand. Not for the first time, his eyes roamed the sleeping figure, a slender frame stronger than most would imagine, but for the softness of his face, all lean, hard muscle. Since coming in from the bush a few months ago, Juli's feet had recovered and were now smooth and brown from five days in the sun and saltwater of Boracay, with no calluses or blisters.

As always, thoughts of Buddy flickered through Larry's head. With Juli naked beside him, this time it was a physical comparison of the two. Despite how he appeared in Larry's eyes, Juli was an ordinary Joe compared to Buddy, who was striking in every inch of his being, who could be a movie star if he wanted. But the ordinary in Juli was the very thing that stirred Larry. He loved the Dumbo ears sticking out from that red hair, the slight protrusion of his snow-white teeth, and the rare clear blueness of his eyes. Maybe it was impossible to ever choose one more than the other.

Eyes roving the plain beauty of this boy from Mandeville, Louisiana, Larry's mind returned to that day in 1958 when he and Buddy were in the fourth grade and for whatever reason, Buddy had followed him home. The memory of that afternoon was sharp as a razor.

Heading home from school one day, Larry had turned around, surprised to see Buddy a short distance behind him. He lifted a hand and waved. "Hi, do you live around here?"

"No, just walking. I didn't feel like riding the bus."

"You sit behind me at school. You're Buddy," Larry pointed out. "I live there," he added, pointing to a house two up from where they stood. "You can come in if you want."

"Okay."

Inside the house, Buddy followed Larry back to a small room off the kitchen where he tossed his school bag onto a narrow bed and told Buddy to sit. In the kitchen, he clattered around in a cabinet, pulling down two jelly glasses and filling them with lemonade from the refrigerator. Buddy sat and studied Larry's small room, littered with books about pirates, Hardy Boys books, notebooks, a compass that showed direction, and a purple PEZ dispenser. A New York Yankees cushion was on the desk chair, and on the floor nearby rested a pair of rumpled underwear.

Back with the lemonade and handing one glass to Buddy, Larry flopped onto the bed saying his mom was at work. He asked if Buddy liked Mrs. Starling.

"She's okay, I guess."

"She sure likes to wallop you with her ruler."

At that, Buddy sniggered and pulled the leg of his blue jeans up to his knee, looking down and rubbing at a spot on his calf.

"Can I see?" Larry asked.

Buddy flung his exposed leg out, propping his foot on the edge of the bed. Larry tentatively reached out a finger and rubbed it up and down Buddy's calf as if to massage away the long-gone sting.

They sat for a while on the tiny back porch talking about *Dragnet*, a TV show they both liked, and then Larry said his dad didn't live with them, that he'd left one day.

A minute or two passed and Buddy asked if he could use the bathroom. Larry told him to just pee off the porch, nobody could see. Buddy sat frozen for a few seconds before asking Larry if he was sure. Larry just smiled and suddenly stood, unzipped himself and rotating his little willy, inscribed a figure eight in the grass. No longer hesitating, Buddy undid his button-fly blue jeans and sent a jet of pee arcing five feet out into the yard. In the next minute they were both tucked in, buttoned up and talking excitedly about *Gunsmoke*.

Larry walked with Buddy to the bus stop and when he was getting on the bus, Larry waved. "See you later alligator," he called.

Buddy waved. "After while, crocodile."

That afternoon was the first of many, and by the third time, the two had become the best of friends. But their play was confined to school and those afternoons Buddy followed along back to Larry's house. Larry's mother was a nurse and was always at work when Buddy was there so he never got to meet her.

When fifth grade came around, Buddy was sent to a different school and didn't see Larry again for seven years, not until that night Buddy pulled into Billups gas station asking for five dollars' worth of gas.

****

Showered and in fresh clothes, they left the hotel, Larry saying he wanted something delicious and all-American, cooked by an American. He insisted they go to the Continental Palace, the big hotel on Dong Khoi Street where the American reporters hung out.

"Whatever, buddy, I'm with you," Juli said, lighting a cigarette and looking out at the lights and nighttime traffic on the big boulevard. Juli had little interest in food, and apart from the need for it, he was happy with C-rats or a hamburger on the go, never one to fantasize about great tasting food.

Larry had studied a map of Saigon in the hotel's tiny lobby and knew they were within walking distance of the Continental. "The first right will take us to Dong Khoi. The Continental should be a half block from there."

A tiny Vietnamese man in a tuxedo led them to a courtyard overhung with trees full of pink blossoms. When the waiter approached the table, Juli asked him what made the courtyard smell so good.

The waiter gestured to the overhanging trees. "It is the frangipani blossoms, sir. The trees have been here for many years. May I bring you gentlemen a cocktail?" he asked.

"Yeah, two Jack Daniels on the rocks," Juli said. When the waiter was gone, he passed a hand slowly over the tabletop. "White tablecloth. I'm gonna shoot his ass if he brings us chopsticks."

"With what?"

With a tiny smile, Juli lifted the front of his aloha shirt to reveal the butt of a 9mm Hi Power stuck in his waistband. "I'm your guard dog, remember?"

"The fuck did you get that?"

"'Nam, son. Easier to buy guns and drugs than noodles of the pork."

"Come on, Juli."

"That big market we went to this afternoon."

The waiter returned with their drinks, passing a menu to both. "Would you care for an appetizer before dinner? I can recommend the strips of deep-fried chicken."

"Bring us a plate of those," Larry said.

They sat silent, smiling across the table, sipping Jack on the rocks while the frangipani dripped its exotic fragrance down on the courtyard. For a few fleeting seconds

Larry felt a Boracay tingle of them being the only two people in the world.

The chicken strips came, and in answer to the waiter's question, they ordered two rare steaks with french fries. Larry asked the waiter for paper and pen.

Back with a sheet of hotel stationery and a pen, the waiter refilled their water glasses and disappeared again. Larry tore the paper in half and quickly wrote his Baton Rouge address and phone number on one half, handing both halves to Juli. "Write down your address and phone number for me."

"Why now?" he said, doing as Larry asked.

"Why not?"

A pretty Vietnamese girl in a white *ao dai* came to the table with a tray of cigarettes slung from around her neck. "Cigarettes?" she asked.

"Pack of Luckies?" Juli smiled up at her.

"Lucky Strike, yes sir. LSMFT," she said, handing him a pack.

Juli gave her a dollar bill and waved off the change. "Wonder where she learned that…what d'ya call it?"

"Acronym." Larry shrugged. "American boyfriend? *Loose Strap Means Flabby Titties*."

"Uh-uh. *Let's Screw, My Finger's Tired*."

The platters of steak and french fries came, along with two bottles of Budweiser. After long swallows of beer, they grabbed the knives and forks, diving in. There was no talk while they went at the thick steaks like two grunts just back from a month in the jungle.

Chewing on a mouthful of beef, Larry smiled over at Juli.

Juli finally pushed his half-eaten steak toward Larry. "I'm full."

Down the road from the Continental was a pocket-sized park and when they were passing a gate leading inside, Juli nudged Larry in through the gate. Half-hidden in the shadows under a tree, their foreheads pressed together, Juli was whispering to Larry.

"Fucking faggots," an American voice snapped out of the dark.

In a split-second Juli spun around, the 9mm pressed to

a soldier's eye socket. "You got business here, mother-fucker?"

Throwing his hands up, the soldier stepped back, stumbling, double-timing it down the street.

****

Farther down Dong Khoi they found a small bar with only a few customers, American soldiers, bar girls clinging to them. A Vietnamese man was behind the tiny bar. They sat at a rickety table bolstered by a wad of folded newspaper under one leg. One of the bar girls strolled toward Juli and Larry, moving to sit in Juli's lap. He waved her off and she turned back to the bar. "You numbah ten cheap Charlie," she grumbled.

Juli went to the bar and returned with two *Ba Muoi Ba*, complaining about soon being back at the hangar.

"Not for long. Two weeks we're back in the world."

"If the paperwork goes through without a hitch."

"What's for you after all this?" Larry asked casually, but feeling an urgency Juli wouldn't understand.

"Not sure. Why?"

"Never really told anyone. I want to open my own classic car shop."

"What exactly is that?"

"For people who want their classic cars rebuilt or repaired." From his wallet, Larry pulled a photograph of the Woody. "This is a 1948 Chevy Fleetmaster Woody Wagon. When I bought it, it was a near wreck and hadn't been driven in at least ten years."

Juli put his finger on the photograph. "You did this?"

"No, my mother did. Who the fuck you think did it? Why you think Rodriguez loves me so much? But look, here's the thing. I wanna do it with you. Be my partner, fifty-fifty."

Juli looked up from the photograph, his eyes meeting Larry's.

"Yeah, I know that's a lot to take in."

Juli laughed. "You think?"

"Well, you know, pimping never goes out of style in New Orleans. And with a classy car…"

"Now you talking."

"You could check up on your girls in a low, slinked-down 1940 Mercury coupe."

"With my gun on the seat beside me."

"Sure, tough guy," Larry said, getting up. "I gotta pee."

Juli squinted. "Wait now, don't stop feeding me the dream."

"Just hold those thoughts."

The toilet smelled like it hadn't been cleaned since the French were in Vietnam, a sheen of puddled urine was on the floor under Larry's boots. At the tiny, stained sink he turned the spigot to wash his hands but nothing came out.

Stepping out into the grimy hallway, he took three steps and the world exploded into white hot smithereens. Hit by a wall of heat and shattered furniture, Larry was knocked back several feet to the floor, deafened by the explosion. Crawling on his hands and knees, pausing to pull out a splinter of wood embedded in his stomach and screaming from the flash of pain it brought, he half stood, fell again and climbed to his feet supported by the door-frame. He was looking for Juli but the tables in the bar were gone, blown away from the center of the room. Ears ringing, he stared at the one chair remaining, untouched, exactly where he had been sitting minutes ago.

In a sleepwalk through hell, Larry's eyes took in the carnage of torn bodies around him.

"Juli! Julian!"

A man missing an arm groaned loudly, struggling with his remaining arm to claw his way outside. Against one wall was the crumpled form of the girl who had tried to sit in Juli's lap, unmoving, her clothes half blown off.

Hearing sounds to his left, he stared blankly at a dozen Vietnamese craning to get a look inside, voices a chatter of singsong confusion.

Through drifting smoke, a broken and bloodied figure on the floor by the bar swam into view. Propped up among scattered stools, the face was a red mask, Larry made out the shirt, the coconuts, hula girls, and splashes of blue, green and yellow and his knees went out from under him. Crawling to the broken form he recognized as Juli, his hands shook violently as he wiped away the blood on Juli's beautiful face. "Wake the fuck up, please God, wake the fuck up!"

He felt something hard under his knee, and Larry scooped Juli's 9mm up from the floor and jammed it under his shirt. He searched for wounds, finding one in Juli's head, the glorious red hair soaked dark with blood. Below his waist was a sea of red. Larry pressed his face against Juli's, kissing him, cleaning the blood from his nostrils, gently touching the now-closed blue eyes, peaceful and unscathed, the fury of a nightmare leaving them mercifully unspoiled. Clamped in Juli's left hand was the photograph of the Woody, now spattered with his blood.

Larry huddled against Juli, trembling and unaware of the steady keening from his mouth and heart. A military policeman squatted beside him, asking if he was okay.

Larry looked at the man vacantly.

"I'm here to help you. What's your name?"

"Juli."

"Juli what?"

"Bentley."

"Are you sure you're okay?"

"Yeah, but you need to help Juli."

"Aren't you Juli?" the MP asked.

Laying a hand on Juli's chest, he said, "This is Juli. Julian Bentley, Big Red One."

From the street outside, curious eyes continued to peer into the shattered bar, watching the American howl with pain, screaming his anger and desolation to an uncaring audience. But all that was quickly beyond him, nothing more than passing faces in dreams to come.

"Let's get you to the hospital," the MP said, urging Larry with a hand to stand up.

"I'm okay. Please help Juli."

The MP stood and went to another MP, the two talking just outside the door. A siren's wail came from down the block and an ambulance made its way through the crowded street, stopping in front of the bar. Two paramedics jumped out the back, running to the man with one arm just inside the door. They put him on a stretcher, carrying him to the ambulance. Back a minute later, they went from body to body checking for signs of life. One of the two went to Juli but seeing Larry's guard dog vigilance, he turned to the MP with a questioning look. Again, the MP squatted beside Larry. "They want you to go with them to the hospital."

"I'm going with Juli," and he placed a protective hand on Juli's leg.

The policeman whispered to his partner once more.

Larry reached under Juli, slipping his wallet out and finding his military ID card, he called the MP back. "Here," he said, handing it over. While the policeman was looking at it, Larry slipped Juli's wallet in his front pocket.

"How about yours? Can I see your ID?"

He took the ID from his wallet and gave it to the MP. Turning back, he slipped the photograph from Juli's fingers and put it in his shirt pocket.

When the paramedics had tended to the other injured and dead, they came for Juli. Larry wouldn't let them near him, fighting them weakly, the pain in his head making him sick to his stomach until a paramedic slipped a needle in his arm.

Part Two

In later life, we see things with a more practical eye, one we share with the rest of society; but adolescence was the only time when we ever learned anything.
— Marcel Proust

Chapter Seventeen

Larry spent two hours in an airport bar before getting a taxi to the French Quarter where the driver dropped him off at the corner of Rampart and Iberville. Uncertain where he was exactly and no idea where his next steps would take him, he leaned against a building, tired, his body still in a distant time zone, strung out, skin crawling with need. He had to find a bar. On Bourbon Street he spotted the Old Absinthe House and went inside, dropping his duffle bag and ruck on the floor by the nearest barstool. The place was nearly empty, only two other people farther down the bar in conversation with the bartender.

Staring down at his ruck on the floor, he didn't notice the bartender. "What's your pleasure?"

"Bottle of Jax." As the man started back down the bar, Larry held up two fingers. "Make it two." He pulled a crumple of bills from his pocket, smoothing them on the copper-topped bar. The bartender returned with two bottles of beer, picking up two dollars from the pile. Larry drained the first bottle.

Taking the small black zipper bag from his ruck, he asked where the men's room was. Following the bartender's gesture, he walked to the back and locked himself in a stall, pulling off his Army coat, hands shaking as he rolled up his sleeve and tied off. The white powder trickled from his last bag into the spoon. From his small bottle, Larry tipped a little water into the spoon, flicking his lighter under it. Juli leaned against the stall door watching him, making Larry's hands shake more, but he slipped the needle into his arm and sank back against the toilet, the flood of deliverance humming in his chest.

Once Larry was back on the barstool, the bartender came down the bar. "Fresh from a year in hell, soldier?"

"Something like that," he said, lighting a cigarette. "You recommend a not too expensive hotel around here?"

"Try the *Maison des Reines*, six short blocks up Bourbon on Dumaine."

"Thanks."

After another beer, Larry hoisted his duffle and ruck and left to look for the hotel. He told the desk clerk he wasn't sure how many nights he would stay, handing over a fifty-dollar deposit. In the second-floor room, he stripped off the clammy uniform and tumbled onto the bed.

He woke with his own smell rank in his nose. After a shower, he dug through his duffel bag for a pair of jeans and a clean shirt and left the hotel looking for a connection. He went to Jackson Square with its crowds, sidewalk artists, and the background few leaning against buildings speaking quietly to passersby. Larry sat on a bench and watched the action for the next half hour, still high and grooving on the scene. Twice, different men sat on the same bench striking up an obvious conversation. Larry sent both on their way with a friendly no thanks wave. He was getting impatient when a guy in his mid-twenties, with a mangy beard and a gold ring in one ear stopped and asked if he was interested in grass.

"That all you got?"

"Depends on what your thing is," he said looking up and down the street.

"Something a little harder."

"Spell it out, man."

"You a cop?"

"Do I look like a fucking cop?"

"Smack."

"Don't have. But for five bucks and a beer I can put you on to someone who does."

"Let's go."

At a small bar on Royal, the guy told Larry to bring a couple of beers to the booth opposite the pool table.

At the table with the beer, the earring guy slid over to make room, saying the man opposite him was Aubin. "He's your guy."

The one called Aubin didn't say anything, only looked hard at Larry. He was a chubby man in his thirties, the top of a tattoo coming up out of his shirt collar. One fat finger stirred the peanuts in a bowl on the table. "You're young for a cop."

"Not a cop. Looking to get some smack," Larry said in

a quiet voice.

"Where's your regular guy?"

"My regular guy?" Larry looked over to the bar, watching the bartender watch TV. "Probably dead. Vietnam, Central Highlands," he said, eyes back to Aubin.

Aubin smiled. "One more customer courtesy of the U.S. Government."

Earring guy said he had to split so Larry slipped him five dollars and sat down again across from Aubin. His beer downed quickly, Larry followed Aubin to a place on Iberville. He bought five bags and the dealer gave him a scrap of paper with his phone number and the initial A. "Don't fucking drop in. Call first or look for me at the same bar. Cool?"

"Yeah, cool. Thanks."

From the dealer's place on Iberville, he looked for something to eat, anything that didn't include noodles or chopsticks. He found a place called Felix's open to the sidewalk and situated under a wrought iron balcony hung with big ferns in pots, one of those New Orleans picture postcard places. It was a popular spot, judging from the number of people inside. He had a bowl of gumbo and a big platter of fried shrimp and oysters, the best food he'd had in the past twelve months.

With a full stomach, nothing in mind, he wandered and ended up at Lafitte's on Bourbon, his fourth bar of the day, the second on Bourbon. Just what the doctor ordered. He sat at the bar, Jack on the rocks, keep 'em coming. Drunk, high, a little beyond conversation, each time Larry raised his glass, he noticed a man at the other end of the bar staring at him. He was young, thirty maybe, in a suit and tie with well-polished black dress shoes. That was a detail Larry noticed right off, a man who took care of his shoes. He liked that. The man continued to stare until Larry motioned him over.

"Where's your wife?" Larry asked right off, surprising the man.

"She...she's in Houston."

He stared at Larry and Larry stared back. "You just looking? Have a seat."

He sat quickly on the stool to Larry's right.

"What do you want to drink? I'll get it."

The man looked uncertain. "Scotch on the rocks. My round," he said, laying some bills on the bar.

Phillip 'Phip' Barndall had been married to Betsy for a year and a half and Larry wondered if she knew about the love of her life, who didn't pull out a wallet photo of wife and child, thank God. Phip worked for a company that bought foreclosed properties, eventually turning them over for big profits after putting people out on the street. Twenty-six and a graduate of Texas A&M, he had short blond hair, wore his tie tightly knotted, and over the next two drinks, slowly worked his leg up against Larry's. He was in New Orleans to buy the houses out from under a few more families in the Tremé district, but he was honest about it.

Larry fended off most of Phip's questions in a friendly way. Old enough to be in a bar? He a student? Live in New Orleans? Girlfriend? Only the last did Larry answer with a resolute *no*.

Somewhere in their second hour at the bar Larry brushed his knuckle against Phip's stubbled cheek, making the man jump, as if the offending touch were red hot.

"Sorry. Didn't think you'd mind," Larry said with a puzzled look.

"You surprised me, that's all." With a quick look around at others in the bar, he whispered to him. "I didn't mind at all." With a look over his shoulder, he brushed his fingers down Larry's beardless cheek.

Once sitting at the end of the bed in Phip's one hundred-dollar a night hotel room, Larry finally asked him to stop straightening up the room and sit down.

"You ever done this before, Phip?"

"What?"

"Been with another guy."

"Uh...once. In college. But we didn't really do anything."

"What do you have in mind now, with me?"

"I don't know. You're beautiful. I guess I want to see you without your clothes."

Larry stood and stripped off his clothes, standing in front of Phip.

"Not sure I know..." Phip whispered, trembling, his eyes devouring Larry.

Larry pushed him gently back onto the bed, pulling Phip's shoes and socks off before loosening his belt. Naked, eyes wide, Phip was trembling when Larry climbed onto the bed. Still riding his high and loose from the beer and Jack Daniels, Larry wasn't a rock-hard partner but that didn't bother Phip, who didn't know what to do other than run his hands across Larry, planting small kisses on his face and chest.

With Phip reluctant to venture below Larry's stomach, Larry took the lead, sliding down the bed and drawing loud gasps from the married barely a year first-timer. Their coupling included some firsts for Larry as well. He'd never felt a rough beard against his face, never run hands through chest hair, and the first time Phip came, Larry choked on the flood of it. But it was all Juli when Phip spasmed and bucked in that same unrestrained way. Catching his breath, Phip said he wanted to see Larry come and Larry said it would take Phip's mouth or ass to bring up that magic. Reluctant at first, he chose to use his mouth. In the end, he couldn't get enough, Larry having to pry him off.

The rest of the night Phip spent wrapped around Larry, kissing him, whispering endearments, murmurs not heard in the drugged-out dreams of his partner.

Larry woke with sunlight flooding the room, alone, the only sign of Phip a damp towel in the bathroom. On top of Larry's neatly folded clothes was twenty-five dollars and a note saying, *Lafitte's at 6 p.m.? Please.* He ordered coffee and beignets from room service before taking a shower and using the toothbrush he found by the sink in the bathroom. Dropping the towel on the floor, he reached for his clothes but then noticed the suitcase on a stand near the bed. Flipping the top up, he looked at the shirts inside still in their wrap from the cleaners, and below them a stack of shorts and snowy white T-shirts, socks folded in the side pocket. Larry slipped on one of the T-shirts, followed by a pair of blue boxers.

Back at the *Maison des Reines*, he slept for an hour before retrieving his black zipper bag and shooting up.

Later, in Jackson Square, he went to the same bench as the day before and sat down to wait. Eventually, the guy with the scraggly beard and earring came by, stopping in front of the bench.

"Hey man, you get what you wanted?"

"You bet. Sit down, I wanted to ask you something. What's your name?"

"Most people call me Shooter."

"Cool. So, do you have any Darvon?"

"I got Darvon. Got something better though, something new called Quaaludes."

"Can I get maybe twenty-five Darvon? And four or five of those new pills to try?"

"Let's walk around the corner to my office," Shooter said expansively.

****

Larry found the nearest St. Charles streetcar stop at Canal and Carondelet. On the streetcar, upon reaching the end of the line, the conductor shook him awake, asking if he was getting off or going back the other way.

"Where are we?"

"You okay, son?"

"Yeah, just dozed off. Can I stay on or get another streetcar back?"

"Sit tight. This is the turnaround. South Claiborne."

He was coasting on a dreamy, sleepy feeling, figuring it was the Quaalude and wondering if he should be mixing that stuff with smack. Maybe not, but he liked the high he was on. Smooth didn't half describe it. He remembered Phip from the night before, who had left him money, half of it gone on pills. Nice guy, clean and strait-laced, smelling like a just-washed cotton shirt in his tight tie and polished shoes. If they ever connected again, he knew what he wanted to do with Phip. Then he remembered the note left with the money but couldn't remember what the note said. He was too fucked up, other stuff crawling through his head.

Eyes on the city rolling past outside the streetcar's window, Larry tripped on the beauty of it all, the new green on the trees, huge stately old houses. He thought maybe he should find a place to live in New Orleans, somewhere in the Quarter. Lost in reverie about the French Quarter and its interesting people, the easy availability of what he needed, the streetcar stopped to let passengers on and off and Larry blinked several times. Just outside the window of the streetcar was a sign over a store, *Buddy's Art Supplies*. Juli was standing inside the store looking out at him from behind the glass door. Just as the streetcar lurched forward again, Juli dissolved. Larry knew he should have called Buddy from California, or at least after getting to New Orleans. Maybe tomorrow.

He got off the streetcar and went into the first bar he saw and ordered a beer, putting folded arms on the bar and resting his head. He roused and drank his beer and when he put his head down a second time, the bartender came over and rapped on the bar.

"Go home, pal."

He stumbled onto the street, aiming himself deeper into the Quarter. What did that fucking note say? The second person he jostled against on the sidewalk shoved him off and he thought again of the Quaalude, telling himself to ease up. Shit was making him wobbly as a slow spinning top.

He sat at a table on the patio at Lafitte's and from the bar brought a beer and a glass of water. Lighting a cigarette and thinking about swimming with Juli, he didn't feel the hand on his shoulder.

"Larry?"

Knotted tie and shiny shoes, there stood the businessman from Houston.

"Oh, hey."

"You came. I left you a note."

"Yeah. Right, I saw it." Phip went to the bar for a drink and returned to sit beside Larry.

After a sip of Phip's scotch, Larry leaned in closer and spoke quietly. "I borrowed some of your clothes."

Phip looked confused. "What do you mean?"

"This morning. After I had a shower at your hotel I borrowed a pair of your shorts and a T-shirt."He plucked at the collar of the T-shirt. "This is yours." He pointed down to his lap. "Shorts, too."

Phip stared at Larry for several seconds. "That turns me on," he said, his voice husky.

"Yeah? What are you gonna do about it?"

Soon after getting there, Larry was asleep on the bed in room 316 at The Andrew Jackson Hotel, wearing only Phip's white T-shirt and blue boxers. Phip stood looking down at him, still in his suit and tie. He sat in a chair and watched Larry sleeping for a long time, before undressing down to his boxer shorts and going in the bathroom to brush his teeth. Slipping the shorts to his feet, he laid down beside Larry, pressing his lips against Larry's. Getting no response, he trailed his fingers down the T-shirt, stopping at the place where the still red scar on Larry's stomach was exposed. With the heat of the body against his, Phip's desire was like a fever, like nothing he'd ever felt before.

Much later, Larry woke, not knowing where he was until he saw Phip beside him, propped on an elbow gazing at him.

"Hey. Sorry I fell asleep. Some pill...knocked me out," he mumbled, groggy.

"No problem. I like lying next to you."

He looked at Phip's hardness. "I guess."

Phip laughed and Larry put a finger to Phip's mouth, working it inside and around his tongue before slipping it wet between Phip's legs.

"What are you doing?"

"I think you know."

"No, I've never done that. I can't."

But he did, and Larry was excited by the coaxing it took, aroused by Phip's timid struggle and the eventual flood of his satisfaction.

They talked for a long time afterward, Larry finally deciding to answer Phip's questions, unexpectedly finding relief in letting his thoughts out, saying things he couldn't say to someone he knew, rambling on about Juli and Vietnam. Phip proved to be a good listener.

"Was this guy over there, a mechanic I worked with sometimes, we called him Dreamer. Used to talk about what a beautiful place Vietnam could be without the U.S.

Army. Mosquitos chewing on his arms, heat rash on fire from sweat and humidity, dodging bullets and he's tripping on scenic splendors. Good mechanic though." Larry rolled his head against Phip's. "Outside the wire one day on a repair run, he got his ticket home. Stepped to the edge of the road to look at some damn flower, toe-popper took off part of his foot."

They went out to a small restaurant down the block, Larry picking at his food, watching Phip eat his crawfish étouffée.

They were drinking coffee and Phip said he would be returning to Houston the next day.

"Will you come back to the hotel and sleep with me tonight?"

"Sure, why not?" Larry said. "Kinda like your scratchy beard against my face."

Phip blushed, sneaking a look to see if anyone had overheard them.

Larry woke that night gasping for breath, with someone holding on to his arm. He tried sitting up but was held back and looking over seeing a face in shadow, he screamed, his heart pounding.

"It's Phip, Larry. You were having a bad dream, screaming in your sleep. Scared me as much as you."

Larry's face relaxed before he sunk back onto the pillow. "Phip, yes. Jesus, I'm sorry." He pulled Phip against him. "Hold me a minute. Can you do that?"

"For as long as you want." He kissed Larry's face.

"Just hold me close."

****

Drunk, high, paying half attention to the man at his left whose conversation he couldn't follow, something about city infrastructure and the mayor who wasn't doing what he should, Larry got up to use the men's room. When he came back, he sat at another stool with no one nearby. Another Jack on the rocks and Larry stared out at the street, surprisingly, his head in a good place. The Darvon was smooth and made him remember the doc at An Khé who handed the pills out like scattering corn in a farmyard of chickens. That prompted the memory of what drug dealer Aubin had said, about him being another customer courtesy of the government.

He left the bar and walked back to his hotel, stopping for two six packs. Naked on the mussed sheets ripe with sweat, he called downstairs and told them the sheets needed changing. Not bothering to dress, he sat in a chair while the woman put clean sheets on the bed between glances at him. He dug a dollar bill from the jeans at his feet, passing it to the woman who took a good look at his nakedness before she left. He popped the beer tab, enjoying the feel of warm foam spilling down his chin and chest. Perk tossing him a warm can of Falstaff, the memory in sync with the movement of his hand to touch himself, warm beer filling a stomach hollow with desire. Juli, over by the bathroom door, watched him.

He slept and later gathered up all his dirty socks and underwear. Slipping on a pair of boxers, he carried the laundry down to the front desk.

"The fuck, man? You can't come waltzing down here in your underwear," The clerk said, catching sight of him.

"Sorry. Can you wash this stuff for me?"

"No, no laundry."

Larry shrugged, and turned back to the stairs. He didn't get far before the clerk yelled at him and pointed to a pair of boxers on the floor.

He dropped the dirty clothes on the floor in his room, opened another beer and stretched out on the bed, the can resting on his stomach.

Larry stayed in the room for two days. On the third, he showered quickly, not bothering with his hair. He sorted through the underwear, picking out what looked and smelled the cleanest. He shot up, chewed up a couple of Darvon, and not much later was in a bar called Erin Rose. Downing half his first beer he noticed a young guy at the other end of the bar, something about him instantly recognizable.

Walking down the bar, he gestured to the empty seat. "You mind?"

The guy turned and looked at him. He shrugged and shook his head.

Casually, looking at the bottles behind the bar, Larry spoke again. "How long back in the world?"

He turned and looked hard at Larry. "That obvious?"

"To me it is," he said tipping the beer up to his mouth, before holding out a hand. "Larry. 5th TACOM, An Khé."

"199th Infantry, Sông Bé. Chandler."

"Fuck me. Another grunt fresh out of the boonies. In the French Quarter of all places, jungle of its own."

"Born and bred here. You?"

"Baton Rouge. Still haven't made it home."

"No better place to weigh that option than here in this jungle."

After a few beers, they went barhopping before ending up at one on Bourbon. The talk was easy and comfortable, digging up memories of the good parts about 'Nam. The buddies, camaraderie, the rare officer you could trust. And those times of being scared so bad you had to squeeze ass cheeks tight not to shit yourself, not one of the good parts, but a little funny now.

Chandler looked around the uncrowded bar. "Think we wandered into a fag bar."

Larry looked around. "That bother you?"

"As long as no one tries to grab my stuff."

"I might," Larry said with half a smile.

"Shut the fuck up." Chandler finished his beer, nodding to the bartender for two more before looking again around the bar. "No shit? You into guys?"

"I'm kind of into you. But don't sweat it. I'm not putting my hands anywhere uninvited."

"Seriously?"

Larry left it there, suggesting they go have a bowl of gumbo, some little place he found a couple of days back. Turned out Felix's was crowded and they had to wait to get a seat. After two bites, Chandler said it was good gumbo, almost as good as his Aunt Belle's. Larry was eating a platter of fried shrimp and tipped a few of them onto Chandler's bread plate.

"Try the shrimp."

Chandler finished his gumbo and ate the remaining shrimp, Larry saying he was full. The last light of day was fading when they stepped outside. The never-turned-off neon became brighter in the dusk, reflected onto the happy faces of people out for a good time as the Quarter came alive.

"Any place you wanna go?" Chandler asked.

"Somewhere quiet with a nice view."

"Let's walk over to the river."

Larry followed Chandler a few blocks until they got to a broad walkway fronting the Mississippi. At that hour it was uncrowded, not more than half a dozen other people drifting past. He and Chandler settled on a bench, Larry lighting a cigarette and passing the pack to his buddy.

"I don't smoke very often but I'll have one. Or there's this," Chandler said, taking a perfectly rolled joint from his pocket, lighting both the Lucky and the joint.

Reaching a hand into his jeans pocket, Larry pulled out a couple of Darvon, offering, "Maybe this. Just the thing for the aches and pains of time under the gun."

Chandler popped the pills in his mouth, chewing them up. "Wasted Vietnam style."

They were quiet for a time, the joint passing from one to the other. Larry stretched his legs out, leaning back against the bench, his T-shirt creeping up above his jeans. Chandler noticed the scar.

"How'd you get that?" he said, carefully lifting the T-shirt another few inches.

"Grenade."

Nothing more was said about it. Both watched the flow of the river, the lights from tugboats and passing ships, each deep into private thoughts.

"One look at the shine on those battered boots told me you were a brother from another place," Chandler said, finally.

"'I saw it in your eyes," Larry answered.

They walked back up Bienville to Royal and from there all the way to Dumaine, a slow amble, neither saying much, passing a cigarette back and forth.

"I'm three blocks up this way," Larry said when they came to Dumaine, looking at Chandler.

Chandler nodded his head and they continued on to the *Maison des Reines*. In the messy room, Larry passed Chandler a warm can of beer. "Find a seat, think there's a chair under those clothes."

Larry sat on the floor at the end of the unmade bed, watching Chandler in the chair at the small desk, thinking he looked nervous. "Everything good?"

"Yeah. Just never done this."

"What? Drink warm beer?"

"You know what I fucking mean," Chandler said. "Toss me another one of those."

Larry underhanded a can of beer and watched the foam run over Chandler's hands. He threw a T-shirt from the floor over to him. "Wipe your hands on that. Wait. Not that one." He tossed another T-shirt and took back the one that had belonged to Juli.

The next morning, they lay side by side on the tousled bed, drinking beer. Everything was good, a still, quiet aftermath of what had been a night of hardball sex. Nothing to talk about, as words only muddied the experience. Chandler turned on his side facing Larry, laying a hand on his stomach, finger tracing the scar there. "I'll write my number down. When you're in the jungle again, maybe we can have a few beers."

He sprung up off the bed and went into the bathroom.

Larry lay listening to Chandler pee.

****

He connected with Aubin again, bringing ten bags back to the hotel. After shooting up, he went to Jackson Square and sat on the bench waiting for Shooter with the Darvon. It wasn't long before the guy sat down beside Larry, speaking too close against his ear. "Anything I can do for you this fine afternoon?"

Larry caught a smell like dirty underwear on the man's breath and eased away from him, the smell too close to his own condition. "Need some Darvon."

"Got a fresh batch, right off the tree." Shooter laughed at the joke. "How 'bout some Quaaludes?"

"Yeah, some of those along with the Darvon."

"You got it. Let's roll." He got up, walking off, Larry behind him.

Larry woke at Café Du Monde. Eyes blinking, he

looked at the girl wearing a paper cap and black bowtie standing at his table. "Sir, you can't sleep here. Please pay your check now."

Taking a sip from the coffee in front of him, he said to her. "My coffee's cold. Can I get hot coffee?"

"Yes sir. I'll bring it to you in a go-cup. Please pay now."

He stood squinting into the sunlight on Decatur, balancing the warm paper cup in his hand. Once more he found his bench in Jackson Square, this time not looking for Shooter at all. He managed a few sips of the hot coffee before he nodded off again, coffee spilling from the tilting cup onto the bench.

He jerked awake when someone rapped hard on the back of the bench, the rest of the coffee spilling into his lap. He looked up into the face of a policeman glaring down at him, asking where he lived. "I'm... I'm staying a few days at a hotel on Dumaine," he managed to stammer, dazed.

"What hotel would that be?"

"It has a French name... give me a second. The *Maison Reines*... on Dumaine."

"You got some ID?"

Larry fumbled out his military identification card, passing it to the policeman.

"Get your ass back to the *Maison des Reines*. Pull your shit together, soldier." the policeman finally said, studying the card.

"Yes, sir. Right away, sir."

The policeman squinted down his veiny red nose at Larry, before snarling at him. "Get the fuck out of here."

****

Mid-afternoon the next day, Larry was in the Golden Lantern, a bar on Royal, three beers in and his high right on point. Quaalude, he thought, Qua-a-a-a-lude. The jukebox was blasting something he liked. He leaned toward a woman two stools down, asking what the song was.

Before she could answer, someone at the table behind

him, called out. "That's Clifton Chenier, 'Bon Ton Rou-let!'"

"I like it." Larry said, as he waved to the table.

The woman came to the bar. "I'm Cheri. Come join us. That's Boo Boo and Babe," she said, pointing to the others.

"Larry," he said, following Cheri back to the table and sitting.

"Hey y'all, this is Larry," Cheri said to the others, who looked up with raised eyebrows.

Babe was a bosomy redhead and talked about a crazy uncle, who a week after remarrying the first of five wives, got his hand bitten off wrestling an alligator in a Morgan City carnival.

"That a true story?" Larry asked, laughing.

"Swear to God," she bellowed, calling to the bar for another round of beers.

Boo Boo was the oldest of the three, mid-forties maybe, balding bullet head, buzz-cut, bristly unshaven face. He chain smoked his Kools, burning off a half-inch of tobacco with one pull. Cheri was full of questions that Larry answered with lies. Told her he was from Covington where he worked at Midas Muffler, in New Orleans to see his mama on her birthday but she ducked out with her boy-friend the day before, leaving Larry to feed her snappy ancient chihuahua. Until she got back, he was stuck at her crummy apartment with the nasty dog.

"You need to boot that animal out the back door," Boo Boo said.

"Mama would be mighty upset. Had that damn thing for the past fifteen years."

More beers appeared and Larry headed to the men's room in back, concentrating on keeping his steps in an unwavering line. When he sat down again beside Babe, her hand found his leg, sliding up to his crotch. Rubbing a fin-ger against him, she leaned in. "Think you spilled a little, baby."

Larry pushed her hand away and went to the jukebox.

Dropping in a couple of quarters, he spotted Juli watching him from the shadows. Pressing the buttons for the Clifton Chenier record and a couple of others, he went to the bar, asking the bartender for a Jack on the rocks. Back at the table, the talk was about leaving and going somewhere else.

"Let's go to my place," Cheri suggested.

"Oh, hell no. You know I can't stand to be around Mary George." Babe said, explaining to Larry. "The sister from hell."

"She's at her boyfriend's place tonight," Cheri assured her.

Once at Cheri's apartment, Larry quaffed another Quaalude and was soon close to passing out. Cheri and Babe were at the dining room table arguing and Larry found a seat on the other end of the sofa from Boo Boo, hardly aware of the man until Boo Boo roared for the two women to shut up. The loudness of his voice roused Larry somewhat, but Boo Boo was ignored by Cheri and Babe.

Larry found the bathroom at the back of the apartment and splashed water on his face. He didn't see a towel, so he dried his face on his shirtsleeves and stood looking out of a window down onto Toulouse Street. When he turned back to the door, Boo Boo was there, glowering at him from the partially open door.

He pushed past the man and walked to the door of the apartment, unnoticed by Cheri and Babe, still caught up in their argument.

He kept stumbling off the sidewalk as he made his way back to the hotel, finally giving up and leaning a shoulder against the buildings and dragging himself along the stone fronts. Back in his room, he saw that the cloth of the left sleeve and shoulder was shredded from his drag along the buildings, his arm scraped and near bleeding. He threw the shirt in the trash can and crumpled onto the bed.

Early the next morning he asked the front desk to place a long-distance call to Baton Rouge, giving the man downstairs the number to Buddy's house.

Chapter Eighteen

Tired and driving home to his apartment, Buddy looked forward to a cold beer and hot shower. His thoughts churned with a carpentry problem. The mantel over the den fireplace at the Dunman Street house was defeating all his efforts to get it right. He didn't think it was a problem of right or wrong carpentry and had a feeling either the architect or a draftsman had screwed up. He was tempted to call his Uncle Dub, ask if he would drive out and take a look at the problem. Buddy wasn't ready to go whining to his boss, Mr. Hargrove. He would find a solution.

Right off of North onto 6th, he cut over to St. Louis where he had been living since shortly before his twenty-first birthday. The apartment provided as much freedom as he wanted and gave his mother and father less to worry about, though he still went to the house for supper one or two nights a week, and every other Saturday to cut the grass and help out with whatever else they needed. He even slept at the house on occasions when too tired to drive back downtown.

Buddy's parents were dealing with a changing neighborhood, new neighbors next door, loud cars, and loud parties with too many girls in and out.

He tossed his keys on the kitchen table and pulled off his shirt, going into the bedroom and stripping off the rest of his clothes. Buddy sat in the tub with the shower pelting hot water down on his back and head. The tension in his shoulders gradually eased and he remembered the mail, hoping he would find a letter from Larry.

The letters from Vietnam had become rare, even after sending his new address to Larry. Only a card a couple of weeks back from some island called Boracay. Two lines, *On R&R. Having a blast. Thinking about you. LPM.* The reverse side showed a white beach lined with palm trees. On first seeing the postcard, a wave of loneliness and desire to hold Larry had come over Buddy and he had unintentionally crumpled the card in his hand. He later smoothed it out and pressed it inside a book. The last letter he had gotten was also a quick scratch of two lines saying his friend had been killed and he would probably be home soon. Now impatient to see if another letter had come, he dried off and, towel around his waist, went out to the mail-box at his back steps. It had a bill from the utility company, a flyer from some place selling mail-order clothing, a statement from his bank, and a postcard. Nothing from Larry.

The bank statement, as expected, told him he was in good shape. The utilities bill went in a drawer. Getting a Budweiser from the fridge, he turned on the TV to a cop show with blaring sirens and tough talk. Sitting hunched on the bed ignoring the TV, Buddy drank his beer and fondled his lighter, rubbing Larry's initials with his thumb. No magic genie appeared in smoke to bring Larry back.

Cutting short the self-pity, Buddy took the empty beer bottle to the kitchen and retrieved *The Art of Woodworking and Furniture Making* from a shelf in the front room. After Larry had left for Vietnam, furniture making had become a serious hobby during the hours not working for Mr. Hargrove. Three pieces of furniture and the cabinets in the St. Louis Street apartment were all Buddy's work. The garage was now his workshop, full of his tools, including a table saw.

* * * *

On Saturday afternoon a week later, Buddy swung by the Pastime for a beer after work. The bar was close to home and had recently become his favorite place to have a beer and sometimes see a friend or two. Several beers ahead, a guy one stool over—said his name was Wiley— was giving expert opinion on how many games LSU would win in the coming season. It got only half Buddy's attention. Wiley was on to coaching problems when someone tapped Buddy on the shoulder.

"Buddy, you sports devil, it's rescue time. Wiley is as dumb as that football he used to throw. Come on over to the table," Bob Wexler said against his ear. "Our cheer costumes are purple and gold lamé."

Buddy was always glad to see Bob, the high school friend he never expected to encounter after graduation but kept running into. And it was Buddy's good luck that he did. Bob had all the qualities that made a good friend, something Buddy only discovered with time, and it was his loss that he hadn't gotten to know Bob better while they were in high school. Like many of his classmates, Buddy had underestimated Bob, not realizing what lay beneath the surface. Often teased in school for being what some called light in the loafers, Bob bore it well, walking past his tormentors with the tiniest expression of disdain. With his thick-framed black glasses and lanky build, he looked like an intellectual, a description not far from the truth. He also had a wicked sense of humor.

Carol and Damien were at the table but the surprise was Cullen Mosley. Buddy hadn't seen Cullen for months, not since their three-day fuckfest back when Buddy had just rented the apartment. And now here with Bob was that same good-looking guy whose startling green eyes Buddy wanted to swim in.

"Look who I found slumming with the sports crowd at the bar," Bob said, pulling out a chair for Buddy and looking around for the waitress.

"Buddy," Carol said, elegantly extending her hand for a kiss from another of her subjects.

"Good to see you, Buddy," Damien said. "I wish Larry were here with us."

"Who's this guy?" Buddy said playfully, looking at Cullen.

Cullen gave his hip a gentle push. "Hey, Buddy."

"How you been, Cullen?"

"What do you hear from Larry?" Damien asked.

"I'm not too sure but he should be coming home soon. Last I heard he was on R&R, having a great time. By the way, I sent him a copy of *Downbeat* magazine with your Bill Evans article."

"That makes me happy. Thank you," Damien said, noticing the waitress. "I'll have another vodka on the rocks. Anyone else?"

"Draft beer for me. So, how's law school, Bob?" Buddy asked.

"I'm hoping before that happens, I will be kidnapped into white slavery by a handsome pirate. Or an ugly one with a great body. Frankly, m'dear, I'm tragically bored by the idea of law."

Carol began telling a long story about a friend in New Orleans who adored being a lawyer, worked for years to get his degree and pass the bar exam, only to get disbarred in his very first year of practice for accepting money and merchandise his client had stolen from Big Barn Appliances.

"For God's sake, who is this person, Carol?" Damien asked.

"Lester Falgout. You met him once."

"I don't think so. The name isn't familiar."

"You met him."

"I don't know the man," Damien said, closing the subject.

After three mugs of beer, an hour of talk, and a lot of laughs, Buddy was ready to go home. Bob was gushing over a book called *Valley of the Dolls.*

"You read it," Bob said to Damien.

"I don't think so."

"Yes, you're the one who gave it to me."

"Hey, everyone," Buddy said, gently interrupting. "It's been a valley of fun but I gotta go." He nodded to Carol and Damien. "Bob, I'll call you soon." He dropped some bills on the table just as Cullen stood up saying he was late and had to leave as well. They walked out to the parking lot together.

"Where are you parked?" Buddy asked.

"By that black truck over there."

"That's my truck."

He told Cullen he was happy they had run into one another and was about to get in the truck and drive off. But that didn't happen. They stood against Buddy's dented fender, talking.

"How's Freddy doing?"

"He's in Mobile for a week. Painting a mural in the lobby of a new building."

"Cool. Sounds like he's branched out. Last time we talked, he was doing commercial art."

"He's doing more painting these days. Even some rich lady's portrait last month."

Buddy nodded, looking around the parking lot at nothing. "You said inside you were late. Too late to stop by?"

"Never too late for that. I'll follow you."

Driving those few blocks Buddy thought about Cullen following him home. The anticipation of getting with him again still brought a stab of guilt over what he knew was about to happen. Betraying Larry again. Being faithful had been easy after Larry left for Vietnam, but as the months piled up, his monkish discipline waned. Sitting next to Cullen at the Pastime, remembering the last time with him at the empty apartment, Buddy tingled with the closeness of him. Each time he looked at Cullen he thought of their weird history, and in a crazy way that added to his desire. Minutes from Cullen being in his apartment, Buddy was turned on.

He pulled all the way up the driveway to the garage, giving Cullen room to pull in behind him. Cullen got out of his car looking up at the old house. "We mostly skipped the talking last time. What's the story with this house?"

"The owner, a man named Otis Laurens renovated the house, dividing it into three apartments, two upstairs, one down. When I was looking for a place, I got lucky."

"Beautiful old house."

"Built around 1920, but well maintained by the family of the original owner. And Mr. Laurens made some modifications when he divided it into apartments. Come on in."

At the back steps, he reached to the mailbox but stopped himself on the chance there was a letter from Larry. He didn't want something from Larry in his hand at that moment.

"This is the kitchen." he said, stepping inside.

Cullen looked at him, laughing. "I wouldn't have guessed."

"The dumb tour guide," he said, twirling a finger at his head. "I forgot for a minute that you've been here before."

"Yeah, but it was totally empty then. No lights or water, remember?"

"I think the ink was still wet on the lease last time you were here." He led Cullen through to the front room.

"Some would call this the living room but it doesn't feel like that to me. I just call it the front room. You want something to drink?"

"I'm good. Can I use your bathroom?"

"Sure. Right there." He pointed to the door in the hall.

Cullen came out wiping his hands on his jeans.

Buddy gave him a gentle push toward the sofa. "Sit down."

Cullen sat at the end. Buddy made a move for the chair but then sat on the sofa.

"Beautiful table," Cullen said, running a hand across the coffee table.

"You like it? Really?"

"What's not to like? I've never seen one like it."

"It's made from floor planks I got from an old, abandoned house on Greenwell Springs Road."

"You made this?"

Buddy nodded and Cullen smiled, kneeling beside the table for a closer look. He ran a hand down one of the legs made from four-inch squared columns before sitting back on his heels and looking at Buddy again. "That is seriously cool, Buddy."

He sat again, narrowing the space between them. "So, you're into making furniture?"

Buddy nodded and immediately leaned closer, kissing Cullen. After a few seconds, Buddy sat back against the sofa, one hand on Cullen's shoulder. "I could show you the bedroom."

"Oh, you have a bed now?"

"Yeah, got pillows, sheets, all that stuff."

Standing at the kitchen sink with coffee and toast the next morning, Buddy pointed to the kitchen table, saying it was another piece of furniture he had made.

"That's impressive, man."

"Want another piece of toast?"

"I'm good, thanks. You mind if I grab a shower?"

"No, go ahead," he said, going to the bathroom to take out a towel for him. "There's shampoo and you can use my razor if you want. I put a new toothbrush with your towel."

"Buddy fucking Hebert. I was always crazy to get in your pants." He slipped an arm around Buddy's shoulder and gave him a quick hug before going into the bathroom.

With the shower running in the background, Buddy washed the coffee cups and plates, dried his hands and went to the bathroom, slipping in the door. Nudging back the shower curtain, Cullen was washing his hair, his eyes closed. Buddy reached out, taking hold of his dick.

Cullen opened his eyes and, smiling, patted Buddy's cheek with a soapy hand. "Come join me."

"Next time."

"That a promise?"

"Yep."

He straightened the bed, tossing the top sheet and bedspread back into place and ignoring the pecker tracks, telling himself he would change the sheets before bed later that night. The phone rang and it struck Buddy as an odd time for the phone. He picked it up, thinking it might be Mr. Hargrove.

Buddy laid the receiver down carefully on the kitchen counter, shaking. Legs unsteady, he sank to the floor, his thoughts scrambled, fingers clutching the piece of paper in his hand with the scrawled name and address of a hotel in New Orleans.

Chapter Nineteen

Cullen came from the bedroom and found Buddy on the floor, leaning against the cabinet, with a disoriented look on his face, the phone off the hook on the counter, pad and pens scattered across the Formica top.

"You okay?"

Cullen held out a hand and effortlessly pulled Buddy to his feet. Smelling of Buddy's lemongrass shampoo, he looked like the Marlboro Man at twenty-one.

"Cullen, I'm sorry. I have to go. My mother called. Go home. I'll...I'll phone you later."

"Is something wrong?"

"No, no. It's just...something I have to do now." Still partly dazed, he bumped into the doorframe going to the bedroom. He turned back to a confused Cullen and gave him a quick hug. "I'll call you. Promise."

Larry was home. Almost. He was at a hotel in New Orleans, waiting for Buddy to pick him up. Rushing through a shower and throwing on clothes, Buddy tore the dirty sheets off the bed and raced to Earl's house in Hundred Oaks, leaving his truck in Earl's driveway. Earl was eating breakfast, and not wanting to involve the whole family, Buddy asked him to step outside for a minute. He explained what was going on and said that he needed the keys to the Woody. Earl unlocked the garage and backed the car out, telling Buddy to be careful driving to New Orleans and back.

Following Florida out to the Circle then south on Airline Highway, he reached for a cigarette and remembered they were on the nightstand at home. At a gas station, he put gas in the car and bought two packs of cigarettes, one of them Lucky Strike.

What a fuck up. Brother, love of his life, home from Vietnam, no doubt landing just when he was rolling around in bed with his dick in Cullen Mosley. Larry had to have known at least a month before when he would be coming home. Why no letter to let Buddy know? Had he written to Earl? But Earl would have called him. Neither could he understand why Larry had called his parents instead of him to say he was back. He'd sent Larry his phone number and new address a week after he moved into the apartment on St. Louis.

Despite the questions in Buddy's head, he was shaking with relief and excitement, knowing Larry was finally safe and out of danger and only a few miles away, as out of danger as someone could be in New Orleans.

The hotel was on Dumaine, between Rampart and Burgundy. Buddy had a general idea where it was, confident he could find it. *Maison des Reines.*

At a little before eleven, driving down Dumaine but finding no place to park, he made a left on Burgundy and spotted a parking lot halfway up the block. At the hotel, he went straight to the front desk. The guy there looked to be Buddy's age, and for some reason was impatient.

"I'm picking up a friend. He's in room 223."

Pointing to some stairs on the right, the man said over his shoulder. "Second floor. Checkout is noon. Any time past that he gets charged for another night."

"Right. Let me pay that bill now."

The man shuffled through a file of cards and after a minute passed over a bill showing a total of more than two hundred. It was in the name of Julian Bentley.

"You sure this is the correct bill?"

"Room 223. Julian Bentley."

"How long has he been here?"

The clerk told him to check the itemized list of charges on the second page. According to that Julian Bentley had been at the hotel for eight nights, used room service five times and made a two-minute call to Baton Rouge earlier that morning. There had been a fifty-dollar deposit paid at check-in. Buddy wrote a check for the charges and took the stairs two at a time.

The room was midway down a dim hallway with a worn burgundy carpet. At the door to room 223, he leaned his forehead heavily against it, breathing in the stale air and knocking. No answer. He knocked again.

A ghost in blue boxer shorts stood in the open door. It was impossible for Buddy to hide his surprise, his confusion and concern, or the relief of having Larry back again. For several beats, he was frozen by a cyclone of emotions.

Larry didn't seem to notice the look on Buddy's face. He seemed half asleep, his eyes dulled.

"Hey," Larry said listlessly.

"Hey." Buddy's greeting was subdued as well.

Larry moved slowly, stepping to Buddy and putting his arms around him, holding him gently and whispering into his hair. "Buddy." And then he was crying, heaving sobs pushing against Buddy's chest.

Buddy kicked the door closed with his foot and guided Larry over to the bed. Arm around his shoulders, he pressed his face into Larry's dirty hair, wiped his face and kissed him.

"Are you okay, Larry? Tell me you're okay."

Larry didn't say anything, just held tighter to Buddy, pushing himself against him. Buddy struggled for the right words. "It's okay. You're back, I'm here. We're together now."

Larry settled and Buddy stared at his friend's frightened and uncertain face, stroking him and again wiping more tears off his cheeks. In all the time he had known Larry, it was the first time Buddy had seen him unwashed, his breath sour. He adjusted his position and Larry grabbed at him.

"I'm not going anywhere, brother. I'm here, I'm not leaving."

Larry pushed Buddy flat on his back and crawled on top of him, mouth against his neck. Buddy felt his breathing slow as Larry's weight settled onto him. Then he was asleep.

Reluctant to move or disturb his sleep, content just to feel Larry's weight on him, he looked up at the ceiling, imagining the terrible things inside Larry that were so evident on the outside. He slept unmoving for thirty minutes before jolting off Buddy. "Juli!" he screamed.

A moment passed, and he looked at Buddy, his breath coming fast, his voice small. "Sorry," he sighed, petting Buddy's face. "Did I scream?"

"Come on, Larry. Get up," Buddy coaxed gently. "Let's take a shower. You and me. Can we do that?"

Larry was docile under the low-pressure drizzle of warm water while Buddy washed him, his fingers tracing the scars of Larry's last year. His back against Buddy's chest, Buddy scrubbed his hair, Larry saying the same thing several times. "Feels good, I love you, Buddy."

All done, Larry turned around and kissed Buddy before sliding down and taking him in his mouth, bringing a gasp from Buddy at the wonder of Larry's mouth on him once again. When it was done, Larry stood again. "Good, Buddy?"

"Better than ever."

Reaching for Larry's hardness, Buddy took it hungrily.

Buddy then dried him off, noticing several small, scabby spots in the crook of Larry's left elbow.

"Shots before I left there," Larry whispered.

"Brush your teeth." Buddy said, wondering if it was true.

From the scattered chaos of the room, Buddy gathered Larry's clothes, putting them in a duffel he found at the foot of the bed. Larry also had a large and dirty khaki brown canvas backpack spilled open by the desk. When he picked up a small black zipper bag on the floor by the bed, Larry took it and stuffed it into the backpack.

As Buddy watched, he put on blue boxers, a pair of jeans, and a lightweight blue sweater over a musty red T-shirt. On his feet were a battered pair of brown leather boots, polished to a high sheen.

At the door Larry stopped. "Can you take my duffel bag down? I have to use the bathroom."

"Sure, I'll wait for you downstairs," Buddy told him, watching his unsteady walk to the bathroom and doing his best to push away his uneasiness.

****

Larry was more relaxed on the drive back to Baton Rouge. Headed toward downtown, he was humming something under his breath. "Where are we going?" he asked Buddy.

"Home."

"You passed it."

Buddy smiled over at him. "A new place. You forgot?"

"I'm confused."

"I wrote you, remember? Telling you I moved to an apartment downtown, not living with my parents anymore. We have our own place on St. Louis Street behind the Old State Capitol."

Larry leaned his head against the window. "Okay."

"We'll be there in a few more minutes."

Getting slowly out of the Woody, Larry looked up at the house. "You live here?"

"We live here."

Larry stood in the kitchen looking around. Finding the bedroom, he dropped the duffel bag on the floor. Taking off his clothes, he fell onto the bare bed, curling up.

"Come on, Larry. Sit in the chair by the window while I put sheets on the bed." He got Larry up and nudged him toward the chair. "Give me five minutes."

First were the clean sheets, then he emptied the ashtray and put the towel Cullen had used in the laundry hamper.

While Larry slept, Buddy unpacked his duffel bag, the smell of unwashed clothes wafting out of it. He put it all in a pile for washing. In the bottom was Larry's wrinkled Army uniform which went on a hanger in the closet. The backpack was on the floor among the clothes Larry had taken off.

Inside, Buddy found the small black zipper bag, swimming trunks, a pair of flip flops, a sheaf of Army papers, two plastic bags with Vietnamese writing on them, and at the bottom, a pistol. He put the plastic bags in one of the dresser drawers. He put Larry's wallet and the papers on top of the dresser along with the black zipper bag. Among the papers was a photograph of the Woody, spotted with rusty smears, and another of Larry with two other soldiers, all smiles, arms around shoulders, standing in front of what looked like a hangar. He didn't know what to do with the pistol. Holding it gingerly by the handle, he couldn't tell if it was loaded. He finally put it in the dresser.

Larry was still asleep at five-thirty. Buddy had washed

and dried his clothes by then and moving quietly, folded everything and put it in the dresser, shifting his own stuff to the lower drawers. Larry's one pair of jeans he folded and put on the floor beside the bed, along with a clean pair of underwear, a T-shirt and socks.

With a coffee and his furniture-making book, Buddy sat in the chair by the window smoking and studying Larry, sprawled in sleep on the bed. He was thinner, with a two-inch reddish scar on his left hip, another on his right arm just below the shoulder, and one on his stomach. His ragged hair fell not quite over the ears.

Unable to stop himself, Buddy went to the bed and leaned down, pressing his face gently into Larry's hair. It was still there, the intoxicating smell of fresh cut grass that caused a stirring in Buddy's jeans. Back to his furniture book, Buddy thought about making a dresser for Larry, one to stand next to the old one he had found in a junk shop and refinished. But his eyes were drawn back to Larry sleeping peacefully, his mind filled with that night at Billups when he was seventeen, ten months until graduation, his whole world tilting with the chance glimpse of his boyhood friend, Larry MacDuff.

At the Billups gas station across from Food Town, seventeen-year-old Larry had been pumping gas into a 1957 yellow Plymouth Fury, his hands smeared with black grease and a hank of dark hair hanging across his brow. The Fury belonged to twin brothers Buddy knew from school. The three of them were coming from a movie and had stopped for gas.

Buddy was in the backseat looking out the window when he saw Larry, recognizing him instantly. Two feet from where he sat, Larry stood gripping the gas pump, his crotch framed in the open window, gazing off at something across the street, unaware of Buddy. Staring at him from the shadowy backseat, Buddy's mind raced with the insane thought of reaching through the window and putting his hand against the front of those dirty coveralls.

The air oily with gas fumes, the hot smell of vulcanized tires and motor oil, dirty thoughts tumbled through his head. He imagined the smell of Larry's hair in that moment, imagined walking in to find him unzipped, pissing in the gas station's smelly, but sexy, men's room with its dented rubber machine hanging crookedly on a wall scratched and scarred with offers and revelations–*Dolores sucked my dick,* "*Blow job call WA-62739.* One proposition in particular intrigued Buddy, scaring him in an exciting way. *Horny 8 inches to fuck your hot ass.*"

Now he couldn't take his eyes off Larry, the little boy all grown up. Still in the chair by the window, Buddy had made some notes and sketches, ideas for the new dresser. He glanced up and saw Larry looking at him. He waggled his fingers, signaling Buddy over. At the bed, he pulled Buddy down beside him, wrapping his arms and legs around him. He struggled to get Buddy's shirt unbuttoned before Buddy took over.

They made love like fevered animals biting and tearing. Buddy couldn't get enough, fast enough, couldn't let go, the feel of Larry's skin under his hands. He had to beg before Larry would fuck him and when he finally did, Buddy was utterly consumed by the strongest orgasm of his life. His lips were sore from Larry's teeth, but he wanted more. An hour later, Buddy couldn't move, exhausted. Larry was an inch away, his breath a delicious tingle against Buddy's lips.

"I put your pistol in the dresser."

"Not mine. Juli's."

Buddy remembered the short letter about his friend's death, likely for Larry a memory of flying shrapnel, exploded bombs, and screams of the wounded and dying.

"I'm sorry about your friend." Buddy looked up at Larry's brimming eyes. "I understand."

"No, you don't. Can't," he said, looking back at Buddy and squeezing his hand.

"I'm trying."

In the front room, Larry opened the door and, leaning against the doorframe, looked out at the street. Turning back to Buddy, he spoke. "How much for this apartment?"

"A hundred a month. Don't worry about that. Get yourself settled and comfortable being home. I have plenty of money."

"You still working for the same guy?"

"Hargrove, yeah."

"Have you seen Earl lately?"

"I saw him this morning."

Larry held out an arm and Buddy joined him at the door. "Your car keys and the key to this apartment are on the kitchen counter below the phone."

Larry pulled Buddy's face against his. "I'm so fucking tired."

"Go back to bed."

"I have to go see Earl."

"He's probably home from the station by now. Go on over, or call."

"Will you come?"

"No, brother. You need to see Earl on your own this time. You wanna stay over there tonight, that's cool. You have a housekey, you can come back whenever. The phone number here I put in your wallet."

Buddy rode with him to pick up his truck at Earl's. Back at the apartment, he made a couple of calls, first to his mother telling her that they were back and that Larry went to see Earl. "Momma, he's real fragile now, cries easily. Tell daddy not to bring up Vietnam. Anyway, I'll call you."

He phoned Bob next and asked him to tell Damien that Larry was home, to pass on Buddy's number to him. The next call was harder. Buddy was elated with Larry being back and sort of wiped out by their sex romp earlier, and impatient for him to come back from Earl's. But even with that, dialing Cullen's number, he couldn't deny the frisson of excitement he felt thinking about Cullen in bed. When Cullen answered, Buddy apologized about rushing him off, told him Larry was home and that he would call again in a week.

He had no real idea when Larry would be back from seeing Earl, maybe not until the next day. He wasn't even sure Larry was comfortable with the idea of living in the St. Louis Street apartment. He might want to live in the garage apartment at Earl's, might even want a different apartment of his own. Buddy figured he would eventually go back to work for Earl. Living with Larry on St. Louis was a dream for Buddy, but possible only if Larry wanted it as well. Though Buddy had enough money for the two of them, earning a good wage, with money in the bank.

Buddy came home from the grocery store with the back of the truck half-full of bags and requiring three trips to get everything inside, another ten minutes to put it all away. A dozen boxes of chocolate pudding went in the cabinet, along with cans of soup and cornflakes. The refrigerator was filled with soft drinks and beer, sliced ham and milk and eggs. Bread was on the counter and there were enough apples and bananas to fill a bowl. There was plenty if either of them got hungry and didn't want to go out.

Buddy had never made chocolate pudding but following the directions on the box. He whipped up three boxes and the milk in one big bowl. Stupid he thought, but he couldn't wait for Larry to open the refrigerator and see the pudding.

While in bed with a ham sandwich and watching *Bonanza*, the sound of a key in the back door could only be Larry. Buddy felt selfishly happy he was back sooner rather than later.

Larry came straight to the bedroom and, saying nothing, dropped his clothes on the floor and climbed onto the bed with Buddy, head on his chest, arm across his stomach.

"How's Earl?"

"Good."

"I didn't think you'd be back so soon."

Larry didn't say anything.

"Did you have supper?"

"Yeah."

Buddy smoothed his hair, toying with his ear. "How come you didn't stay longer?"

"Missed you."

"You okay with this place? Think you can be comfortable here?"

"Where else would I go?"

Buddy moved the plate with the half-eaten ham sandwich to the bedside table. On the TV, Hoss was beating up a bully in Virginia City. "Want me to turn the TV off?"

"I don't care."

"How'd you get this scar?"

"What scar?"

He rubbed a finger across the welted pink line on Larry's hip. "This one."

"Shrapnel."

Eventually, Buddy turned off the TV and the light. Larry's head was still on his chest but Buddy wasn't sure if he was asleep. He'd hardly moved since getting in bed.

"Larry?"

When he didn't answer, Buddy eased out from under his head and went to the bathroom. Coming out, he found Larry looking in the refrigerator. Spotting the chocolate pudding, he took it out, setting the bowl on the table and looking for a spoon.

"Left drawer."

Buddy sat across from him in the dark apartment, deliriously happy, watching Larry shovel spoonfuls of pudding in his mouth. "Can I have some?"

Larry filled the spoon and held it out to him.

"Don't leave me," he said, watching Buddy swallow the pudding.

"Why would I ever do that?"

Larry ate one last spoonful of pudding, fed Buddy another and getting up, returned to the bedroom. Buddy left the spoon in the bowl, returning it to the refrigerator. Back in bed, he pulled Larry close, his chocolatey mouth against his neck, Larry's grassy hair in his face.

He lurched awake later with Larry screaming, hands on his head, elbows in front of his face. "Get him off me, Juli!"

"Shh, shh, it's okay. I'm here. Buddy's here." The clock hands on the bedside table glowed 2:25.

Larry sat rocking on the bed, head down and keening, staring at the floor.

"Do you want some water?"

"Don't go."

"You can come with me." Buddy helped him off the bed and walked him to the kitchen, an arm around his shoulder.

At the table, the glass trembled in Larry's hand. Buddy put a hand under it, guiding it to his mouth.

Chapter Twenty

It was obvious to Buddy, Larry was out of whack and clearly not himself. He seemed frail and scattered, lifeless and uninterested in anything but hiding. Buddy let it go for ten days. Larry was mostly sleeping, eating whenever, whatever he found in the refrigerator or cabinets before sitting on the front porch and smoking or diving back into bed. Some days he stared zombie-like and unseeing at the television. Bath habits were iffy, and a few times, Buddy threatened to sleep in the back bedroom, an empty threat as it turned out.

Sensing it was time, on his tenth morning in the apartment, Buddy threw the covers off Larry and opened the wooden blinds, shocking Larry awake with an explosion of sunlight that hit him like a flashbang. He pulled Larry out of bed by the feet, sending him to the shower. He hadn't asked for much, allowing Larry to wallow in misery up to a point, but that was over. Out of the shower and in fresh clothes, Buddy led him over to the levee, forcing him to walk a mile and back in the bright morning sun. Back at the apartment and unaware that Larry was jonesing, Buddy hustled him into the truck and off to the grocery store to load up a cart with the healthiest food he could find. Larry's lack of appetite worried him. He was also certain Larry was using something when his head got too crowded.

When they got home from the store, Larry locked himself in the bathroom. Buddy was busy in the kitchen with making coffee and scrambling eggs. While they were eating breakfast, Buddy explained that he was setting some limits. Larry was going to start eating right or there would be hell to pay. It was a Buddy Larry had never seen, and he was cowed. But thanks to Buddy, he was finally able to get up and out on his own.

Two weeks after his time in New Orleans, early on one Sunday morning, Buddy made them a breakfast of oatmeal with sliced banana, toast and coffee. After eating everything put in front of him, Larry told Buddy he had to go out and would be gone for a few hours.

"You want me to go with you?"

"No. I'm going to visit Juli's parents in Mandeville."

"That's an admirable thing to do. You think you can be back in time to have supper with my parents? They're expecting us."

"I can be back for supper. I want to see your momma and daddy. It's time."

Buddy was washing up the breakfast dishes and from the bedroom, Larry called, asking where his uniform was.

"In the closet."

"Fuck." Larry muttered, looking at the wrinkled uniform.

Buddy stuck his head in the door. "I have an iron. I can fix that. You go on and shower. It'll be ready when you're finished."

In his ironed uniform, with a gym bag borrowed from Buddy, and flying high on his last bag of heroin, Larry said he would meet Buddy at his parents' house later.

****

Larry cut over to Florida Street and turned east, heading for Covington, the drive a little over an hour, chain-smoking all the way. He hadn't figured out yet what or how much he would tell Juli's parents, but he wanted them to at least know their son had not died alone, that Larry was by his side. By custom, two soldiers from the 1st Infantry out of Fort Hood would have visited the house, but he didn't know what they might have told the parents about Juli's death. As Juli's best friend, he would give them what measure of comfort he could for the son they lost.

In Covington, he turned south toward Lake Pontchartrain and reaching Albert Street in Mandeville, stopped at a gas station and called the Bentley house, telling them he was in town. Juli's mother gave him directions to their home.

They were standing in the front yard of a small gray-green clapboard house with a good-sized front porch, the yard enclosed by a Hagen fence. At their feet was a hunting dog, its ears pricked as it watched Larry get out of the car and move toward the gate. Juli's mother and father stepped forward, meeting him at the gate. Sensing their friendliness toward the stranger, the dog wagged its tail and moved up to sniff at Larry's legs.

"Mr. and Mrs. Bentley, I'm Juli's friend, Larry MacDuff."

They both extended a hand to shake, inviting him inside. Larry was momentarily thrown by the blue eyes of the father, so like Juli's. Mrs. Bentley said the spotted dog was Buster, Juli's dog. He knelt and ruffled its ears and scratched its muzzle.

"Can I offer you some coffee or iced tea?" Mrs. Bentley asked, gesturing to a chair.

"No ma'am, I'm fine, but thank you."

On the mantel over a fireplace that housed a gas heater was a large, framed photograph of Juli in his uniform. Larry studied the photograph, fighting to hold it together and keep his face composed before turning back to the parents.

How did you and Juli meet?" Mr. Bentley asked.

"We were in basic together at Fort Polk, sir. Friends from the first day and we became what the sergeants call battle buddies. In Vietnam, we were at the same base camp in An Khê. Juli was my guard dog. That's what we called any Big Red One infantryman guarding mechanics outside the camp perimeter. I was a mechanic. Juli watched my back outside the wire."

"You spent a lot of time with Juli?" his mother asked.

"Yes, ma'am. We lived in the same hooch, the shelter where we bunked. Together most the time. Juli saved my life in two different firefights."

His mother cried quietly, blotting at her tears with a shredded tissue pulled from an apron pocket.

No one spoke.

"It should have been me," Larry said quietly.

"No, son. I know you did everything you could for our boy." Mr. Bentley's voice was husky, the light puddled in his brimming blue eyes. Juli's eyes.

From the gym bag, Larry brought out the plastic bag

from Ben Thanh Market. And from his coat pocket, Juli's wallet. "I took this for Juli's military ID. I gave the card to the MP but kept the wallet." He passed it over to Juli's father. "The afternoon of that day, Juli bought these for you," he said, handing the plastic bag to Mrs. Bentley.

Tears unabated, she peeked inside the bag, taking out a blue velvet box and finding the silver pendant on its delicate chain. Shimmering in Larry's memory was Juli showing him the pendant and asking if he thought his mother would like it. Mrs. Bentley laid a finger on the pendant in its box, asking if Larry would fasten it around her neck. She passed the plastic bag to her husband and turned, lifting the hair off her neck while Larry closed the loop on the chain, his hands jittering. Juli had gotten his father a silver money clip in the shape of an elephant.

They sat talking in the living room, a place filled with light from the windows but weighted with loss, the quietness a sound all its own. Larry asked if it was okay for him to see Juli's room. Mrs. Bentley took him back, telling him not to mind the dog, to take all the time he needed.

The dog was curled up at the foot of Juli's bed, eyes watching Larry. He brushed a hand across the bedspread, then the pillow, for a moment laying his head where Juli's once rested. Sunlight caught a collection of plastic toy soldiers on the desk in front of a window. They were the faded green of Juli's fatigues. Picking up one of the figures, Larry's knuckle tipped over its neighbor. Carefully righting it, he slipped the other one into his pocket.

Across from the bed, Larry slid the top drawer of the dresser open and looked down at the neat stacks of snowy white BVD briefs. He had never seen Juli wear anything other than boxer shorts, sometimes white, other times Army green or camouflage. Closing the drawer, he looked up, seeing his face in the mirror over the dresser. Wedged into the edge of the frame, a strip of three pictures from a photo booth hit Larry like a blow to the heart. The top picture was a goofy-faced Juli. Below that a half-smiling Juli, the face strongest in Larry's memory. The third picture showed a serious Juli, Larry's guard dog, mouth a straight line, the arresting blue eyes reflecting a defiant, flinty glare. Fitted into the opposite frame of the mirror was the photo of a girl, pretty with slightly crooked teeth, her brown hair pulled back in a ponytail. Prudy, Larry guessed.

Larry knelt at the foot of the bed, looking into the big, brown eyes of Juli's dog, scratching an ear gently. "I miss him, too, Buster."

Rejoining Juli's parents in the living room and holding out the strip of photos, Larry haltingly asked if he might keep them.

Mrs. Bentley stepped in to hug him. "Of course, you can, son." She passed Larry a slip of paper on which she had written directions to where they had laid Juli to rest. "It's just five minutes from here should you ever want to visit him."

Getting in the Woody, Larry gave a final wave to Juli's mother and father standing just inside the gate. Starting the car, he looked again to the house. Juli stood on the porch looking back at him, hands stuffed into his front pockets.

****

The causeway across Lake Pontchartrain got him to New Orleans in less than an hour. He found his way to the apartment in the French Quarter where the dealer lived, the one who'd sold him heroin several times. Before getting out of the car, Larry changed into jeans, tucking Juli's 9 mm in his waistband under his shirttail.

The dealer opened his door only a few inches, looking out at Larry, not saying anything.

"I was here a few times, couple of weeks back, remember?" Larry said into the narrow opening.

"The soldier, right?" the man said finally.

"Yeah. Can we do some business?"

"Didn't I fucking tell you to call first?" After another pause and shaking his head, the man said, "Fuck me. Hold on," before shutting the door in Larry's face.

He waited long enough to wonder if the guy was coming back but then the door opened. A downward glance from Larry showed a pistol jammed into the front of his pants. He gave a long look up and down the street before gesturing down the long hallway and following Larry to the messy kitchen that still smelled like onion soup.

He took two bottles of Jax from the refrigerator, passing one to Larry. "Same as last time?"

"A little more."

"How much more?"

"Twenty-five?"

That got his attention. "You got the bread?"

"How much?"

"Eight per bag. You buy thirty-five I can knock it down a little. Two-forty-five."

"Deal." Larry fanned the cash onto the dirty table. He had checked his wallet before leaving Buddy's apartment and found a hundred dollars more than he remembered having. Buddy must have put it there. It could only have come from him. "What's your name again?"

The man looked at him with a squint. "Aubin. And keep it to yourself." He scribbled a number on a scrap of newspaper, handing it over. "Don't lose it this time. And fucking call first," he said, going off to another room and coming back with a cigar box. From one end of the box, he counted out twenty-nine small glassine envelopes of heroin. From a plastic bag he measured out twenty milligrams on a scale, transferred it to an envelope, and doing it again five times, wrapped the thirty-five glassine envelopes neatly in a plastic sandwich baggie. "You want a taste?" he said, picking up the money and passing the bag to Larry.

Larry was sitting at the kitchen table in a wobbly chair, just past the first golden rush of his freebie. His eyes were on Aubin opposite him, the syringe an inch away from the vein in his arm. A loud pounding echoed down the long hall from the front door, jolting them both. Aubin dropped the syringe, lurching out of his chair and looking wildly down the hall to the door before swinging his gun to Larry's head.

"Cocksucker! Who the fuck you brought to my door?" His eyes flashed back to the front door, the gun swiveling from Larry to the hallway. He moved slowly down the hall to the door, the gun extended in front of him.

The thought hit Larry with the force of a trumpet blast in the ear. Police! Crashing through the door with thirty-five bags of heroin and a 9mm stuffed down his jeans, Larry stumbled to the rear of the apartment. Looking for a back door and finding it, he hit the door like a fullback slamming into a defensive line. It didn't budge. Stupidly, he rattled the handle before kicking it as hard as he could. It sprang open to a weedy garden littered with trash and walled by a six-foot wooden fence that he scrambled over. On the other side was a narrow alley leading out to Robertson, Saint Louis Cemetery on the other side. Dodging traffic, Larry ran inside the cemetery and sprinted down the path to a group of big mausoleums, finally collapsing from view behind one of them.

He sat catching his breath, adrenaline pumping through him. Fucking ripped on H and someone beating down the door, and the dope dealer pushing a gun in his face. He hunkered behind the mausoleum, playing the scene over in his head, trying to settle his nerves but finally laughing because he was free and alive and very stoned in the City of the Dead. About to step out onto the path, he read the name carved into the stone of his mausoleum hiding place.

Savinien LaSalle, born 1876, died 1937. Delivered to the Lord by His Will.

Taking a zig-zag route back to the car, the streets of the French Quarter were a sparkly carnival. The free fix was cooling Larry's head and he was once more on top of the world, despite the post-panic tremor in his hands that he couldn't stop.

At a phone booth, Larry dug a dime from his pocket and called the number Chandler had given him. He answered on the third ring and said he would meet Larry at Rampart and St. Ann in ten minutes.

Larry left the Woody parked on St. Ann and walked with Chandler back to his house, or as he called it, his parents' house.

"They here?"

"The old lady is visiting her sister in New Iberia, my pop's at work. Come on in."

He followed Chandler back to a small bedroom in the back. Telling Larry to sit, Chandler went to the kitchen and came back with two bottles of Jax. Seeing Larry still standing and snooping around the room, he gently pushed him onto the bed, passing over one of the beers. Around the other side of the bed, Chandler stretched out, his back against the headboard. "Make yourself comfortable," he said, patting the bed. "What brings you back so soon?" He clapped a hand on Larry's leg just above the knee and squeezed.

"Needed some Darvon," Larry answered, holding out two pills.

Chandler popped one in his mouth, crunching it up and washing it down with a swig of beer.

Larry swallowed the other one. "Besides, I wanted to see you again."

"Yeah? How come?" Chandler's hand moved up to Larry's belt.

"Maybe I like wrestling with grunts from the 199."

Walking back to the Woody with Chandler beside him, Larry's skin tingled. Chandler's smell was on him, his saltiness in Larry's mouth. Before Larry drove off, Chandler leaned in the window, his face close. "Don't lose my number."

****

Larry drove back to Baton Rouge with the radio loud, bopping in his seat to Marvin Gaye's "It Takes Two," and thinking about Perk, picturing him back in Lime Sink, Georgia, clapping his hands and grooving to Marvin. He often thought of Perk, fantasizing about his smooth coffee and cream skin.

Circling onto Florida Street off Airline, Larry couldn't remember what time Buddy said supper was, finally deciding fuck it, he'd go straight there, whatever the time. For the last mile, windows down, he belted out "There's a Kind of Hush" along with the radio, Herman's Hermits singing and swinging all up in his head, all the bad shit magically hushed.

Parking in his old spot across the street, Larry walked around back, a little disappointed not to see a flourishing garden, not even a few rows of strawberries. He sat on the steps looking out at the yard, head swirling with memories of all he had missed in the eighteen months he'd been gone. He saw Mr. Hebert on his knees trimming a tomato plant, telling him, "A garden is like the lost and found. Lose your worries, find yourself." He saw him wiping his face and lifting a glass of iced tea, saw him also falling to the ground, and later his pale figure in a hospital bed.

"Larry?"

Mr. Hebert had come out and in an instant Larry was up, arms thrown around the man he loved like a father. Unable to stop himself, he cried with the comfort of being at this house again with Buddy, his mother and his father.

"Welcome home, son. Lord, we've missed you." An arm around Larry, he guided him into the kitchen. "Look who I found."

The surprise made Mrs. Hebert almost drop a pan of biscuits. "Oh, my goodness! Larry, Larry." She went to him with arms open, pulling him into an embrace.

Larry kissed her on the forehead. "Makes my day seeing you, Mrs. H. I've thought about y'all just about every day."

"Just stop now before I cry. Clyde, take Larry out to the den while I get him a beer."

"Beer?" he said, surprised.

"Buddy told me to buy beer."

"Stretch out, son. You want the TV on?" Mr. Hebert said, pushing him toward the couch.

"No, sir. I'd rather talk to you."

"What d'ya think of Buddy's new apartment?"

"It's pretty cool. Full of stuff he made himself."

Mrs. Hebert brought a bottle of beer and a bowl of shelled pecans and sat in the chair across from Larry with a beer of her own.

"Thank you, ma'am."

"Furniture. That's his new hobby. Mother, did you hear Dub say that Buddy's cabinet work in the apartment could bring him a lot of work if word got around?"

"Yes, and I'm proud of him."

"You been feeling okay, Mr. Hebert?"

"I'm good. Can't complain. Been missing my helper out in the garden." Gesturing toward the backyard. "As you no doubt saw…"

The front door opened with Buddy yelling about the

people next door. "Call the police on those asses next door! How come Mr. Roberts on the other side hasn't said anything to 'em?" Buddy said from the kitchen. "He's a state cop." Coming into the den, Buddy rested a hand on Larry's chest before ruffling his hair. "You good, brother?"

"Never better."

When Earl and his wife arrived, they all enjoyed a reunion of sorts, Buddy's mother serving beer to all but her husband and asking Earl if he'd prefer a highball. Buddy was relieved that all talk skirted anything to do with Vietnam. When Larry said he was hungry, Mrs. Hebert called everyone to the table. "Larry, you sit over here next to me across from Earl and Eileen. Buddy, you're at the end opposite your daddy."

Mrs. H. kept the table full of Larry's favorites, meat-loaf and mashed potatoes, biscuits, butter beans and stewed squash with tomatoes, and later there was warm apple pie with her strong dark coffee.

"Eating your momma's meatloaf, I feel every time like I've died and gone to heaven," Larry said in bed later that night.

"I can ask her to make us one. She told me you look skinny." Buddy turned Larry's arm, and as he touched the needle marks there, a look of concern passed over his face.

Larry fell asleep, mouth against Buddy's neck, arm across his chest.

Chapter Twenty-One

From the door, Buddy tossed a pair of jeans out to Larry who was sitting in his boxers on the front steps.

"Might freak out the neighbors. Better put those on."

Buddy was making coffee when Larry came back inside. Leaning his face into Buddy's hair, he said, "Hey."

"I gotta work today. I left the address where I'll be on the counter in case you need me. It's not far, over behind the capitol, off the lake."

Out of the shower, Buddy found Larry in the window chair in the bedroom reading his book on furniture making. "Coffee's ready. You want some?" He brought a cup to Larry, setting it on the table at his elbow. "Got any plans today?"

"Might go and talk to Earl, see if he's got any work for me."

"He's not going to say no to that."

"Unless he already has a full crew."

"He'll let someone go to bring you back."

"What are the notes and drawings in this book?"

"Some ideas for a chest of drawers."

Before leaving, Buddy called his mother and told her Larry was raving about her meatloaf, and when she had the time, could she make one for him? He filled his thermos with the rest of the coffee, told Larry he would be home around five-thirty, and rumbled off in his old truck.

A little before eleven, Damien called the apartment, surprising Larry, saying he was working at home and inviting him to come over.

Larry straightened up the bedroom and washed the few dishes in the kitchen sink before taking a quick shower. Before getting dressed, he sat on the edge of the bed and took out his kit. He packed up his troubles, falling back onto the bed, a surge of soothing magic running down his arms and legs.

Afterwards, he followed Damien's directions, taking Government all the way to the old airport, a right on Lobdell and left on Sevenoaks. Damian's was a yellow house on the righthand side.

Shoeless in dark brown socks, camel brown corduroys and a mint green polo shirt, Damien stood in the doorway looking out at Larry. "You're a welcome sight, Mr. Mac-Duff," he said.

Damien led Larry back to a sunny room lined with record shelves, that he called the music room. He gestured to the sofa.

"You're thinner," he said, looking Larry up and down.

"That's what Buddy says. I read your article about the jazz pianist, Bill Evans, in *Downbeat*."

"Bored to death, were you?"

"Just the opposite. I want to hear his records."

"That's easy." From one of the record shelves Damien chose an LP, placing it on the turntable.

It caught Larry by surprise when music poured into the room from speakers mounted in the four corners near the ceiling.

"This album is *Waltz for Debby*, recorded in 1961 at the Village Vanguard. The first track, "My Foolish Heart," is an old 1949 movie soundtrack song, much better without the silly words," Damien said, joining Larry on the sofa.

Larry was silent for the duration of the track. This was his first time hearing Bill Evans and, not really knowing what to expect, the romantic opening with a hummable melody surprised him. He had expected something discordant and abstract. From the other end of the sofa Damien watched him, finally leaning closer and handing him a joint. Before sitting back, he brushed his fingers through Larry's shapeless scruff of hair.

"Scott LaFaro on bass, Paul Motian on drums. LaFaro never got to hear the recording, he was killed in a traffic accident only ten days after recording the album."

"That's a bummer."

"Evans went to college at Southeastern in Hammond. He has a brother who lives here in town, and the Debby in the album title is Evans' niece."

They were quiet for the remainder of the album. At the end, Larry asked Damien to play more.

"This one is called "Peace Piece" from *Everybody*

Digs Bill Evans, 1958." Damien said, pulling another LP from the shelves.

He was saying something else Larry missed, everything fading away behind the music, a slow-moving stream of notes that tingled the back of his neck. At the end, he asked Damien to play it once more.

"Evans said once that the idea of 'Peace Piece' came out of a Leonard Bernstein tune called 'Some Other Time' from his musical, *On the Town*. I'll get the Evans album for your birthday." Damien said, as the last notes faded.

"Can I see the album cover?"

"Okay, I get it now. Two different spellings," Larry said.

Laying aside the record jacket, Larry pulled Damien closer and mentally replaying the party at Bob's not long after they'd first met, kissed him.

"Wow."

"I kinda like you."

They sat against one another, captive to the Bill Evans Trio, the occasional low appreciative sound slipping involuntarily from Larry's throat.

"That baby blue looks good on you." Damien said, commenting on Larry's T-shirt.

Eyes falling to Larry's left arm, he lightly rubbed the needle marks in the crook of his elbow, then went off to another room. He was back a moment later, applying alcohol to a cotton ball and swabbing the marks on Larry's arm, before putting a small bandage across them. "There."

"Show me the rest of your house."

The music surrounded them, this time from speakers in the bedroom. Cross-legged on the bed, Larry looked at Damien standing a few feet away. This was only the third time he'd seen Damien, spent any time with him, but that night of the party at Bob's house lingered in his mind. He didn't understand it then, and even now didn't get it, but there was something in Damien he liked. Something he hadn't figured out, something comfortable. His intelligence and the way he talked, always correct, never cursing, never sounding like what Larry was used to and unlike the vernacular sloppiness he was familiar with. Damien was always neatly dressed in what Larry guessed were expensive clothes. Looking at him now five feet away, in nothing but Jockey shorts, he was slim like Juli but without the hardness of muscle. He had brown eyes, reddish-brown hair and small, dark nipples against his pale skin, a combination of aspects that appealed strongly to Larry.

Over the next hour, Larry experienced a new kind of arousal, one his partner might have described as a cool jazz-adagio of erotic play that left them finally spent in physical communion, body to body in the rumpled sheets.

"Does Buddy have a turntable at the apartment?" Damien asked.

"I don't think so. Haven't seen one."

****

Larry was polishing his boots when Buddy came in the back door.

"What's that?" Larry asked.

Buddy extended the platter, foil crinkled around it. "Meatloaf. My mother made it for you."

"Two nights in a row? We're living high on the hog."

Setting the meatloaf on the counter, Buddy pulled off his T-shirt and, leaning into Larry, the familiar smell of sawdust and sweat radiated off him, Larry taking greedy gulps of it. Tossing the shirt aside, "Everything good today?" Buddy asked.

"I went over to Damien's earlier. Listened to a couple of Bill Evans albums."

"He's the guy in that magazine article, right?"

"Yeah, jazz pianist. Totally cool. He graduated from Southeastern."

"Really? He from around here?"

"Damien didn't say."

Larry called Buddy's house to thank his mother for the meatloaf. She told him to come over anytime, she didn't want him going hungry. Larry promised he would come for lunch.

Out of the shower, Buddy put the meatloaf in the oven to warm up. "What else do you want? We have lettuce and tomatoes."

"I want a meatloaf sandwich."

In bed later, Larry was reading a book, while Buddy was watching *Mission Impossible*. He turned it off halfway through, staring at the blank screen and pulling at his long hair. He got up, went to the kitchen and came back with a beer, sitting on the edge of the bed facing away from Larry, smoking and worrying the label on the beer bottle.

"Larry, will you tell me about your friend, Juli?" he said, his back to Larry.

Larry squinted over at him before turning his eyes back to the book.

Buddy turned to face him. "I know he meant a lot to you."

"You don't know anything about it."

"You're right, I don't."

Larry closed the book and lay on his side, facing away from Buddy. Turning off the light and leaving the room in a pale wash of ambient light from outside, Buddy went to the chair by the window. The occasional thud of his beer bottle against the table was the only sound. Some time passed before Larry spoke, the words barely audible. "I loved Juli."

"I sort of guessed that much."

Larry swung his feet slowly to the floor. "I loved him and he died right in front of me. What else, Buddy? Did we do what you and I do? Yeah, that too." Going to the window, he looked out. "I was scared and Juli was there."

"Actually, I always thought he liked girls. He used to talk about one named Prudy, tell me what he liked about her. At the start, Juli was just a friendly guy in the bunk next to mine," he added, after a stretch of silence. "You were in my head, but you weren't there. I was scared shitless. But I was lucky, really. Juli was Big Red One and they put his ass in the boonies from day one. He was tough. You didn't fuck with Juli. He was gentle as a lamb and hard as nails. He got some stand-down time back in An Khê, and we met up again. Somehow, he wrangled a job in the maintenance hangar with me, and started riding shotgun outside the wire, me and him and Perk."

Larry told Buddy how they got in some serious shit one day in Indian country, that he'd have been a dead fucker without Perk and Juli, how he got the shrapnel in his hip, his baptism of fire. He told of watching the life leak from Trout's eyes. He stopped there, going to the kitchen for a beer and coming back. He sat on the floor by Buddy, smoking, staring into the dark. "Charlie got in through the wire one night. Fuckers love to come at night. I was in a foxhole with Juli and the world exploded." Like it did every time Larry thought about it, his heart bounded. "I killed a sixteen-year-old boy and I see his eyes in my sleep every night."

Buddy put a hand on his shoulder.

"I was fucked up after that. The sergeant let me slide, and I found something to help manage my head, the pain in my hip. Me and Juli went for R&R at a small island in the Philippines. When it was over, we flew back to Saigon." He looked up at Buddy. "By that night he was dead."

Larry sat on the floor at Buddy's feet, Buddy in the chair, the two men were thousands of miles apart, each looking for the way back.

Lying against one another that night in bed, Larry's eyes fastened on things far away, Buddy's mind spun, trying to plumb the unspoken parts of the story he'd just heard.

"What did he look like?"

His eyes on the ceiling, seeing things not there, a slight smile curled the corner of Larry's mouth. He reached into the drawer of the bedside table and took out the photo with Perk and Juli, passing it to Buddy. "Juli had big ears sticking out from his head. Blue eyes, like his father's, I discovered. His hair was the color of cinnamon, and he had a scar on his left shoulder, the first place I ever touched him. We were the same height, but Juli was lanky with hard muscle. He could kick ass in a firefight, was scared of nothing." He slipped the cigarette from Buddy's fingers and took a couple of drags. "When we were on the island in the Philippines, I coaxed him onto the back of a motorbike. I was doing some daredevil stuff and managed to scare him a little. It was not easy to do." He passed the cigarette back to Buddy. "I never figured out what he saw in me."

"So, all said and done, brother, where does that put us?" Buddy asked.

"We'll have to figure that out, I guess. I've never stopped loving you for one second since that night at my house on North Street four years ago. I never stopped thinking about you, even when Juli's shoulder was against mine. I've thought hard about what Juli meant to my connection with you. I love you, Buddy, but I loved Julian Bentley, too and he's gone now." They lay still, looking at one another in the dark.

"I'll go if you want me to. But I don't want to live without you." Larry said, after a while.

****

When Larry got up the next morning, Buddy was gone. He made coffee and took their dirty clothes out to the washing machine in the garage. On the kitchen table, he found a note under the saltshaker. *Gone to work. Home the usual time. RWH.* He sat thinking about Buddy, wondering if they were all right, hoping Buddy wouldn't ask for more confessions about him and Juli. He wanted to be alone with his thoughts about Juli. He was a private part of him not to be broached, something to keep close, polishing with a grief he feared might never diminish. He was revisiting memories of Juli, keeping them alive. Clinging. A two-fold betrayal, twice as bad? And Damien the day before? What would that do to Buddy?

Larry made the bed, straightened up the apartment, and moved the clothes to the dryer. After a shower, he tied off his arm and played out his small ritual with the white powder, savoring even in the preparation that feeling of leaving his body. He was hanging suspended for a time in a life less cluttered, where everything inside and out was at harmony. Drifting through the apartment, he left some of the cleaning chores half-finished before driving off in time to see Earl before lunch.

Earl saw him pulling in and came straight to the Woody, leaving a man bent under the hood of a green Chevy Malibu.

Earl threw an arm around his shoulder. "Goddamn, it's a pleasure to have you back," he cried out, loud enough to be heard across the street.

"Yeah, I missed your gnarly ass, too."

Laughing, Earl called to the man in the bay. "Loomis, put this car in back, slot that says *Woody*. "Come on in the office," he said, grabbing Larry's arm.

There was the cluttered counter and battered desk with the bevel gear paperweight. A different calendar hung on the closet door, but it was all the same, felt and smelled the same, and Larry realized how much he had missed the place.

"So, when can you start back?"

"Work, you mean?"

"Hell, yeah, work. I need you, Larry." Gesturing first to the bay, then the pumps outside, he complained. "I can't trust either one a them yokels out there."

"Maurice gone?"

"Yeah, the fool got married, moved to Gonzales."

"Well, whenever you say, I'll be here."

"Lemme juggle the schedule, I'll call you tomorrow. How many hours you want?"

"All you got." Copying it from the slip in his wallet, Larry wrote down the number at the apartment. "I'm staying with Buddy at his place downtown on St. Louis."

They jawed for a while before Larry left for lunch at the Hebert's house. Parking spaces at the lumber mill were all taken, so he parked in front of the house and went in through the screen door around back, calling out for Mrs. Hebert..

"Come on in, Larry!" she answered, coming into the kitchen. "Clyde will be here in a little bit. You want some tea?"

"No, ma'am, I'm good. Your meatloaf Buddy brought home is appreciated. Thank you for that."

She was just taking roast beef sandwiches out of the refrigerator when Mr. Hebert came in the back door. "Hey, son. You doing okay?"

"Hanging on."

"Every soldier coming home has a time of adjustment. I can remember not wanting to talk much, didn't matter what."

"Yes, sir, I believe you're right. Buddy's helping to pull me together."

"Well, enjoy taking it easy for a while. You damn well deserve it."

"Maybe, but I'm gonna start back with Earl soon. Anything y'all need done while I'm here? Think I might enjoy cutting your grass."

"The big box in the bedroom needs moving to the attic. Can you manage that?"

"Sure, I'll do it now."

"No, sit down. Lunch is ready. You want milk or tea?"

"Okay if I have a beer?"

"I'll have one with you." She got two bottles of Jax from the refrigerator.

"What does Buddy do for lunch?" Larry asked.

"I think he stops at one of the take-out places downtown on the way over to the house they're building. You want more Thousand Island for your sandwich?"

"This is perfect. You sure there's nothing I can do out in the yard?"

"No," Mr. Hebert said. "But I wish you'd see what's making a noise in the engine of our Chevy."

"I can do that."

"Now, Clyde, don't put the boy to work."

"Not a boy any longer."

"You still thinking of starting up your own business fixing old cars?" Mrs. H asked, putting some salad on Larry's plate.

"I had a friend who was gonna do that with me. He didn't make it back, though."

"Oh, son, I'm sorry to hear that. So sorry." In a quieter voices she said, "I'm starting to think those hippies on TV yelling about us getting out of Vietnam aren't all wrong."

"One of 'em spit on me at the airport in California."

"I hope you boxed his damn ears off!" Mr. Hebert snapped.

Larry didn't know why he had said that about Juli, about doing the car business with him. He had only just mentioned it to Juli when their world blew up. It was an evaporated wish that something good was going to keep them together when they got home. He was still clinging to Juli.

After lunch, he carried the box up to the attic and

drove the Hebert's car around the block, listening to the engine. Pretty sure he knew what the problem was, he drove across the street to the station.

"Go on and put it in the bay," Earl said. "Whose car is it?"

"Mr. Hebert's."

Larry let the engine warm up a little longer before revving it hard. His ear was cocked to the engine sound when the man he'd seen earlier came into the bay asking how long he was going to be.

Larry glanced at him. "Long as it takes."

"How long, you think?" He swiped at his nose. "I need the bay. Have to get to work on that blue Mercury over there." He was leaning in the window of the car.

Too mellow to take the bait, Larry spoke quietly. "Get the fuck out of my face. Take it up with Earl."

Earl walked up behind the guy. "Back off, Loomis, before you get your ass handed to you. Take your lunch break. Sorry, Larry. What's going on with the Hebert's car?"

"Engine knock."

"I'll take care of it and have Loomis drive it over to the house in an hour or so. You go on."

"I don't mind doing it."

"Go on. Tell Mr. Hebert an hour."

Back at the house, Mr. Hebert was napping on the couch in the den and Larry told Mrs. Hebert about the car. He was getting in the Woody when she brought out a stack of Buddy's washed clothes.

Two boxes were sitting in front of the door at the apartment when Larry got back, one of them big. Seeing Buddy's name on the labels, he figured it was something he had ordered. He carried both boxes inside and thinking Buddy wouldn't mind, opened the smaller box. It had an envelope with *Larry* written on it. Inside was a card with just two words: *Enjoy! Damien.* He pulled out three Bill Evans LPs, *Waltz for Debby, Conversations With Myself,* and *Everybody Digs Bill Evans.* The big box held a turntable, amplifier and two speakers. After opening it, Larry called Damien, who told him it was a welcome home present.

He surveyed the front room. The table against the bedroom wall seemed like the best spot to use. He wired everything up, placing the turntable and amplifier on the table. He put one of the speakers in the bookcase and the other against the wall. He tucked the wires neatly behind the bookcase, and under the table. *Everybody Digs Bill Evans* went on the turntable first and, sitting on the floor among the boxes, Larry listened again to "Peace Piece." Its meditative calm, the repeated phrases and serene melody stirred thoughts of Damien Marsleigh before spinning Larry back to Buddy and back again to Damien.

Chapter Twenty-Two

Home from work, tired, and sweaty, Buddy heard music in the front room. Looking around, he saw the turntable and sound system with two speakers. He picked the card up off the coffee table and looked up to see Larry standing in the kitchen doorway.

"Pretty cool, huh? It was here when I came home from your house."

"Why would Damien send us a stereo?"

Larry shrugged.

"I don't get it."

"Me neither. Big surprise."

"Did you call Damien, ask what gives?"

"Yeah. He said it was a welcome home present."

Buddy remembered Bob telling him that Damien had family money from a patent his father held for some gizmo in airplanes. He figured the guy must be rich.

"Are you mad?" Larry asked him.

"No, Larry. Just wondering about any strings attached."

"I don't think so. Maybe he's just trying to share some of what he loves."

That got a slight frown from Buddy. "That's what you think?"

"What else?"

Still puzzled, Buddy pulled Larry against him. "I like having music in the apartment. What's this playing now?"

"Bill Evans, the guy I mentioned hearing at Damien's the other day. You like it?"

"Yeah. You washed clothes. Thanks," he said, noticing the stacks of folded clothes.

"What's wrong with you? You don't have to thank me."

"Okay." Going to the bathroom, he said, "Could you look at my truck? Something's off. It's been overheating the past couple of days."

"Could be the water pump. I'll look at it tomorrow.

You take the Woody to work."

"What you told me about Juli? Pretty much been on my mind all day," Buddy said, later that night, speaking against Larry's ear.

"I don't wanna talk about Juli anymore."

"That's just it. We don't have to talk about Juli. I respect your feelings and won't bug you anymore about him." He put a hand against Larry's heart. "Is that okay with you?"

Larry nodded and rolled over, throwing an arm across Buddy's chest, his mouth against his neck.

****

In the middle of the night Buddy woke to the sound of Larry whimpering.

"Wake up, brother. You're dreaming. Shh, I'm with you."

Larry's dreams were often bad. Some nights he screamed or cried out. This time, the sweat poured off him, his heart jumping out of his chest. "Lie still. I'll be right back."

Buddy brought him a cold, wet cloth and a glass of water. Larry was sitting on the edge of the bed, head in his hands. "Here. Drink this," Buddy said, as Larry's whole body trembled against him. "I don't know much about this kind of thing but you can't be the only one who came home with bad dreams. Can't one of the doctors at the VA give you some pills to help?"

"The VA is fucked up. I have medicine. Just can't take too much of it, too much is bad."

Buddy had heard things, stories about guys coming home from Vietnam. He knew about what they called shell shock. He'd also heard that some guys came home with drug problems.

"What kind of medicine are you taking?"

Larry didn't say anything.

"Larry?"

He held up his left arm and with a finger touched that spot Buddy had noticed and wondered about many times. And then everything fell into place. Buddy knew. The full realization was a wrecking ball at full velocity. A few seconds passed with Buddy processing it, before he asked, "Where do you get it?"

"A guy in New Orleans."

"It's dangerous, Larry. You could kill yourself."

"I know. I'm careful."

"Yeah, but it gets worse. You'll need more and more, right?"

"I know."

"How long?"

"After K'bang. Last February."

"Oh, shit, Larry." He held him, rocking on the edge of the bed until Larry fell asleep. At seven, Buddy called Mr. Hargrove, saying he had a bug or something and was taking the day off. Back in bed, he pulled Larry against him and they slept until a little before ten. Not long after waking up, Buddy noticed Larry was sweating again, and irritable.

"Come on, stop grumbling. Get up. I'll make some coffee. You hungry?"

"No." He found his cigarettes and, pulling on jeans, went out to the front porch.

Buddy saw the tremble in his hands as he paced up and down the porch.

"When are you going to work?" Larry said.

"I'm taking a day off."

Buddy saw the movement of Larry's eyes, flicking from right to left, a slight crease in his forehead. "That's okay with your boss? You can do that?"

"Yeah. What's wrong? I wanna be with you today."

"Why?" He looked out the back door instead of at Buddy. "You afraid I'm gonna shoot up?"

He was suddenly up against Buddy. "Because I am, Buddy. I am, and you're either with me or not."

He pushed off Buddy, getting his black zipper bag from the dresser and taking it into the bathroom. He didn't bother closing the door all the way and Buddy stood in the hall looking at him through the partially open door. Sitting on the floor, Larry fumbled inside the bag, taking out an eyeglass case, a strip of rubber, bent spoon, small bottle, some cotton balls and a small envelope of what Buddy guessed was heroin. From the eyeglass case came a syringe, all the things Larry needed to chase away the demons.

"Come sit with me. It's better than way." Larry said, seeing Buddy at the door.

Cross-legged on the floor, his hands resting on Larry's knees, Buddy watched every move, not missing a single detail of the cooking, the cotton ball, the look of concentrated desire on Larry's face as the syringe drew the heroin into the barrel. He saw Larry's tooth biting down on his bottom lip as he moved the needle to the bulging vein beneath the rubber tourniquet. Larry's hand trembled as the needle got closer. Buddy reached out, steadying it until Larry found the vein and very slowly depressed the plunger. He watched Larry's mouth open, his eyes closed, until the needle slipped out and he sank back against the bathtub, a purely beatific look passing across his face, sunlight erasing shadow. Stunned by the transformation, it was in Buddy's eyes like watching an angel come to life.

"Jesus," he whispered.

"Even better," Larry whispered back.

Chapter Twenty-Three

Larry was back at Billups working full shifts and managing it well. Buddy called Earl asking how it was with Larry back at the station, and Earl said it was like he'd never been gone. He conceded Larry was the best mechanic there, even teaching Earl things he hadn't known about engine maintenance. Larry had been missed and Earl felt the station was better having him back. Earl told Buddy that he'd bought a beat up 1950 Ford F1 farm truck, just for fun, something for Larry to tinker with, a side job for him to piddle around with in their spare time at the station. According to Earl, Larry was on his way to turning it into a dream truck for car collectors.

"I'll be honest with you, Buddy. Larry is wasting his skills at my gas station. He deserves to be working in his own shop, being his own boss. I surely don't intend to hold him back when he decides to take that step."

It eased Buddy's heart hearing Earl say that. He had never doubted what Larry could accomplish, he just worried about the drug addiction, something he never said a word about to anyone. Though Damien had mentioned it, recognizing it the first time he'd seen Larry after his return from Vietnam. Damien had actually made Buddy feel a little better about Larry's use of heroin, saying he knew what to look for and how to steer Larry through his hazardous condition. In one of their conversations about it, Damien had explained that the cost of addiction was often what led addicts into threatening situations, adding that he would never let that happen. Buddy said that he too would make sure it never happened. And so for the time being, Buddy felt they could manage it, the two of them protecting Larry from himself.

On another front, Buddy was becoming more involved with Cullen Mosley. It wasn't a case of diminishing love for Larry, more of a physical attraction, what he'd heard someone once call, *thinking with his dick*. For both of them, he and Cullen, it was never more than anything but two friendly companions getting together for some fun. The truth was, Buddy couldn't get enough of a naked Cullen. Sometimes he felt as if he could spend the entire day in bed with Cullen and never tire of it. He didn't know the why of it, but Cullen was a sexual maestro, a grandmaster who could bring Buddy to whimpers or shouts of gratification, depending on their sexual scenario.

This time, he and Cullen had taken the day off to meet and drive out to Belle Helene. They agreed to meet at the Pastime, leaving Cullen's car in the parking lot and driving out River Road in Buddy's truck. When they met in the lot, Buddy discovered Cullen had brought along a gym bag of what he called toys.

Buddy sensed in Cullen a mood, a sense of mind he hadn't seen before, quietly garrulous and telling Buddy things about their days at Alan Shepard High he had never guessed at.

"I once talked to my friend Freddy about you, Buddy. Told him all about our fights and my being the king of assholes to you, admitted finally that I wanted more than anything to do with you what we only got around to a few months ago. Hell, Buddy, if I could have gotten over my fear in high school, I would have jumped your bones in a second. You were my fantasy. Probably surprises you, huh?" He leaned across the seat and gave Buddy a sloppy kiss on the cheek. "So, when we get to this place you're taking me, this crumbling manor house of yore, you can open my bag of toys and pay me back for all those times I made life miserable for you at Alan Shepard."

He lit a cigarette and put an elbow on the open window, gazing out at the bucolic sights of River Road, and didn't say another word.

The next time Buddy saw Cullen after that afternoon at Belle Helene, he told him they had taken it a little too far that day and maybe they should dial it back. "Where did you learn all that stuff anyway?"

"I'm not really sure, Buddy. Sometimes I think it was always there, somewhere in the back of my mind. You remember that day in Phys. Ed. class you and I got into it and Coach Riggs came running out to break it up? At first, I didn't understand it, only later that night thinking about it in bed, did I see the truth of it. That whole time we were rolling around on the ground, you on top of me, pounding on me, my busted lip gushing, from the first punch of that fight, I got a boner. No kidding, you smack me in the mouth and I'm thinking how close we were in those minutes and how great it felt."

"How did you learn that stuff about ropes and getting tied up? And the handcuffs."

"I saw it in a magazine and thought I might like it."

"And do you like it?"

Cullen was slow to answer and Buddy didn't force it. They sat through a red light before Cullen answered. "I liked it when you did it to me at that old place on River Road."

"I don't know Cullen. I'm not sure I can share that feeling with you. I like it when we can go at one another freely without being tied down. I want the feeling we are both active in what's going on. I can't feel that when one of us is restrained by handcuffs or tied up with rope. I'm sorry, I'm just trying to be honest. The handcuffs and tying us up just isn't what turns me on."

"Okay, Buddy. I understand that. We don't have to do it."

It wasn't until they were parked in front of Freddy's house that Cullen again brought up the past, telling Buddy of another time in high school, a time that involved him as well. "That day I sat across from you at lunch with a bloody nose, it was me that started the thing with the big football player. I was looking for it, provoked it. It had nothing to do with that big goofus and all to do with my insecurity over liking guys and getting fucked for the first time the night before. Under all that was the difficulty of admitting I had liked it. It hurt like hell, but I liked it." He smiled at Buddy and grabbed his hand. "And then we went out to your car and I told you my big secret."

"I remember that day. You and I were better after that talk."

Freddy came out the front door and seeing Buddy's truck, went over to say hello to Buddy and tell Cullen he was off to his studio. "How are things with you, Buddy? You and Cullen go in and have some of that brisket on the stovetop. I gotta run. I'll see you guys later."

"I'll call you," Buddy said as Cullen got out of the truck.

Chapter Twenty-Four

One Saturday evening, Buddy and Larry were having some friends over to the apartment for a party. Larry spent a couple of hours putting a high gloss on the natural wood cabinets and the furniture while Buddy gave the place a rigorous cleaning. Damien came early with a stack of records, wanting to get the music set up and arranged in the order of his playlist. With the few albums in Buddy's and Larry's collection, they needed Damien's help, as he would surely provide the right soundtrack.

Larry was washing his hands at the kitchen sink when Buddy returned from the store, juggling a heavy bag of booze and another of peanuts, chips and pretzels, dumping it all on the kitchen counter. He looked Larry up and down, and asked if he planned on wearing what he had on for the party, saying the jeans and T-shirt were kinda grubby. Submitting to Buddy's frown, Larry changed and put on a clean pair of jeans and an aloha shirt.

After changing clothes, stepping over to Damien poring over his playlist at the turntable, Larry told him to stop worrying. "Everyone will love the music."

"Hope I haven't made a mistake with Betty Carter."

"Who?"

"Never mind. I'll tell you later." He looked from one speaker to the other, shaking his head. "You really should replace these Pioneer speakers. They're terrible. My mistake."

Buddy had found another chair to go with the one by the window in the front bedroom, so now there was the table and lamp with a chair on either side. The old lamp had been replaced by a brass banker's lamp that Bob had seen at an estate sale and gotten for Buddy. The new bedcover was one of Buddy's finds, something like an Indian blanket, mostly black, white and red.

The apartment looked good. Most of it was Buddy's handmade furniture and cabinets. He had an eye for what made a room look just right, a good sense of color and pattern and the skill of matching things to create a tasteful and comfortable look. Damien and Bob had both commented on it.

"Fifteen minutes is too long, Bob. The cheese will be dripping." Bob and Denise were at the stove, fussing over the nachos she had just put in the oven. Buddy was getting a beer for Jay, his friend from work, and a cola for Jay's friend, Arthur. Cullen and Freddy were on the sofa talking to Carol and the couple from upstairs, and in the bedroom, Damien was pressed up against Larry saying he looked high as a kite.

Damien was right, he could always tell. At that moment, Larry was golden on his second fix of the day. Underneath that high, he fended off a worrisome tingle about using twice a day, fixing morning and night for the past three months and wanting more. Each time Larry saw his dealer in New Orleans, he came home with a wallet lighter by three hundred dollars. So far, the money hadn't been a problem. He was working full-time at Billups and Buddy was still in the habit of leaving money in his wallet. Now Damien was also cautioning him about using, but also slipping money in Larry's pockets, money he knew would be used for smack. He explained it by saying the money would help keep his addiction less complicated. The other side of that reasoning was that it gave Larry the freedom to buy more, to stockpile heroin with never a shortage and no need to scrimp.

Only a week ago, on an afternoon they were in bed, Damien had made the comment that desperate love and addiction made for a bad partnership. Later, putting on his jeans after a shower, Larry found two hundred-dollar bills folded inside a pocket. Now, kissing Larry on the ear, Damien whispered that when it became time—and there would come a time—he knew a good place for getting off drugs. It was scary stuff that Larry only half-heard, thankful at least Damien hadn't thrown the word rehab in his face.

Larry was now falling for Damien. Buddy controlled his heart as he always had, as Juli had for a short eighteen months. But now Damien did as well. Yeah, it was addiction and desperate love all around. But it was another of Larry's secrets that each time he was in New Orleans he got together with Chandler. It was his Vietnam connection and he needed the commonality that seeing Chandler provided. Somewhere in those brief couplings were words and gestures that kept Juli alive for him.

Damien gave Larry a push. "Go on back to the party. Buddy will be looking for you."

Buddy wasn't looking for Larry but was instead at the kitchen sink with Cullen Mosley standing close, both men laughing softly, in a chummy moment. Larry knew that he was the last person to question Buddy's faithfulness. In the front room, he sat down next to Jay, Buddy's work friend.

"Hi, I'm Larry."

"Hey, man. Jay."

"Buddy said you guys work together. Gotta say, as soon as you walked in the door I had a flashback of my friend Perk, guy who lives in Georgia."

"How's that?"

"I don't know. You look a little like him maybe?"

"And there I was, thinking we all look the same," Jay said, a smile in his eye.

"Clarence Perkins, we called him Perk. Saved my life once or twice."

Damien came from the kitchen stirring his drink with a finger.

"What's this music?" Larry asked him.

"Betty Carter, "Heart and Soul," from a 1963 album called *'Round Midnight*."

"Have you met Jay?"

"Damien Marsleigh, Jay. A pleasure." He held out a hand.

"Cool music, man."

"Damien writes for some of the jazz magazines."

"You fellas need something to drink?" Damien asked, ignoring Jay's impressed look.

"I'm good," Larry said. Jay held up his still full bottle of beer.

Damien checked his watch and moved to the turntable. Looking at his playlist, he took the top LP off the stack and, slipping the record from its sleeve, passed a cloth over it. Betty Carter faded away, followed a moment later by John Coltrane's "On Green Dolphin Street."

"Most white folks never heard of Betty Carter," Jay said to Larry.

Meanwhile, Bob and Buddy sat talking in the bedroom at the table by the window, Bob with his usual vodka martini pointed to the nearest chest of drawers.

"I made it after Larry got home. He needed one of his own," Buddy said.

"What kind of wood is it?"

"English walnut. I chose it because it's resistant to decay. Solid, durable, not too heavy, bonds well. I'm trying to build with fewer nails. Mortise and tenon. The Japanese do it very well."

"Do you ever sell your furniture?"

"Never tried."

"I would buy a chest of drawers like that. Name your price."

"You serious?"

"The cabinets, the coffee table, that bed over there, and the kitchen table, right?"

Buddy nodded in response.

"You have skills, Buddy. Make a chest of drawers like that for me and name your price."

"All right, I'll make one for you."

"Good. Now I have to check on Carol."

"She and Arthur, Jay's friend, were in the other bedroom last time I looked."

"Biggest fag-hag in the world," he said, shaking his head. "First time she met Larry she drooled. But then, Larry is definitely drool-worthy." He picked up the copy of *In Cold Blood* from the table.

"Larry's reading that. Damien loaned it to him," Buddy said.

"Nice bedtime reading."

"What's it about?"

"Murder."

****

The small bedroom at the back of the house wasn't used often by Buddy and Larry and, for that reason, was sparsely furnished. The only furniture in the room was a brass bed centered on one wall, with small tables and lamps on either side. On the floor at the foot of the bed was a bright Navaho rug in wide bands of red, green and white. The walls were a pale pumpkin, empty of decoration, and the two windows had dark wooden blinds in place of curtains.

Carol and a young black man, Arthur Marks, sat on the bed, an ashtray between them. Arthur was Jay's cousin, one distant enough to become a little more than just cousin. He was dark-skinned with wire rimmed granny glasses and he'd had his eighteenth birthday only a month earlier. Talking about Paul Gauguin and the paintings he'd seen at an LSU art exhibition, his voice carried true excitement. An exhibition catalog of Gauguin's work open in his lap, he said he was struck by the orange-brown skin tones of the two women and one man in a painting called *Three Tahitians*.

"Especially in contrast to the red of the woman's sarong," he said.

Carol lit another cigarette, studying Arthur before blowing a plume of smoke to the side, and looking down at the catalog. "Marvelous how he placed the man facing away from the viewer, showing his full bare back."

"Yes, yes, and how the eye is drawn from the male figure to the green fruit in the woman's hand."

"You have a good eye," Carol said, another long look at him. "Maybe something in art after high school, Arthur?"

"Money for college will be tough," Arthur said, with a slight grimace. "And my grandmother wouldn't understand majoring in art. I'll have to find some kind of job." Leaning in a little closer he added archly. "God save me from bricklaying or plumbing."

Jay appeared, leaning in the doorframe. "S'up cuz? You hitting on this lady?"

Arthur smiled when he saw Jay. "Yeah, we'll probably get married."

Carol laughed, getting up, saying she needed to use the powder room.

"Somebody barricaded himself in there," Jay said. "Powdering his nose, maybe."

"Then I'll make myself a cocktail while I wait." She smiled at Arthur, touching his cheek.

Jay sat beside Arthur on the bed, arm around his shoulders. "Everything good, little man?"

"I like it here. We don't have to pretend."

"You talk to that guy, Freddy? He's an artist. Guy in the white shirt."

"Can I have another drink?"

"Go get you one, you're a big boy. And find that guy Freddy."

Arthur kissed Jay on the cheek and went to the kitchen in search of vodka.

Buddy turned from the refrigerator and spotted him. "You look lost. What I can I get you?"

"Vodka?" he asked, his voice soft.

"That's easy. You want ice?"

"Please. I like your apartment."

"Thank you." He held the vodka out to Arthur. "Did you see the front bedroom?"

"I didn't know if it was okay to go in there."

"Sure, it is. There are chairs by the window. Sit down, wander around, have a look if you want."

Leaving Freddy in the front room talking to Denise, Cullen came into the kitchen saying he needed some air. Buddy nodded and, looking to the front room, saw Larry listening with concentration to something Damien was saying. He slipped out the back door behind Cullen.

Sitting on the back steps, they caught the faint sound of Miles Davis from inside. Looking down the driveway to make sure they were alone, Buddy turned back to Cullen, bringing their mouths together.

"Can we go in the garage?" Cullen hinted.

"Can't turn on the light."

"We'll manage."

Little more than dark silhouettes squeezed between half-built pieces of furniture and Buddy's table saw and worktable. Buddy tore at Cullen's jeans, shoving them down roughly and pushing Cullen face down on the worktable.

"Do it," Cullen grunted. "Hard."

Buddy spit in his hand and smeared it on himself,

pushing his full length all at once into Cullen. Spurred by his deep-throated howl, he clamped a hand over his mouth. But secrecy and the risk of being caught by friends nearby increased their passion, making both of them vocal. With a grip on Cullen's hips, Buddy pulled him back fiercely, emptying himself. Running with sweat, his chest heaving, he collapsed on top of Cullen. Then lifting himself, he rolled Cullen over, sinking his partner's hardness into his mouth, holding on when Cullen spasmed under him.

They stood in a clinch, breathing hard, jeans around their ankles.

"Jesus, Buddy. You drive me wild."

"Yeah, yeah," Buddy said and laughed. "But I need a cigarette."

They sat on the floor behind the table saw smoking, and between drags on a shared cigarette hands wandered, and mouths met, Cullen biting him.

"I want more of you," Cullen said against Buddy's hair.

"It could turn out that way." Buddy said, barely audible.

Later that night, Larry and Buddy stood on the front porch, waving off the last of their friends. Tom and Aubrey went upstairs to their apartment, calling thanks. Back inside, Larry began collecting glasses and paper plates, taking them to the kitchen.

"Leave it," Buddy said. "We can do all that in the morning."

"No. It will leave glass rings on the furniture." He picked up a beer bottle beside the sofa.

"We'll have to open the windows to get the beer hall smell out of the place," Buddy said.

"Good party, huh?"

"It was, yeah." Buddy emptied the ashtrays into a bag, taking it out to the garbage can. "You think Freddy was hitting on that young friend of Jay's? Pretty boy with the granny glasses?"

"I didn't notice. Damien was the den mother from hell, on my ass most of the night."

"Good for him."

"Right."

Turning and giving Larry his full attention, Buddy spoke gently. "He has a point."

"Okay. I'm tired. Let's go to bed."

He didn't ask him about the sawdust on his jeans.

Chapter Twenty-Five

Coming home and seeing Larry's car in the driveway, Damien thought little of it. Larry had his own key, coming and going as he pleased. Damien had spent most of the day at the university music library and was tired, looking forward to a drink. Pausing in the hall and idly flipping through the mail, he called out, "Larry, it's me."

In the kitchen, he drank a glass of water before heading back to the bedroom. Eyes on the mail in his hand, he was halfway across the room before he saw Larry on the bed and froze, the mail falling from his hands. Larry was unconscious, his face pale, lips bluish, the rubber tie-off around his left arm, and the needle still in place. Larry was slumped among the spilled contents of the black zipper bag, several bags of heroin, spoon, and cotton balls. Among the tools of his addiction, oddly out of place, was a green plastic toy soldier.

In another second, Damien was at the bed and screaming for Larry to wake up. He slipped the needle from Larry's arm and stuck a finger in his mouth, feeling for anything blocking his breathing. He tilted Larry's head back, pinching his nose closed. His mouth over Larry's, he breathed slowly two times, waiting, and breathing once more into his slack mouth. Each time, Larry's chest rose and fell. Damien pulled him off the bed and, with an arm around his shoulders, walked him around the room, getting Larry's legs moving, loudly cajoling him to wake up. He rubbed his knuckles against Larry's sternum, pinching him in an effort to rouse him.

At the moment when Damien's fear peaked, Larry's eyes fluttered, and he managed a wheezing breath.

"Come on, Larry, breathe...breathe!" He patted Larry's cheek and pinched him again. Finally, after one ragged breath, then another, Larry gasped, his eyes opening wide.

"You scared the hell out of me, Larry!"

Damien quickly got a pot of coffee going, hurrying

back to the bedroom. Larry was sitting on the floor, head down, his breathing irregular, fighting to find a rhythm.

"Come on. Get up, Larry, one more waltz around the room. Come on." He got his hands under Larry's arms, lifting him to his feet.

Larry was crying, asking Damien not to be mad. "I'm sorry, Damien. Mistake...I made a mistake. I'm sorry."

"Just breathe. Save the apology for later. You're going to be okay."

He settled Larry in an armchair and went back to the kitchen for the coffee.

"Drink this...come on, drink it up."

After two scalding mugs of coffee, Larry was breathing steadily, sitting in the music room and staring out the window. Damien was at the other end of the sofa, turning over in his hands the plastic toy soldier.

"Give it to me," Larry said.

Damien handed it to him. "Something from when you were a kid?"

Larry didn't answer, his eyes locked on the tiny figure, head moving.

Damien moved closer and pulled Larry's head down on his shoulder. "You're okay. I love you. You know that."

Damien put everything back into the black zipper bag, holding it open to Larry but when Larry refused to let go of the tiny toy relic, he took the bag to the bedroom closet and put it inside a small wall safe behind the clothes. From Larry's wallet he removed all the bills but a five. The cash went into an envelope with Larry's name and then into Damien's safe. He folded Larry's scattered clothes and took them into the music room. "More coffee?"

Larry shook his head.

"Music?"

"Bill Evans."

Damien put on *Time Remembered* and went to the kitchen, filling a small bowl with chocolate pudding. "Open your mouth."

Larry's mouth dropped open and Damien slipped a spoonful of the pudding in. He handed over the bowl and spoon and sat again, watching Larry prod the pudding with the spoon before eating a small amount.

"Do you want to go home later, or stay here? I'll call Buddy either way."

"Here."

Damien called Buddy, downplaying what had happened and hoping he wouldn't panic. Buddy wanted to come over, but Damien suggested it wasn't a good idea and might upset Larry more. He was okay, though still shaky and wanted to stay where he was for the night. "Let's get together tomorrow evening and talk about Larry's problem. I have a plan."

He hung up, relieved that Buddy was agreeable. Chances were good Buddy was aware of what was between him and Larry, but Buddy's first concern would always be to help Larry. Of that, Damien was certain.

****

Apart from the bluish flicker of light from the television tuned to *Green Acres*, the bedroom was dark. The sound was low and though his eyes were open and on the TV, propped against Damien's shoulder, Larry's face was expressionless and unseeing of the fish-out-of-water Gabor character. Damien was not paying attention to the television either, his mind revolving around the next day's phone calls and preparation. Deeper down he grappled with the guilt of financing Larry's addiction over the past months, knowing now he had made it too easy, with the foolish belief that an adequate supply of what he needed would protect Larry from the seamier elements of heroin addiction. The accident that afternoon had come in large part out of the abundance of dope Damien made possible. That, and Larry's growing need for more.

Something not even his best friend, Bob, knew—though he might have guessed it—Damien was no stranger to what drugs could do, and he knew the ins and outs of heroin use and abuse as well as anyone, knew from personal experience. In his case, it was a lesson learned from a substance that was a best friend and ultimately the teacher of destructive black magic.

In the last year of high school, Damien's actual best

friend was a cousin on his mother's side, a girl of average looks with a wild streak always edging toward more dangerous fun. Mona was the kind of fearless teenager who would try anything once, and a lot more if she liked it. She was good at talking Damien into anything, even her bed. That experiment taught Damien once and for all which direction his male member pointed.

Other experiments he liked more, especially those involving drugs. Cousin Mona liked it all a little too much, and employing her usual slippery wiles, talked Damien into trying heroin. And he loved it, but Damien knew they were playing a dangerous game. Mona had no notion of giving up the high of a lifetime and soon found she couldn't. The afternoon's experience with Larry brought back those lost months of shooting too much heroin with Mona. There were three near-fatal ODs for Mona before her parents got her into a drug rehab facility. The third time, Damien had found her barely conscious with a needle in her arm, choking on vomit, her face a bluish purple.

A month out of rehab, she was late for class one morning and Damien went looking for her. He found her in the school parking lot, dead in the backseat of her car. After that—always a mystery how he managed it—Damien was able to detox with the help of Sheila and Ben, friends since grammar school. Damien had learned well about drugs, rehab, and heroin ODs.

"Come on, handsome. Let's get you cleaned up." Damien nudged and finally pushed Larry off the bed, half dragging him to the shower. Scrubbed clean, Damien stood over Larry while he brushed his teeth, then sat him at the kitchen table, prodding him to eat a plate of scrambled eggs.

"How're you feeling?"

"Shitty."

"Eat. You'll feel better."

At ten o'clock, Damien gave him two one hundred milligram Librium tablets with a glass of orange juice.

"That all I get?" Larry growled, knowing the answer already.

That night, beside Larry in bed, Damien was propped on an elbow watching him sleep. He had seen Larry's addiction grow over the months he had been home, and the pain of seeing him unconscious on the bed earlier had shaken his own carefully maintained defenses. That day back in March when Larry had come to the house for the first time, he'd spotted the needle marks, the obvious signature of a drug user. It was a big jolt to Damien's own foundation and the belief that he had left all that behind. The subsequent lovemaking that first afternoon with a drug-fueled Larry, Damien remembered as a Bill Evans kind of love, an improvised progression of two chords in complex variation dissolving into grace notes. And with its final glorious shudder, he realized just how far he could fall with Larry MacDuff, ex-soldier and junkie, the possibility of them both slipping into longtime heroin addiction.

****

By six the next morning, Larry was awake and tossing about under the bedsheet. Awake himself, Damien recognized the first tremors of a scorching need. Out of bed, Larry began pacing in front of the TV, repeatedly scratching his neck. Damien went to the music room and put Paul Desmond's *Two of a Mind* on. Ignoring Larry's complaints, and unnoticed by him, Damien got the black zipper bag from the safe and went into the bathroom, preparing a fix but cutting the amount by two-thirds. Putting the black bag out of sight, he took the syringe back to the bedroom and motioned Larry to sit on the edge of the bed. Larry's face came alive, eyes locked on the prize. He grabbed the rubber tie-off from Damien and quickly wrapped it around his arm, holding the arm out to Damien.

Moments later, Larry fell against the pillows, his tension melting, whispering to Damien that it wasn't enough. Ignoring the complaint, Damien swabbed his arm with alcohol.

He cleaned the syringe and put everything back in the safe again. Larry had moved to the music room and, from the sofa, asked for coffee. Damien brewed the coffee and made waffles, taking both to Larry, and with his own coffee went to the telephone with his address book. He called Buddy, catching him before he left for work, and reminded him that he would be at the apartment with Larry at five thirty.

Arrangements with the rehab facility were straightforward. Bring Larry in at ten the next morning. He made a list of things the woman said Larry would need during his stay, with another list of items not allowed.

Larry had finished his waffles and wanted more coffee. Damien refilled his cup and sat beside him. "What do you know about Bill Evans?"

"Only what you wrote in that magazine."

"Bills Evans has something in common with you."

He shrugged.

"In 1958, when he was playing with Miles Davis, he picked up a heroin habit. It was his way of blurring the world. For Evans, reality was too brutal at times and heroin is the remedy that helps him cope when life hits too hard."

"Maybe that's why I like his music so much," Larry said in a barely audible voice.

Damien inched closer to Larry, laying a hand on his shoulder. "Larry, I know where your head is now. I'm guessing you hear that and say there's no way I could understand, but I was once where you are now. I've been there. I know what you're feeling." Their eyes met and held, Damien nodding a definitive yes. "Buddy loves you very much, as do I. The thing is, the mistake you made yesterday...one more like that and I might not be there. Buddy might not be there. You know that. It was a close call, damn near a deadly one, and neither Buddy nor I can risk that happening again. We're getting you some help." Once more their eyes locked. "So, here's what's going to happen. Tomorrow morning, Buddy and I are taking you to a place where you'll stay for a while. They're going to help so that you can come home well."

"What does that mean?"

"You're going to kick your habit. Get well. Get off the junk."

Larry gave a husky, one-note laugh. "And the shit in my head?"

"They will help you with that. Without shooting heroin into your arm. I'll keep you comfortable until you get to the facility. Later today, we'll go to the apartment and talk with Buddy. The three of us."

"What about my job? Earl?"

"We'll handle all that. Buddy will talk to Earl. Your job will be waiting when you come home and Earl will support you, and so will everyone else."

Larry sat slumped on the sofa, silent and broken, tears leaking from his eyes.

****

Late that afternoon, Buddy met them in the driveway at the apartment and, stepping into the kitchen, put his arms around Larry. "I was worried, brother. You scared me."

"I'm sorry. I'm stupid. I love you." Larry clung to Buddy.

Damien filled a glass with ice and made himself a vodka martini. He had the black zipper bag, Larry's wallet, and the envelope with Larry's cash, putting all three in a kitchen drawer. "You want a beer, Buddy?"

"I'm good."

"Larry? You want anything?"

He shook his head.

They sat in the front room, Larry and Damien on the sofa, Buddy on the coffee table.

"Tomorrow morning, Buddy and I are taking you to a place in Lafayette called Greener Pastures. You'll stay there for six weeks."

Larry tilted forward, face in his hands.

Buddy winced at the sight. "They're going to help you, Larry. They helped Damien's friend."

"It's a good place, they do good things. It's out in the country with horses, even a swimming pool. You'll have your own room with a bath and shower. And after the first week, we'll be able to talk on the phone," Damien explained.

Going to the kitchen drawer where he'd put Larry's black bag, Damien called back to Larry, "Why don't you and Buddy lie down for a while?"

"Come on, Larry," Buddy said.

Damien came with the syringe and Larry sat up holding out his arm. His body reacting to the reduced doses, he was on edge and wanting it as quickly as possible. It was less than he hoped for, but still enough to produce a transformation in his face. He sank into the bed, limp with relief.

Buddy and Damien sat by the window talking quietly, Damien explaining how he was using only a third of the heroin Larry's system was accustomed to. "Enough to calm him, not enough for the rush he craves. Once he checks in at the facility, he will go cold turkey with mild sedatives. He will be climbing the walls for a few days and cursing you and me as heartless devils."

"And tonight?" Buddy asked.

"He'll be edgy by eleven, and I'll give him two Librium to carry him through the night. Before we leave in the morning, we will give him a going away present of the heroin he's accustomed to, so he is in happy shape when he checks in. Meanwhile, you be nice to him in bed tonight."

"He may be happier sleeping between you and me."

"Now you're getting kinky, Buddy Hebert."

"Thank you for this, Damien." Buddy reached over laying a hand on Damien's. "I didn't know what the hell to do. Now, I do need to ask, what kind of money are we talking about?"

"Taken care of."

"But that's not right."

Damien lifted a hand, palm out. "For now, it is. We'll talk details later."

****

Damien woke with Larry shaking his arm. "Damien, please. I need it now. Please?"

He looked over at the clock, it was almost seven-thirty. Buddy was asleep on the other side of Larry. Damian got up and went to the kitchen—Larry begging him to hurry—and cooked a full bag of twenty milligrams, returning to Larry on the edge of the bed, jiggling a leg and waking Buddy. Damien passed the rubber belt to Larry and he whipped it quickly around his arm.

"Fasten your seatbelt," Damien said, depressing the plunger.

Buddy, fully awake by then, turned over to see heaven bloom in Larry's face.

"First time I saw that, it made me want to try it."

The night before, Buddy and Damien had packed a small suitcase. Larry had enough clothes to last a week between washings. Damien had brought along a pair of pajamas, something Larry had never owned, also a pair of slippers. Buddy had put a comb, shampoo, toothpaste, and toothbrush in a small bag. A razor wasn't allowed. There was a blank notebook to use as a diary or journal. And Juli's swim trunks. Damien said they would stop on the way and buy two cartons of cigarettes. He wasn't allowed to have his lighter.

Larry was leaning back on the bed pillows, a slight smile playing on his face, and Damien told him they would put money into his account at Greener Pastures for any extras.

"Do you know everyone's phone number?"

"Everyone but Doug McClure," he said in a dreamy voice, making Buddy and Damien laugh.

"What do you want to wear today?"

He thought about it. "Aloha shirt, blue jeans, tennis shoes, no socks. And Buddy's underwear with the little boxing gloves."

"The toy soldier and photo booth pictures are in your suitcase," Buddy said quietly.

Buddy made coffee and toast, and twenty minutes later they locked up, following Scenic Highway to the bridge. It was a little over an hour to Lafayette, Larry comfortable in the backseat singing a song from one of Perk's tapes, Dionne Warwick's "You'll Never Get to Heaven If You Break My Heart" under his breath.

"You good, Larry?" Buddy said, turning for a quick look in the backseat.

Larry grinned. "Look who I'm with."

After taking Buddy's suitcase and the bag with his cigarettes out of the Woody, Damien told Buddy. "Best to get all the lovey-dovey stuff out of the way here in the parking lot." He stepped in and hugged Larry, gave him a quick kiss and walked off toward the entrance. Turning back, he called out. "Don't overdo it, you two."

"I love you, Larry MacDuff." Buddy said, hand at Larry's face.

Inside, an orderly took Larry's suitcase and cigarettes while Damien went through the process of getting him checked in.

Close against him, Larry gripped two of Damien's fingers. "I'm scared," he whispered.

"It'll be okay," Damien whispered back. "My promise."

Part Three

Each has his past shut in him like the leaves of a book known to him by his heart, and his friends can only read the title.
—Virgina Woolf

Chapter Twenty-Six

From his place on the couch, Larry saw three horses inside a fenced pasture, heads down, nibbling the grass. He envied their unbothered calm, their insouciance, their peacefulness. His eyes drifted to the doctor's large, scrolled oak desk with its orderly arrangement of knick-knacks, the Dundee orange marmalade jar filled with pencils and pens, a baseball with the fading signature of yesteryear's homerun king, the neat stack of blue gray patient folders, and the green telephone with its row of buttons across the bottom. A framed photograph faced inward, and unable to see it, Larry imagined a wife with big hair and a double chin. To the right of the desk, in bookshelves that lined the wall rested a book that caught his eye. He remembered the title from a conversation at Damien's, Bob talking about the movie version and a scene with Burt Lancaster and Deborah Kerr kissing in the wash of ocean surf.

Only vacantly, Larry heard the doctor speak.

He sat in a brown leather armchair, legs crossed, a closed notebook resting on his knee, black fountain pen in his left hand. "I asked what you were thinking."

"Playing in the ocean surf with someone I loved."

"Tell me more about that."

"No," Larry said, holding up a cigarette and asking for a light before turning to look out the window again.

There was a long silence. Patterns of sunlight flared and blinked on the shiny brown leather couch he was stretched out on, head cushioned on one arm, the ashtray balanced on his stomach. The doctor leaned forward in his chair, passing Larry a book of matches.

Clayton Remick was a thin, bony man with large-framed tortoiseshell glasses that magnified his eyes. His loosened tie and unpressed trousers were in opposition to the starchiness of others hired by the facility to keep patients calm and orderly. Even the old woman who swept and mopped the common rooms was neat in her butter-yellow uniform.

Whereas something on Dr. Remick's tie hinted at what he'd eaten for breakfast.

He tried again.

"How long were you in Vietnam, Larry?"

"Too long."

"Okay. How about a word—a single word—that relates to your time there?"

"Juli." He pointed to *From Here to Eternity* in the bookshelves. "Can I borrow that book?"

"Which one?"

"Just over your head. *From Here to Eternity*."

"One condition. When you finish reading it, you'll talk about it in our time together."

Larry shrugged. "Sure."

****

At a session later in the week, Larry sat, chin in hand, studying the coffee cup on the doctor's desk, unable to figure out why he had that particular cup. It seemed odd, and his interest in it annoyed Larry. It was a large white mug with the words *Shrink by Day Chef by Night*.

"Do you cook?"

The doctor looked up from his notes. "Sorry?"

"*Shrink by Day Chef by Night*, the cup."

"A joke gift from my wife. Actually, I'm useless in the kitchen."

Larry nodded, barely hearing his answer. Juli was standing out at the fence, arms resting on top, watching the three horses graze. The gray one lifted his head, looking back at Juli.

The doctor closed his notebook. "So, what did you think of the book?"

"It was pretty good. Great title. Lots of characters, a lot going on. The main character, Prewitt, is a resilient guy. Simple man really, always the underdog, always fighting, always something trying to break or destroy him. Finally does."

"Violence is an integral part of the book. What did you make of that?"

"That's interesting. Prew resists pressure from his

captain to box for the company team but his whole life is mostly violent and destructive."

"Did you find the violence in the novel true to your own Army experience?"

"Not really. Many characters in the book are bullies, not my experience."

"But you did experience violence, no?"

Larry gave a long look out the window. "Yeah, I experienced violence." His voice was quiet.

"How did your reactions differ from the characters in the book?"

"All right, Doc. You're not going to fucking leave me alone about this, are you? That's the game here, right? Should I tell you what it feels like tearing red hot shrapnel out of your own body, or being so scared you piss your pants, mortar shells blowing up around you, making you deaf to screamed orders? If I tell you what it feels like to shoot the heart out of a sixteen-year-old boy, plunge a metaphorical knife into my guts and brains so you can slosh around and bloody us both, if I do all that, will you then leave me alone about the fucking violence? I'll even put the big cherry on top and tell you what it feels like to have someone you love die with his blood soaked into your skin, and the holy-as-Jesus fix afterward that is the one and only goddamn salvation." Going to the window and leaning his forehead against the glass, Larry looked with full eyes at the horses, envying their calm, taking deep breaths, trying to find some of his own. "I'm in this fucking place because of all that shit." The scratching of his finger against the glass was the only sound in the room.

The doctor let the silence play out.

"A jazz pianist I like said his heroin addiction helped blur the world. Sounds about right," said Larry.

"The sixteen-year-old boy? What are the reasons behind his death and your part in it?"

"He was trying to kill Juli and me."

"And where did that happen?"

"In the boonies, a place called K'bang. In a foxhole."

"Who put you in that foxhole?"

"The lieutenant."

"Was the lieutenant a bad man, you think?"

"No," Larry remembered how kind and efficient he was. "Good man. A good man trying to save the men under his command."

"So how do you fit into this not-so-great scheme of things?" The doctor got up and joined Larry at the window. He leaned against the frame, looking at him until Larry turned his head that rested against the glass. "What happened in that foxhole was *imposed* upon you, Larry. That boy's death was not your fault."

"I blew his life away. I can't stop seeing his eyes."

"You will, Larry. That's the direction you're moving." Touching Larry's shoulder, the doctor added. "That's enough for today. Same time tomorrow."

Something in the word *imposed* gripped Larry, something in the doctor's eyes invited trust.

****

Back with his head resting on the couch arm, Larry was looking at the green-shaded brass banker's lamp on the left-hand side of the doctor's desk. It was a twin of the one on the table by the bedroom window in the St. Louis Street apartment.

"What's bothering you?" the doctor asked, without looking up from his desk.

Larry stopped jiggling his right foot. "You cut my meds."

"Guilty as charged." He closed the file folder and got up, moving to the armchair with his notebook. "Why do you think I did that?"

"I don't know, Doc. To torture me?"

"You don't need that third pill anymore."

"Says the doctor who wonders why I can't stop jiggling my fucking foot."

"Trust me. That will go away."

"What? My foot?"

The doctor laughed. "Let's get started." He gestured to the tiny figure Larry was worrying in his hand. "What's that you have? A toy soldier?"

Larry didn't say anything.

"Tell me about it. A child's toy? Why do you have it?"

He knew the doc wasn't going to let it go, like a dog with a bone. "It belonged to a friend of mine."

"Some history there."

"It was Juli's."

"You've mentioned that name a couple of times. He was in the foxhole with you."

"Bingo. You're a good listener, Doc."

He waited. "Juli?"

"Julian Raine Bentley." He shook a cigarette from his pack. "Light?" adding a moment later. "Please." He stared into the flame for a few seconds before dropping the match in the ashtray. "Juli was someone I loved with every ounce of my being." He looked over at the doctor. "Does that shock you? Yeah, Doctor Remick, I loved Juli, more than life, and wish the grenade had killed me, too."

"I'm sorry you lost Juli. But it's good that you're still alive. And just so you know, there are no distinctions regarding love in this room, Larry. Something my mother taught me, corny maybe, but I've never forgotten it. Love doesn't come with boundaries." He resettled himself in his chair. "Will you tell me about the toy soldier?"

Recalling that day at Juli's in Mandeville, Larry's heart raced and he lit a second cigarette from the butt of the first. After a deep shuddering breath, he told the doctor about getting home from 'Nam and going to visit Juli's parents. Told him how he was shaken by the identical eyes of father and son, the same blueness that had held Larry captive, and at the same time strengthened him during the bad days and nights over there.

"I met Juli's dog, Buster. I was surprised by that because Juli never mentioned a dog." Remembering the doctor's question, he looked again at the toy soldier. "Mrs. Bentley said I could see Juli's room. Standing there, the first thing I saw was Buster curled up on the bed. Waiting for Juli, I suppose. I noticed a squad of toy soldiers lined up on his desk." Holding up the small figure, he continued. "This one was leading the charge, just like Juli. Without thinking, I put it in my pocket." He tapped the cigarette out in the ashtray.

"Tell me how Juli died."

"Going for the throat, huh, Doc?"

"Hard memories, but you need to talk about them. Riding the pain over and over does no good. Embracing the pain and not letting it conquer you is the answer."

"We were finishing up our R&R in Saigon, a layover before returning to An Khê. We had something to eat and afterward went to a small bar on Dong Khoi. I was riding a heroin high. Juli thought the smack was for my hip but it was way more than that. We hadn't been in the bar long, I had to take a piss and went to the bathroom in back. When I stepped out of the bathroom, the building was rocked by an explosion, flames and debris flying everywhere. Knew right off it was a grenade. Ten feet down the hall, I still caught some of the flying splinters."

He lifted the Big Red One T-shirt Juli had given him, tracing again the scar from the wood splinter he had pulled out of his stomach, knowing he would have welcomed a hundred splinters if it would have saved a drop of Juli's blood.

"At first, I saw four or five bodies crumpled against the wall, and a chair untouched, standing in the center of the room. Guy with one arm gone." He looked out the window in the doctor's office for the gray horse, feeling the heat and deafness of that day, the sting of the wood splinter, the concussive shock of the explosion, all flaring in his chest. The rest came out in a husky croak, his ears dulled to his own voice. "Juli was just below the bar. Blood. So much of it. I recognized his shirt. Below that...not much left. Shredded. Emasculated. I couldn't catch my breath, my hands were slippery, full of Juli. After that, I don't know. Somebody shot me full of morphine."

The doctor waited quietly.

The fog, the smoke and destruction around him in the doctor's office settled slowly, leaving him with a gritty red image of Juli on the floor of the bar.

Doctor Remick leaned forward, asking if he would like a cup of coffee.

"A pill to go with it, Doc?"

Chapter Twenty-Seven

"Your file indicates your mother is deceased, Larry. May I ask, is that a recent event?" Doctor Remick said, looking over the top of his glasses at Larry on the leather couch.

"November 16, 1964. Traffic accident."

The doctor let the silence play out, waiting to see where Larry went from there. He was able to see from where he sat that mention of his mother hadn't wrought any serious change to Larry's face. If anything, he thought he detected a slight smile.

"She was my mom but she was a friend, too. I miss her all the time, but I'm glad she didn't have to witness what I was like after coming home from Vietnam, or even worse, see her junkie son ODing on heroin and shipped off here to Happy Pines."

The doctor laughed. "I hadn't heard that one."

"Anyway, mom is gone but at least she didn't have to see me in this place." That thought settled for a moment. "I don't know. She might've been able to handle it. She was a nurse." He sat up. "Can I have a light, Doc?"

Lighting his cigarette and looking down at the floor between his feet, Larry continued. "Her being a nurse and all, she was always levelheaded, you know. Cool and collected. I only found out about a month before the accident that she had a boyfriend. He was married, had a couple of kids, I think, a doctor at the hospital. Mom never said so, but I could tell she was crazy about him. I know because he came to the house one night, came to pick her up. They were going out to supper somewhere and I could tell by the way she looked at him. What's that corny old expression? I read it in a book once. *She had stars in her eyes.*"

He got up and moved to the window, looking out. "Good for her. I don't think she ever felt that way about my dad." He tapped on the glass. "But what do I know? Maybe she did when they first got together. Anyway, the doctor came to the funeral. I always wondered if it was the rain or a boyfriend-related distraction that got her killed."

Larry came back to the couch. "For a long time, I felt bad about our last conversation, thinking it wasn't what it should have been. But you never know do you? Never think it's the last time you're gonna speak to your mom. I came home late that afternoon and found her at the kitchen table eating something Buddy's mother had sent over. She was laughing about my wild hair, saying I looked like a mop head, needed a haircut. She knew I hate going to the barber. I went to my room to change clothes, about to leave for work at the gas station and she asked me about Buddy. I told her he was going to cut my hair after work. She laughed again and I kissed her on the cheek...left for work."

"Two hours later she was dead. Killed in a car accident on the way to her shift at the hospital."

Doctor Remick watched Larry for several moments, reading the loss on his face. "I'm sorry, Larry. That's hard for a boy...what?" Looking down at the file, he went on. "Seventeen years old? I'm guessing your father wasn't around at the time?"

"Nah, he ran off when I was five. There one day, gone the next. I never said it to anyone, not even Buddy, but from around the time I started working in Mr. Hebert's garden, I always thought of him as my father, wanted him to be my father. No one knows that. You're the only person I ever told. Odd about their name. The runaway dad's name is Clyde, same as Mr. Hebert."

"That is curious, yes. You mentioned Buddy in relation to your mother and also in relation to Mr. Hebert. What's the connection there?"

"Remember that dwarf song from the old Snow White movie, Doc? *We dig dig dig dig?*"

Palms held outward, the doctor nodded yes. "Guess I have that in common with the dwarfs."

"Anyway, I should have mentioned Buddy before. Buddy Hebert is the most important person in my so far short, but fucked up, life. Mr. Hebert is his father."

"Tell me about Buddy."

"Buddy came before Juli. I fell hard for Buddy when we were high school boys. It really started when we were in the fourth grade together, best friends even then. It became something more when we were older."

"Where is Buddy now?"

Larry put a finger on his heart. "Right here." A moment later. "But I guess he's at home in our apartment. Or maybe at work. He's a carpenter."

"Was he there when you came home from Vietnam?"

"Yeah. Buddy rescued me. Tried his damnedest, but I was a full-time handful. I broke his heart with my drugs."

"You're on the way past that now, Larry. Let's stop for today."

****

Dr. Remick was talking about what the Army and their doctors called battle fatigue or shellshock. He left his chair to sit on the other end of the couch from Larry. "There are various names for it, some of which have come to us from wars fought long ago. There's nothing new about soldiers coming home from war damaged by what they've seen and done in the chaos of battle. The Greeks and Romans experienced it in ways similar to modern soldiers. They had their own names for the condition." Going to the bookshelves, he took down a book and opened it to facing pages, each a full-page illustration. Both were paintings of Civil War soldiers, one riding at the back of a wagon, glassy eyes fixed on the cannon-pocked road, the other sitting amidst the horror of a battle at its finish, his face a mask of devastation.

"In the aftermath of the Civil War the condition was called soldier's heart. Many of those damaged soldiers looked for relief in alcohol, laudanum or morphine."

Passing the book to Larry, Dr. Remick went on. "We know more about the condition today and have more effective ways of dealing with it. Primarily, why you and I are here."

"Tell me about this…soldier's heart."

"Some of what you went through during your time in Vietnam was incredibly stressful. You know that already. What happens as a result of that stress is a chemical change in your body. When these terrible things happen, your nervous system reacts to the stress and goes into survival mode. That reaction is fueled by adrenaline. When the stress is removed, the numbing effect of adrenaline subsides and your body chemistry returns to normal. You follow me so far?"

"Yeah, I think so. But why does the pain of a bad experience return after it's through, months ago?"

"In some cases, including your own, the memory remains disruptive long after the triggering event. The memory and stress return but without the battleground effect of adrenaline to numb it. What we're doing here together will provide the tools and answers to tame these memories and disruptions without medication, without heroin."

Larry let the silence stretch out. Lighting another cigarette, he went to the window, looking out to where the horses usually were. They were missing from the picture on that morning. The tree just over the fence still shimmied in the breeze, a viridescent pasture bathed in light. But the horses were gone, and Larry wanted them there. It was a soothing, pastoral picture, absent of any sharp threatening edges, but by Larry's estimate at least, a part of the total calm was missing. The horses weren't there.

"Where are the horses?"

"I'm sorry. What about the horses?" the doctor said, raising his head from his notebook.

"Most of the time there are three horses in the pasture outside this window."

"I believe you're right, yes. And?"

"Maybe just my opinion, Doc, but I think the horses are sort of like your unrecognized assistants. My guess, most of the people who come in here are edgy, and a little frightened. The horses help out with that. They have a presence out there over the fence that's like an extra dose of the pills you feed us, a relaxing sight to look at while digging around in your guts with a Ka-Bar."

Doctor Remick stepped to look out the window, stretching his neck for sight of the horses. Seeing none, he turned back to Larry. "That's a damn astute observation, Larry."

****

There was the next time, and the next time, and the time after that. Larry had lost count. Now the doctor was talking about dogs, saying that Larry had mentioned Juli having a dog back home in Mandeville.

"Yeah, Buster. A brown and white hunting dog."

"Have you ever had a dog, Larry?"

"No. I don't remember much about my dad, but he didn't like dogs. Guess that's why we never had one at home when I was a kid."

"Any resentment there?"

"No. I imagine my mom would have let me have a dog if I'd wanted one. After my dad was gone, the lady next door had a dog I used to play with sometimes."

"I'd like to talk about your dad. The other dad, the one you wanted."

"Mr. Hebert?"

"He's the one. Isn't that what you said?"

"Yeah, he's the one. I don't think even Buddy knows what all Mr. Hebert has given me. He taught me all about backyard gardening, but that wasn't the half of it. And all the time he treated me like a son. He could say the simplest thing, just casual like and I wouldn't realize 'til later that he was teaching me something."

He said no more for a while, looking out the window at the horses there, showing no sign that the doctor was in the room. The silence played out until Larry turned as if seeing Doctor Remick for the first time.

"One afternoon Buddy and I were out back, having a smoke by the pecan tree. Mr. Hebert was showing my boss, Earl, around the yard. He and his wife had come for supper. I was looking at the two of them there by the side of the house, looking at the cap Mr. Hebert was wearing. It was cold that day. And then, Mr. Hebert was falling, crumpled to the ground. Earl told me to stop yelling, to help him sit Mr. Hebert up. Course, Buddy was there. We got him in the car and raced to the hospital two blocks away. It was a heart attack. That hit me almost as hard as it did him. But he got through it."

"What was it that drew you to Buddy's father?"

"I was aligning the wheels on Buddy's car at the station

and when I finished, I drove it over to his house. Buddy was mowing the grass, shirtless, dripping sweat, my eyes devouring him. He introduced me to his daddy who was working in the vegetable garden. I stayed for supper with Buddy and his parents. It was real special. I don't know, a week or two later I asked if I could help out in the garden. After that we used to work there every Sunday. Sometimes after we finished and washed up, Mr. Hebert would take us to the Piccadilly for lunch. I love Mr. Hebert, Doc. Wish I could call him daddy, like Buddy."

****

Larry's time at Greener Pastures had come to an end. He was going home. Despite the earlier reservations about digging around in his head with a mind doctor, Larry had eventually found what he needed with Doc Remick. He had taught Larry ways to handle the aftermath of those months in Vietnam and the loss of Juli.

Doctor Remick got up from his desk and moved to the armchair across from Larry. "A few days ago, I asked if you'd ever had a dog. I brought it up for two reasons. Something you said a while back about the horses out in the pasture." He gestured to the window and the one horse visible from where they sat. "The other reason relates to studies that have been done in recent years about the therapeutic effect dogs can have on people dealing with the stress of wartime experiences."

Reaching for a magazine on his desk, he tossed it to Larry on the couch. "Take this with you and read the article on page seventeen. That might explain it better than I can. The point of what I'm saying is, I think it would be good for you to have a dog. The article there will make clear why many veterans have responded well to having a canine best friend."

"Yeah, sure. I'll read it. Kinda like the idea. Buddy would love a dog."

"Everything tells me you're going to be okay, Larry. I'll say it again, you have to work hard at it. Remember the triggers we talked about. Now, I'm happy to ship you out of here, young man. I believe some people showed up and are outside waiting to take you home. Go and say hello and get yourself and your bags out of here."

Extending a hand across the desk, he shook Larry's hand. "Good luck to you, son. Call if you need me." Taking a book from his shelves, he passed it to Larry. "Something you might like."

Chapter Twenty-Eight

"Cool car," Larry said, opening the back gate of the Woody.

"I kind of like it, too," Buddy answered, putting Larry's suitcase in the wagon space. Closing the gate, he held the keys out to Larry. "You wanna drive?"

"No. I'd rather sit in back looking at you for the next hour."

Damien held the front door open waiting until Larry said he would ride in back. Turning out of the parking lot onto the road, Larry pointed ahead. "Pull over for a second where that big oak tree is."

While Damien and Buddy waited, he went to the fence where the gray horse looked out at him from the other side, calm and unafraid. Forearms on top of the fence, Larry studied the horse's withers as he cropped grass. He stepped closer to Larry's extended hand and nudged his fingers with his muzzle, inviting Larry's touch. Caressing the horse with the back of his fingers, he was surprised, it was the softest thing he'd ever felt.

"Goodbye, blue eyes. Thanks for all the help."

Back on the road he turned to look back. "Face-to-face with doctor number two."

"What's that mean?" Buddy asked.

"Let's just say he's a medicine horse."

"You're going to have a mane like a horse if you don't get to a barber soon." Damien said, noticing Larry's hair.

"I want a mane just like Buddy's."

"Guy on the build site started calling me the hippie. Another one came up with Miss Hebert. Something tells me he won't call me that again." Buddy said, glancing back at him.

Ear always open to song cues, Damien sang. "If I had a hammer, I'd hammer out a warning…"

When they got home, Larry started toward the back steps at the apartment and Buddy said, "Let's go in the front."

The door flew open and shouts of welcome and applause burst from inside. Halted in the doorway, Larry flashed a nervous smile at the group of friends standing beneath a *Welcome Home* banner. In front was Buddy's mother and Carol, and in the chair beside them, Mr. Hebert. Behind them was Bob, with Earl standing at the door to the kitchen. Mrs. Hebert hugged him tightly, and in a choking whisper said she'd missed him. One by one they welcomed Larry back, even Earl giving him a quick unexpected hug. When the hubbub quieted a little, Buddy's mom spoke. "Everyone, there's a mountain of food in the kitchen. Plates on the counter. Please help yourselves."

While that was going on, Larry knelt beside Mr. Hebert's chair wanting to explain himself but before he got a word out, Mr. Hebert put a hand to his shoulder. "It's all good, son. We're glad to have you back."

Larry felt something poking at his back and turning around got a big wet tongue in the face. From somewhere had come a big puppy. "Whose dog?" He looked up at the others gathered around him.

Smiling, Carol laughing, they all shrugged or looked confused, before Buddy knelt, pulling the dog between them. "Someone told me you wanted a dog. Was he wrong?"

The earlier conversation about dogs with the Doc came back to him, and pulling the puppy closer, Larry nodded. "No, he wasn't wrong."

"Dr. Remick called me a few days back and suggested it. I found a family out on the Old Hammond Highway near Millerville that had some puppies."

The dog was grayish brown, with darker brown spots, a white chest and socks. It had a big head with floppy brown spotted ears and pale blue eyes. Buddy said it was a Catahoula Leopard Dog, four months old.

"What's its name?"

Buddy shrugged. "Guess it doesn't have a name yet."

Larry tipped his head to get a look at the puppy's gender, then gripped his head in both his hands, the dog's eyes looking back at him. Juli's middle name came to mind. "Raine. That's your name, little fella."

Earl came with a plate piled high with fried shrimp

and oysters, passing it to Larry and holding the dog back from the plate. "Something told me you might be hungry for some fried oysters."

"Top of my list. Thanks, Earl." Their eyes caught and held. "I'm sorry, Earl. I was fucked up. I'm working on it."

Earl handed him the loaded plate and brought his mouth close to Larry's ear. "We all fuck up, wrestle demons at one time or another. I could tell you a few stories about that. But just so you know, I'm proud of you."

Finishing the shrimp and oysters and carrying his plate to the kitchen, Larry found Mrs. Hebert taking a bowl of Cole slaw from the refrigerator. When she closed the fridge, he coaxed her into a chair at the table.

Putting down the bowl, she took one of his hands in hers. "What is it, Larry?"

"I just wanted to tell you I'm sorry for any worry or trouble I caused. I didn't mean to involve y'all in my problems."

"I hope you will always involve us in whatever troubles you have. You're family to us." Leaning across the table, she kissed Larry's cheek.

****

Buddy led Bob out to the garage and flicking the light on, gestured to a tall chest of drawers fragrant with the smell of English walnut and wax.

Bob's hands flew to his face. "My God, Buddy! It's the most gorgeous thing I've ever seen." He went to the chest, running his hands over it, caressing the glossy wood.

"My first piece done completely by mortis and tenon. Not a nail, screw or staple anywhere."

Bob smiled at Buddy. "Oh, you gorgeous devil!" In the French fashion, he kissed Buddy on both cheeks, landing a third full on the lips.

"I'll take it over to your and Spencer's place in the truck tomorrow."

Meanwhile, in the apartment, Larry rounded up the puppy and took him out to the front steps. He sniffed around in the grass awhile and squirted a stream of pee onto a hydrangea bush before climbing the steps and sitting beside Larry, who was smoking a cigarette and thinking the doctor was right again.

Earl came out the front door, and after surveying the view toward the Old State Capitol, sighed. "I sure do like this downtown neighborhood." He sat on the steps next to Larry and lit one of his L&Ms.

Larry glanced at him. "Little while ago you said you had fucked up. You trying to make me feel better?"

Earl scratched the dog's ear, looking down at his shoes. "I'll tell you a story not even my wife knows, Larry." He blew ashes off his cigarette. "I wasn't always Earl Thompson." He gave a soft laugh and shook his head. "Rode some bumpy highways before Korea. Can't count the troubles I've had with the law. I was the first, and only, child of a mean, hard drinking daddy who regularly beat the tar out of me. By the time I was sixteen, I was dishing out beatings to other people when I wasn't stealing cars. One night I picked the wrong ride."

When Earl said a former Texas Ranger had whipped his ass for stealing his car, Larry turned, eyebrows lifted in surprise, and studied Earl's face as he told his story.

Earl found himself behind bars for assault and battery and attempted car theft. That wasn't his first rodeo and he ended up doing two years in Big Mac, the Oklahoma State Penitentiary. A month after he got out, he hooked up with another bad boy and they robbed a string of liquor stores in Missouri.

"I got away with the robberies because of bad police work. Came down to Louisiana and got me a set of forged identity papers. Joined the Army under the name of Kenneth Earl Thompson, and at the age of twenty-four was in Korea. And like you, I had a hard and brutal time of it. But the Army gave my life structure. I came back to Louisiana determined to make up for all the bad shit I'd done when I was younger." Earl let a long silence pass. "It wasn't long after that I got lucky and met Eileen."

He took an envelope from his pocket, smoothing it out with his fingers. "I want to talk about your mother for a minute. I didn't say anything about it before you went overseas, mainly because nothing was settled and the lawyer had to comb through the paperwork and finally get a ruling on what belonged to you. Since I was your guardian after her death, everything with the lawyer came through me. Upshot of it is, it's all done now and you've got a little money left to you in your mother's will. It went directly into a bank account in your name."

He passed the envelope to Larry. "This letter is from the lawyer and you can take it to the bank and claim the money held there in your name. It's a little under $25,000. Being held at the Louisiana National Bank on Third Street.'

Larry was stupefied, unable to believe his ears. Between Earl's story, and on top of that the stuff about a will and money from his mother, he was knocked sideways. He didn't know what to say or think and was unable to form any intelligible thoughts.

Earl went on. "Pretty good timing if you ask me. Later today, along with Buddy and Damien, I want to take a drive and show you something. Something to think about."

He finished quickly, pushed off with hands on his knees and stood. "Could be something you'd like to try."

****

With the talk and laughter of the others as background, in the bedroom Damien unpacked Larry's suitcase, setting the dirty things aside to wash and putting the rest in Larry's chest of drawers. He put the suitcase in the closet and took the toiletries to the bathroom.

Larry sat on the edge of the bed watching, his nerves firing. "You unpacked my stuff."

"You can't live out of a suitcase."

"Why not at your house? I thought..."

"And you thought right," he said, sitting beside Larry. "Let's for a moment not think about ourselves." He looked at Larry. "As much as I want you with me, for now you need to stay with Buddy. It's the right thing to do. I like and respect Buddy and I know you love him. Give him some time. As long as it takes. Don't be too quick in walking away from Buddy. You owe him that."

"You're right. Like always."

Bob and Carol said their goodbyes and were off. Mr. Hebert had stretched out in the back bedroom for a nap. Coming out to the back steps where Earl, along with Buddy, Larry and Damien had gathered, Mrs. Hebert said they should go on, she would finish in the kitchen and lock up.

With Larry behind the wheel in the Woody, Earl said to take Government to Park Boulevard, south to Perkins Road. Buddy and Damien were in the back with the dog.

At the corner of Cedardale Avenue, Earl motioned for Larry to pull over and park.

The four of them stood in a paved forecourt on Perkins Road, surveying the property and the building on the lot. A large sheet of white paper taped to the window glass said, *Property For Rent*.

"I put a deposit down so it's yours if you want it. You have a week before that deposit expires."

Larry looked at Earl. "You serious about this?"

"As a goddamn heart attack. Damien, explain it to him."

"The three of us want to finance a start on your classic car business." Indicating Buddy and Earl, he went on. "We think you can make it work. Earl knows the car business and he's sure of it. Most of all, we know you. You have our faith and trust." He laughed. "And our money, too."

Larry squatted, a little dizzy, looking first at the ground to get his balance, then to the empty building in front of him. He remembered the money Earl said was in the bank. Finally, he looked up at Earl.

"Just so you know, MacDuff, I got two old cars at the station with owners waiting for you to get to work. I'm pretty sure there'll be another one there in two weeks. If I were you, I'd start hiring some help." Earl stared back at Larry. "You ready to get to work?"

Chapter Twenty-Nine

That night, Buddy and Larry were once more seventeen-year-old boys discovering one another for the first time, exhausting themselves before falling asleep, their breath a tandem rise and fall, bodies slipping automatically into practiced alignment, as easily as birds falling into formation.

With the light from the window little more than a pale hint of morning, Buddy woke to Larry's erection pressing against him. Pushing the puppy off the bed, he shifted to accommodate an urge he recognized. As a result, he had to hurry his shower and coffee before rushing off to work.

After letting the dog out in the backyard for a few minutes, Larry returned to the tousled bed. Burying his face in Buddy's pillow, he slept for another hour with Raine's head across his feet.

He found some egg salad in the refrigerator and spread it on toast, Raine's eyes following it to his mouth. Taking some sliced ham from the fridge and cutting it up, he put it in a bowl for the dog. Three cans of dog food stood on the counter and Larry made a mental note to buy more. After Raine had gulped down the ham, Larry took him out to the backyard again and sat on the steps with his coffee, watching the dog nose about in the grass. He was thinking about Dr. Remick. "Thanks, Doc," he whispered.

Buddy's mother had straightened, dusted and vacuumed the apartment after the party yesterday. With Bill Evans playing in the background, Larry pulled the sheets off the bed and emptied the laundry basket, carrying it all outside to the washer and dryer. He had a shower, clipped his nails, and put fresh sheets on the bed.

Last was the ritual of polishing his boots. After six weeks of nothing but tennis shoes and slippers, Larry was happy to be back in his familiar boots, though Raine got his first taste of discipline when he tried chewing the top of a boot.

Waiting for the dryer to finish, he sat with the book

Dr. Remick had given him when he left Greener Pastures. It was one called *Lord of the Flies* by William Golding. At the end of the first chapter, he considered the pre-teen English boys stranded on their primitive island, struggling without grownups to create order out of a threatening jungle. It wasn't far from the dilemma of young soldiers trying to stay alive in another jungle he remembered.

He folded and put away the clothes and called Damien to say he would be over later. He said nothing about the dog, but figured Damien would be okay with Raine in the house. Larry wanted to get the puppy used to riding in the car and being at Damien's. It wasn't his plan to leave the dog waiting, alone in the apartment. He had a sidekick now.

****

Before going to Damien's, Larry had a private thing that needed doing, and drove in the direction of Buddy's house on Apperson. Two blocks past Apperson, he cut over to North Street and the gates of Roselawn Cemetery. He followed a curving gravel road to a cluster of live oak trees in a back corner of the grounds, leaving his car on the edge of the road. He walked back to his mom's spot under the trees. The ground had been well-kept, but Larry knelt to brush the fallen leaves from the flat stone marker. A splotch of bird droppings whitened the gray stone and spitting on his fingers, he rubbed it clean. Just above the marker, a bunch of withered brown flowers rested on the grass somehow making Larry think they had been put there by his mom's doctor friend. He didn't know what made him think that. Larry had never known all that much about the guy. The flowers were dry and crumbling and he put them aside to throw away.

With his pocketknife, Larry made a deep cut in the ground a couple of inches above the stone marker, and with two fingers widened the cut. From his back pocket he brought out the silver pendant and chain he had bought for this very purpose at the big market in Saigon. He dropped it into the hole, pushing it deeper into the dirt before working the grass back into place, disguising the spot. "I love you, Mom," he said, hand against the stone.

He let Raine out of the car, giving him time to sniff about and take a whiz. The dog picked up the trail of Larry's scent, leading him over to the tree and straight to the marker, sniffing the grass at the spot where Larry had buried the pendant. Before he could start digging, Larry picked him up and carried him back to the car.

When he arrived at Damien's house, Damien carried a bowl of water to the back door. "Let Raine play out in the backyard. With the fence he'll be okay. I have some papers you need to sign. They all concern your new business."

He set the bowl on the ground by the steps, Raine following him out.

Damien explained the papers. "We all knew you would want to do this, so part of it was pretty much in place before you saw the Perkins Road property. Earl called to tell me he went to the realtor's office this morning and put down two months' rent. He got a lease that needs your signature. You'll have to get that from him. The papers here are related to forming a corporation. I will co-sign everything having to do with the bank loan, easier all around since I have established credit. You need to open a personal checking account at the bank I use. The money in your current bank can be transferred to the new account. I will deposit three thousand dollars to make it look a little healthier."

"You don't have to do that, Damien. I'm not sure if Earl told you, but I got money from my mother. That means I have a lot to put into this. It's in the Louisiana National Bank downtown."

"That's perfect. It will make getting a business loan much easier. We'll also open a corporate account at that bank. If everything goes smoothly, you'll soon have access to the loan money and be able to start hiring and setting up the shop with all the tools and equipment you need, plus remodeling the space for the work you'll be doing there."

"It's kind of overwhelming. Are you sure we're ready to do this?"

"Better question. Are you sure *you're* ready to do this?"

There was a moment's pause before he nodded his

head slowly. "Yeah, I mean I want to, and think I can do it. I just worry about the money you and Buddy and Earl are putting up."

"Don't. It's going to work, Larry. We all believe in you and see it as an investment."

He leaned across the desk, putting his arms around Damien. "How did I ever find you?"

"I might ask the same about you. Now read these papers and when you're sure you understand everything, sign in the places indicated. You should be back at the apartment when Buddy gets home. Did you talk at all last night?"

"Mostly just fucked."

"Well, that's good, too."

Still a little anxious about it all, Larry fixed his eyes on the papers Damien held out. After Damien had explained the parts he didn't fully understand, Larry signed in all the places Damien indicated.

****

It was happening a lot faster than he ever thought, the notion of having a classic car shop, a dream since the early days with the Woody and those hours spent immersed in restoring the beauty and mechanics of something old. Earl had really been the one who encouraged and nurtured the dream, and now here he was stepping up again to help with a substantial amount of investment money. Buddy was a big part of it too, not for a second backing away from the opportunity to help. Larry knew Damien was the catalyst for making it all happen, the one with the financial freedom allowing him to underwrite a deal for Larry that, whatever its risks, wouldn't damage him greatly. He wasn't so naive as to think it could all be done with just the money his mom left, but at the same time, that money gave him the feeling the business would be his.

At the kitchen table in the apartment, Larry wrestled with the numbers he had scribbled in a notebook. Raine was on the floor gnawing on a leather chew toy Larry had gotten for him, along with a supply of dog food. And then Buddy was coming in the back door dropping his tool belt on the floor and leaning in to snuggle Larry's hair. He pointed to the page of numbers. "What's all that?"

"I'm trying to make sense of the numbers. Projected costs, finances, bank loan."

"Ask daddy to help. You know he will."

Buddy's words sent a flush of heat down Larry's body, like walking past an open fire.

Daddy.

His and Larry's.

He got up and opened a cold bottle of Budweiser, passing it to Buddy and standing behind the chair to massage his shoulders. "Supper later at the Piccadilly?"

"Lemme shower first. Get in with me?"

"Maybe." He leaned down with a naughty smile and nibbled Buddy's ear, breathing in the familiar musk of sawdust and sweat.

As he got into bed with Larry one night about a month later, Buddy commented "Clean sheets. Nice."

"Needed changing after last night. I'm beat," Larry said, turning out the light.

Buddy pulled Larry's head onto his chest, promising not to instigate anything and wrestled a foot from under Raine.

With the soothing cadence of the heartbeat against his cheek, Larry listened to the nighttime sounds of the old house, the familiar hum of the refrigerator, the ticking of a clock, footsteps overhead.

"I need to tell you something." Larry reached up, gently tugging on Buddy's earlobe. "You awake?"

"Mm. What?"

"You know how I feel about you." Buddy didn't say anything. "You awake?"

"Yeah."

"You and me since we were ten. That's never gonna change. A hundred years old, I will still put my head on your chest and say, 'I love you, brother.' Never gonna change."

Buddy's voice a whisper. "But?"

"It's something I need to—"

"Just say it, Larry."

"I need to stay with Damien for a while."

"Because you love him?"

"I don't know. Maybe, but that doesn't change how I feel about you."

"Sounds a little like what's called a modern arrangement."

"I didn't go looking for it, Buddy. It just happened. A bolt out of the blue. That make sense? Maybe I do love Damien. He's been good for me."

"And I revere him for that. Think, too, that he's the one that can make your dream about the car shop happen. Earl and I only put up a little money. Damien and you—"

"This is not payback for that."

"Okay."

"Damien fills a need I didn't know was there. Maybe him being a few years older has something to do with it, I don't know. He makes me feel safe, like I need his guidance. I need Damien, Buddy." His head still on Buddy's chest, the heartbeat beneath his ear was a steady comfort in Larry's ear, but he feared his words were a knife cutting straight into that heart.

"Are we okay?" Larry said, putting his mouth against Buddy's.

"I can't tell you it doesn't hurt, Larry. Can't tell you I haven't noticed you growing closer to Damien. I suspected, as you already know. I respect your feelings, love you nonetheless. We'll be okay. We'll always be okay." He pulled Larry closer. "Nothing changes about the car business. I'm still in."

Chapter Thirty

The days were crowded with the work of getting a business up and running. From early morning to late afternoon the garage was crowded with workmen remodeling the space. Larry spent hours perusing tool and equipment catalogs, only to have Earl or Mr. Hebert tell him to look again, find a better alternative. Earl sent mechanics looking for work. For use with the business, Larry bought the red farm truck off Earl, the one they had restored at Billups when Larry went back to work. He needed it to haul equipment and tools. He spent two or three nights a week with Mr. Hebert, his patient voice explaining why Larry could or couldn't afford to do this or buy that, pointing to a column of mind-numbing figures backing up the reason why. He was tired all the time, but beneath that was the growing feeling he could pull it together, make it all work.

In July, Larry hired a high school kid interested in mechanics as a part-time helper. He had gone back to his old high school and talked with Mr. Roland, the mechanics teacher there, asking him to recommend a student in need of an after school and weekend job. Two days later, he got a phone call from a senior in Mr. Roland's class asking about the job. He didn't have a car so Larry picked him up in front of the high school the next afternoon and took him for a hamburger at Hopper's. His name was Wesley Trahan, said to call him Wes.

"Okay, Wes. Call me Larry. I have a question I'd like you to answer. Tell me where your head is when it comes to a car engine."

"All I can say is, there ain't nothing I'd rather be doing than taking apart an engine and putting it back together again. Not since that first time, when my daddy stuck my head under the hood of a 1955 Chevy Bel Air."

"And if you could have any car, what would it be?"

"A 1965 Mustang GT Mecum."

"I wouldn't want to screw up your schoolwork, but I need someone maybe three or four afternoons after school and on Saturday, maybe the occasional Sunday. Can you do that?"

"Yes, sir. I sure can."

"Don't call me sir, Wes. I'll pick you up Saturday morning at ten. Where do you live?"

More difficult, busy weeks crowded against one another while buying, hiring, and monitoring a business— a dream—coming to life. The kid Wes had turned out to be a big help, he had a good head for cars. Buddy handed over the Ford farm trunk, let him drive it home each day. He cared for it like it was his own.

Separate from the business, more than a few times Larry froze, feeling the absence of Buddy. It was as if stepping into a cold winter wind, a sudden need for the feel of him, the smell of him. He was happy with Damien, but missed Buddy on the gray days when rain pounded down and the work was hard. It became more comfortable as time passed, for Larry as well as Buddy, the separation gradually taking on shades of what Buddy had called a modern arrangement. He lived with Damien, spent most of the time away from work with him, but that didn't stop Larry from getting together with Buddy at the apartment on St. Louis. Damien knew and gave it little thought. No questions asked.

Larry and Damien were watching television one night when someone knocked on the door. Raine leaped off the bed, dashing to the front door. It was Buddy. Stepping inside, he hugged Larry, one hand ruffling Raine's ears. "Hey."

"Hey."

Kneeling to nuzzle Raine, he looked up. "Am I interrupting?"

"No, come on in. Damien's in back." He led Buddy inside.

On Larry's heels, Buddy held out a small cardboard box. "Brought you a little something." Once in the music room, Buddy nodded to Damien. "Hey, Damien. Sorry to bother you guys so late."

"Don't be silly. How about a beer?"

"Sure."

Damien went off to the kitchen and Buddy passed the

cardboard box to Larry.

Inside was Juli's toy G.I. toy, now set into a block of teakwood, the area around its legs and feet modeled to look like a rice paddy. On the front edge of the block was a small brass plate engraved with Juli and in smaller letters below his name, Big Red One.

A surge of emotion overwhelmed Larry. "Buddy, Buddy... what to say?"

Damien returned with Buddy's beer, leaning in to look at the toy soldier.

Larry reached for Buddy and kissed him. "Thank you, Buddy. Thank you."

Larry walked Buddy back out to his truck, leaning in the window and talking for another minute, finally putting his fingers against Buddy's lips before he backed out of the drive.

Damien came out of the bathroom and found Larry at his chest of drawers deciding on just the right spot for Juli's toy soldier. He finally settled on placing it to the left of the framed photo strip of Juli. He lightly brushed a finger across the middle picture, the smiling one.

Stretched out on the bed, staring up at the ceiling, his eyes sparkled with old thoughts of Juli.

"You okay?" Damien asked.

"Sure." He reached for Damien's hand.

"When you look at that photograph something in your face changes. Every time."

He rolled closer to Damien. "You know what I think about when I look at Juli's picture?"

"Tell me."

"Always the same. I remember us bare-assed in paradise, rolling in the surf of a blue-green ocean, under a hard blue sky, laughing and crazy in love."

Chapter Thirty-One

Larry was at the bottom step with Raine, combing through his coat looking for fleas. "I saw in a magazine the other day they have what's called a flea collar for dogs." He spoke into the dog's face. "Just what you need, Raine."

They were at the St. Louis Street apartment, sitting out on the front porch. "Think I found some good flooring for the office at your shop," Buddy said. "You know what acacia wood looks like?"

"No."

"I have a book inside with a picture. Anyway, my Uncle Dub told me about a man in Denham Springs that has a load of acacia flooring he's willing to let go for a low price. He's got about a hundred square feet which is just right for the office. If you like it, Wes can drive out and pick it up in the truck. I'll try to get it laid next weekend." He noticed Larry's attention to the dog. "Did you hear what I said?"

"Yeah, that's sounds good. Give me the address, I'll send Wes to pick it up. How much?"

"Three-seventy-five."

"I think your daddy will okay that. He's got me on a tight leash with spending."

"How's business?"

"Might have a new customer, a guy wants to restore his '56 Packard. Not definite yet. I'm going lie down for a while. Come on, Raine."

Larry had been staying at Damien's house for about six weeks, but neither he nor Buddy had said anything about it to Buddy's parents. Both had the feeling it would upset them and it was easy to get around since Larry was at St Louis Street much of the time anyway. There was nothing there that would alert them to Larry sleeping somewhere else on most nights, so they let the pretense go on.

Cullen was now spending more time with Buddy and despite himself, Larry harbored some jealousy over that. More than once, Larry had gone to sleep wondering if Cullen was at the apartment and what he and Buddy were doing. Such thoughts made him wonder if his jealous feelings about it were part of what Buddy called a modern arrangement. He and Damien had a good thing in bed and Larry enjoyed sleeping with him, but no one could make Larry's body sing like Buddy. He had never felt with anyone else the oneness he felt with Buddy. Not even with Juli. Buddy had a lock on that and Larry was feeling the ache of living without it.

He woke with fingers combing through his hair, which was at that point only an inch or two shorter than Buddy's. Larry opened his eyes, Buddy against him on the bed, mumbling into his neck. "I miss you."

"Miss you, too."

****

On Wednesday, Larry drove over to the Heberts' to discuss the shop numbers with Mr. Hebert. He went in through the back screen door as usual and found Mr. Hebert napping on the couch in the den. Mrs. Hebert wasn't around, out shopping he guessed, or maybe at the golf course. Not wanting to wake Mr. Hebert, he sat quietly in a chair across from the couch, noticing then the total quiet of the house. In that stillness Larry sat, watching Buddy's father sleep. He looked so peaceful, one arm behind his head, the other hanging off the edge of the couch, right leg bent at the knee. The late afternoon light found its way through the windows behind the couch, softening his features and leading Larry to wonder how old he was, thinking he would ask Buddy later. Not for the first time, it struck him how comfortable it was there with Mr. Hebert. One day Buddy had opened a door into his world, and Larry experienced the richness of feelings that came with all of it, a big part of which was the coziness and acceptance he'd found in Buddy's family. Looking at Mr. Hebert's face, untroubled in sleep, Larry took comfort in his nearness.

Mr. Hebert stirred, and looking over to see Larry, he scrubbed his face with his hands and apologized for falling asleep.

"No need. I can come back tomorrow if you're tired."

"See if there's any coffee on the stove, would you?"

He brought a cup, black, the way Mr. Hebert liked it and told him about the flooring Buddy had his eye on. Mr. Hebert commended Larry on finding such a good deal and Larry told him it was Buddy and his Uncle Dub who found it. "Wes will drive out in the truck and pick it up on Friday. Buddy says he can put the floor in this weekend."

"Did you add that boy's name to the insurance on that truck like I told you?"

"Yes, sir, I did. He's all covered. Anxious now to get his nose under the hood of the next car we get to work on. Kid's a bully for work."

"How's the new mechanic working out?"

"So far, so good. No complaints. He's one Earl recommended."

"Okay, let's look at your shopping list."

Mr. Hebert got his record book and they moved to the kitchen table. Larry took a folded piece of paper from his pocket. "You're not going to like it."

The list included an additional floor jack, another creeper, three pairs of goggles, coveralls, and fifty gallons of floor cleaner. From his back pocket, Larry took a catalog and pointed to the coveralls on one page. "I like these black ones. We get the mechanic's name stitched in red on the left pocket and Classic Vibe in red on the right." Classic Vibe was the name he and Earl had decided on for the business. "We can order the plain black coveralls and have a local seamstress put the names on. I like the black because they won't show grease as much, won't look so dirty."

"All right. Go ahead and order them." He looked at the next item on the list. "How long will fifty gallons of floor cleaner last you?"

"Nine months, maybe a year."

"Bring me the receipts. And be sure the boy gets one from the fella with the flooring in Denham Springs." He closed his record book. "You oughta go out to the garden and pick a few tomatoes to take back downtown. We got a bumper crop this summer." Mr. Hebert said, closing his record book.

****

With Wes helping, Buddy got the floor laid in the office on Saturday. Larry walked in just about the time they finished. "Wow! That's fucking beautiful."

Buddy dug a can of wax out of his carry-all, passing it to Larry. "Can you get a coat of this on it before Wes and I bring the desk over tomorrow? My mother has one of those electric floor buffers. Maybe you can borrow it."

The desk was waiting in Buddy's workshop. He had built it from a stash of ash gotten at a used-lumber auction a few months before. Larry had yet to see the finished piece.

After Buddy left, Larry got a couple of clean rags and began applying wax to the new floor. Wes sat in the doorway smoking and talking about the new Pontiac GTO. From what Larry guessed, he was liking his job. Say one thing about Wes, he was no slacker. He liked driving around in the red farm truck and kept it looking and running top notch. Once Larry okayed it, he had some guy paint *Classic Vibe* and the shop phone number on the truck's two doors. Black letters with a white outline against the hot rod red of the truck.

"Let's you and me drive over to the Hebert's house and borrow that floor buffer," Larry suggested.

Wes drove, Larry giving him directions.

"Okay if I have next Saturday off? My little brother has a baseball game, I told him I would go."

"Sure, Wes, that's no problem," Larry said as they tuned onto Apperson. "Didn't know you had a little brother."

They weren't long back from their golf game, Mrs. Hebert with her feet up enjoying a beer, Mr. Hebert with a glass of iced tea. Larry introduced Wes and Mrs. Hebert told him to sit down. She got up and went to the kitchen and came back with a beer for Larry and a cola for Wes. She asked about his family and Wes said they lived up on Madison, north of Fairfields, that he had a little brother and four little sisters.

"My gracious. That must keep your mother busy."

"Yes, ma'am."

"What's your daddy do?"

"He works up at the plant, Standard Oil."

"You working for Larry, I figure you must like fooling with cars."

"Yes, ma'am, I plain love it."

Larry said, "Buddy and Wes put the floor in today. Looks good. I came over to see if I could borrow your floor buffer."

"It's in the hall closet. Keep it as long as you like. I don't need it," Mrs. Hebert said.

"How was your golf game today? Wes, Mrs. Hebert is the women's city golf champion," Larry said.

"You wouldn't believe it if you'd seen me today. I hit two balls in the water."

Before they left, Mrs. Hebert took Wes into the kitchen and gave him a piece of pineapple upside down cake. Larry got the buffer from the closet and put it in the back of the truck.

"Drop me off at the shop and you can go on home," he said when Wes came out. "I'll see you tomorrow. You're helping Buddy, right?"

"Yeah. We have to carry your desk from the garage to the shop."

"I forgot to tell you, that guy from Port Allen is bringing his old Chevy in Monday morning."

"Damn! Okay if I cut school and come to the shop?"

"No. Go to school. The Chevy will be at the shop at least a week."

Back at the shop, Larry called Damien to say he was staying downtown that night.

Coming in the back door he was greeted by an excited Raine, Buddy at the table eating a sandwich. "Hey. I didn't know you were coming."

"Is it okay?"

Buddy smiled. "You want a sandwich?" he said, moving to get up.

"I'll make it. Sit. Did you feed Raine?"

"Yep."

"I saw your folks. Went over to get the buffer. Your momma gave Wes a piece of pineapple upside down cake. Know what he said when we were driving back to the shop?"

"Best pineapple upside down cake I ever ate."

"What else, huh?" Larry said, laughing. He leaned to nuzzle Buddy's ear. "That floor is beautiful. Thank you, Buddy."

"There's something for Raine on the counter under the phone."

It was a thin clear plastic dog collar. "A flea collar. Where'd you get it?"

"Raine's regular vet has them now. They're brand new, he told me."

"Cool."

Later, after a time for two, Raine was allowed back on the bed and Larry returned to an earlier issue, coming right to the point. "I miss you. Can I come stay for a few days?"

"Why even ask? You have a key. This apartment is as much yours as it is mine."

"Yeah, but do you want me here? What about Cullen?"

"What about Cullen? Cullen's not even on the same plane as you. Cullen is a distraction, or in words I recently heard, a sex toy."

Larry didn't say anything to that, and Buddy went on. "Forget Cullen. What about Damien?"

"Damien's not you. I want you."

"So, what's the problem? You have me. You've had me all along. I'm not the problem, Larry. This is something *you're* going to have struggle through. Where you are right this minute is forever an open door to you. Here or here," he said, pointing to his chest and the room. "You frustrate me with this question. I want to hug you, kiss you, and I also want to slap you awake."

Between them, the sleeping dog whimpered, ears twitching in a dream.

"Look, you gave Raine a bad dream."

Chapter Thirty-Two

Early September brought the hard heat to south Louisiana, the usual summer pattern of heavy rains, high humidity, and aggressive tiger mosquitos that dive-bombed in late afternoon. Grasshoppers bounded, fire ants built their mounded nests, and on many humid mornings, neighborhoods swarmed with hungry mosquito hawks, darting and hovering like squadrons of tiny helicopters. By ten Sunday morning, the temperature was already eighty-seven degrees. Wearing only Juli's swim trunks, Larry was in the backyard at Damien's working on his new bike, a Kawasaki Catalina 250, one exactly like the bike he and Juli had rented that time in the Philippines.

He was adjusting the clutch when Damien came to the backdoor and stood, watching him work. "You're not riding that thing over to Buddy's later, are you?"

"No, we're going in the Woody. But I'll take you for a ride if you want."

Damien held up a stop-sign hand, going back inside.

When Larry came in later, Damien was listening to a John Coltrane album called *Ballads*. A week ago, Larry had discovered the album in his T-shirt drawer with a note from Damien saying, *Welcome to Coltrane*. Lifting the note off the record jacket brought the shock of seeing the cover was signed by John Coltrane.

"I wanna tell you something."

"Keep those grease-blackened hands off me and this bed," Damien yelped when Larry sat beside him, the dog jumping up right behind him.

"I looked at a '59 Cadillac Eldorado convertible the other day. The man selling it isn't asking a lot. The Continental has been giving you trouble, so how about I buy the Cadillac and fix it up for you, paint it pink like the one Elvis drives?"

"My old Lincoln is fine."

"No, it's not. The transmission is on its last legs. The Cadillac won't cost you a penny."

"I'll think about it." He laughed. "A pink Cadillac convertible would actually be very cool."

"Super cool."

He combed his fingers through Larry's hair. "What time are we going to Buddy's?"

"Sometime after three."

"Who's going to be there? You know?"

"Just us guys. Bob, Spencer, a few others. If you're taking any records over, put one of the Coltrane albums in the stack."

"What do you know about John Coltrane?"

"Not much. He died last year. That was too bad."

****

In his garage workshop, Buddy ran a soft cloth over a small piece he had just finished for one of Bob's customers. The completion of a project, large or small, always brought a sense of satisfaction he found hard to describe. The only person he could communicate this feeling to was his Uncle Dub, inarguably the person who shaped and nurtured Buddy's love of crafting things out of wood. It was impossible to dispel the countless hours of his boyhood across the street at the lumber mill, perched on a worktable watching his uncle shape raw wood into cabinets and staircases, deaf to the daylong roar of planers and giant circular saws, his focus solely on the hands of his uncle turning simple wood into beautiful shapes. Best of all were the times when his uncle signaled him closer to explain the function of a combination square, a router or another of the tools that Buddy saw as enchanting objects, magical in the changes they effected on wood. The small wooden chest beneath his hands now was the realization of a dream guided by his Uncle Dub.

As for the chest, a woman browsing in Bob's store had spotted a similar one Buddy had made as a birthday present for Bob and expressed an interest in it, wanting to know if it was for sale. Told it wasn't, she asked if it was made locally and Bob gave her Buddy's card, saying he would call and ask. It was a miniature *kiritansu*, a chest of drawers made from paulownia, a wood not easy to find in

Louisiana and constructed without nails or screws. The woman would likely be shocked at the price, but Bob was certain she would pay it. Buddy wasn't worried. He knew it was something he could easily get a good price for elsewhere. He had a growing list of customers and the woman wasn't the first sent his way by Bob. Some months earlier Bob had opened an antique shop with his friend, Spencer. The business was doing well, a combination of Bob's good taste, his friend's connections, and a choice location on Jefferson off Government. He kept a stack of Buddy's cards in the store.

Buddy ran a hand over the small chest one last time, leaving it where it sat on the worktable.

Cullen was at the sink scrubbing a skillet when Buddy came in the back door.

"Good timing." Cullen dried his hands. "I put some scrambled eggs and toast in the oven for you."

"Any coffee left?"

Cullen poured a cup, passing it to Buddy and taking the eggs from the oven. "Sit down and eat."

"Gotta go pick up the ribs and baked beans before long. Did you buy beer?"

Cullen pointed to an ice chest in the corner. "And two six-packs in the refrigerator."

Buddy was getting in his truck when Earl pulled in behind him. He got out of his Pontiac with a large bowl covered in foil. "How are things, Buddy?"

"Great, Earl." He pointed to the bowl. "I could have run over to your house for that."

"I figured you wouldn't want to have to deal with Helen. She'd likely make you pay in grief."

"Good as her potato salad is, it might be worth it."

"Better get it in the refrigerator. Hot out here," he said, walking back to his car.

"Sure you don't wanna come back this afternoon for some ribs and corn on the cob?"

"Appreciate it, Buddy, but I gotta be at the station. Short of help today."

In the kitchen, Buddy handed the potato salad to Cullen. "Put that in the fridge, will 'ya? I'll be back in under an hour."

Buddy's father was pulling weeds in his garden when Buddy arrived. "Hey, Daddy. How's the garden doing?"

Taking off his straw hat, he met Buddy at the steps. "Been missing my helper."

"He didn't come over this morning, huh?"

"No, he didn't. Is he all right?"

"Yeah, busy I guess. Got all the work he can handle."

"I reckon. His books show he's making a little money."

Buddy caught his mother in the kitchen, standing on a chair reaching to the top cabinet shelf. "Momma, get down from there before you fall. What are you looking for? I'll get it." He gripped his mother's waist and her hands on his shoulders, helped her down.

"That big platter on the top shelf."

He reached up bringing it down.

"That's for your barbecued ribs. You can take the baked beans in the pot. Just be sure you bring it back. It's my gumbo pot." She washed the platter. "There's a lemon pie in the ice box."

Buddy took the pie out, cutting a slice and sitting down.

"What are y'all having for dessert?"

"Hadn't thought about it. Nothing, I guess."

"Pick up some ice cream on the way back to the apartment."

"This pie's good. Might be the best you ever made."

His mother rolled her eyes at that old tune.

"You and Larry come for supper one night this week," she said through the car window, before he drove off.

****

Buddy and Cullen had rigged a canopy over the picnic table in the backyard, one side attached to the roof of the garage, with two posts ten feet out in the yard. The table was another of Buddy's projects and unlike the usual picnic table, was a comfortable fit for four people on each side and one at either end. Around the table were Bob, his friend Spencer, Damien and Cullen, and Buddy's friend from work, Jay, with his cousin, Arthur. Spencer was telling a shop story about

Bob and a customer, a woman interested in a ceramic piece.

"It was an Art Deco black panther figurine. Beautiful lines, made by Royal Haeger. Bob found it at an estate sale in St. Francisville. We priced it at twenty dollars." He placed a hand on Bob's shoulder. "Can't remember what you paid for it."

"Twelve dollars."

"Twenty was too much she said and she stared at Bob, waiting for him to knock down the price. Price was firm, couldn't sell it for less, Bob told her. She said that was ridiculous and put it back. She browses a while longer and in five minutes is back to Bob, offering fifteen for the piece. 'Sorry, can't do that, ma'am.' So she left. Well, obviously possessed with having this little bit of Deco, she's back in thirty minutes, this time offering seventeen. Bob picks up the panther, bobbles it and then drops it. Shattered. 'Oh, my. I guess it's broken. Sorry,'" He says to the woman,

"A fishwife from hell," Bob said blandly, looking around the yard. "Where are Buddy and Larry?"

Standing at the foot of the bed in the front bedroom, Larry had his arms around Buddy, the fingers of one hand in his hair.

"I miss you." Larry pulled him closer. "That guy treating you good?"

"Cullen? Yeah. Not the same person he was in high school. But none of us are."

He felt Buddy's familiar hardness against him. "Can I come stay with you a few days?"

"We've been over this Larry. You don't have to ask. You've got a key."

Damien leaned into the doorway. "Hey, you two. They're asking about you outside."

"Well, hell. Just when we were about to strip down and get smutty," Larry said.

"Ooh, can I join in the fun?" Damien said with a wink.

As Larry went past him into the kitchen, Damien held Buddy back. "I know you're going to think I'm a fussy old woman, Buddy, but seeing Larry on that new motorcycle he bought scares the hell out of me. He drives that thing like a daredevil set on doom. I'm afraid he's going to kill himself. Talk to him, please."

Buddy nodded and called out to the picnic table from the back door. "Who needs a beer or a drink?"

A few minutes later, Buddy squeezed in beside Bob. "Y'all hungry? Ready to eat?"

"In a while," Damien said, echoed by the others.

"Great picnic table, Buddy," Spencer said.

"What do you expect?" Bob said. "You think he's just a common nail-banger?"

"Bob, come see the finished chest for Mrs. Bordelon." He went to the garage, Bob and Arthur following, Larry going as well, wanting to see Buddy's latest piece of work.

Bob looked at the chest closely, opening the two smaller drawers on top, then the larger one below. He ran a hand over the whitish paulownia one last time. "What are you charging her?"

"I thought one-twenty."

"Not enough," Arthur quickly tossed out.

"Arthur's right. One-seventy-five. Not a penny less."

"You sure?"

"Buddy, it's gorgeous and handmade, not to mention constructed using some exotic Japanese technique. I'll take it to the shop, call Mrs. Bordelon, and tell her to come pick it up. One-seventy-five. Probably break one of her elegant fingernails grabbing her checkbook." He looked at Arthur. "Am I right, Arthur? You know Mrs. Bordelon." Bob explained that Arthur was working at the shop now and was friendly with the woman.

"Oh, she'll pay one-seventy-five, won't hesitate for a second."

Bob held Larry back as they were leaving the garage. "Larry, I don't know if Damien has said anything but our friend Carol is not well. I thought you should know."

"I'm sorry to hear that. Is it serious?"

"Unfortunately, very. It's cancer, cervical. They found it in June. I spoke with her mother last night and she's back in the hospital."

Larry didn't know Carol all that well, nothing like Bob and Damien, but he'd liked her from the first and hated what he was hearing. "That's a fucking bummer. Can we visit her? Where is she?"

"Parish General. I'll see if and when we can visit."

Larry stood looking down at the wood shavings on Buddy's worktable, thinking about the smart and beautiful Carol he had known all too briefly.

"Carol has always liked you," Bob said, hand on his shoulder.

The news came at a bad time for Larry. Only the week before he had called his friend Chandler in New Orleans, and unexpectedly got his father instead. Two days before Chandler had put a gun in his mouth and pulled the trigger. Larry knew the story, it was familiar, shit that happened sometimes with vets who hadn't had the luck he'd had. Not for the first time, he said another thank you to Doc Remick. But now there was Carol, and that hurt, too.

Damien and Cullen came out carrying the ribs, baked beans, and potato salad, Bob behind them with a platter of corn on the cob. Larry followed with a round of fresh drinks.

Not much later, the food was down to a pile of scraps and everybody was stuffed. Raine was at the back steps chewing on a plate of rib bones. Cullen and Buddy lay sprawled in a shady spot of grass, smoking, and Bob and Spencer were cleaning up in the kitchen. Arthur sat against Jay on the sofa, cleaning his glasses, and Damien held up two LPs, asking Larry, "Paul Desmond or John Coltrane?"

"Coltrane."

A soft glow of twilight colored the apartment's front room. It was the best time of a hot summer day and everyone was in a comfortable sprawl around the room while Buddy made coffee and Cullen brought out bowls of strawberry ice cream. "There's coffee for whoever wants it."

A minute later Buddy came from the kitchen with two bowls of chocolate pudding. He sat with Larry and Raine on the floor, passing one bowl over.

They leaned against one another with their favorite pudding, quiet together. "Damien's worried about you and the motorbike. Says you drive like a daredevil."

"That's the fun of it."

"Like it was yesterday, I remember that afternoon at your house the first time. Eleven years ago? Two little boys side by side, peeing off your back porch."

"I remember. Remember hoping we would be best friends and walking to school the next morning, I couldn't wait to see you again," Larry said.

Buddy reached over with a finger and wiped a spot of chocolate from the corner of Larry's mouth.

Epilogue

On a Sunday morning in the summer of 1971, Larry crouched in the backyard garden at Buddy's house spraying the cucumber plants under Mr. Hebert's direction. The spray was a homemade concoction of water, baking soda and dishwashing detergent aimed at stopping the powdery mold graying the leaves. The squash plants were free of mold, but were susceptible and next to be sprayed.

Working the garden with Buddy's father was always a balm to Larry's spirit until it had been put on hold by the demands of building a business, and work that swallowed all his time. He appreciated even those few cherished hours on Sunday mornings when the garden and Mr. Hebert waited. The garage still kept him busy but he had finally turned the Sunday work over to his man Friday, Wes. Raising his head to look above the tomato plants at Buddy who was cutting the grass, his mind spun back to that first time at the Hebert house and the sight of a shirtless seventeen-year-old Buddy running with sweat, a spatter of cut grass sticking to his arms and stomach. It had taken his breath away as he stood dumbfounded beside Buddy's mother.

Remembering it now, he thought there was a good chance she had easily read the hungry gaze directed at her son. Minutes later, as she poured him a glass of iced tea in the kitchen, he had held onto the chair back to stop the shaking in his knees.

"It's as hot as Hades out there," she'd said.

As if to prove it, he'd felt the heat radiating off Buddy standing an inch to his right, chest heaving with breath. Invited to supper on that day long ago, Larry happily ate two helpings of mac and cheese, another of string beans, both things he didn't like, but made easier by the feel of Buddy's knee against his under the table.

****

During the past couple of years, usually no more than once a week, Buddy retreated to his workshop for some quiet time alone. Having learned to read Buddy's mood long ago, Larry left him with his thoughts on those days. Buddy might be focused on a project and resent any distraction, or he might be between projects and simply enjoyed wandering in his thoughts or daydreams.

Now he swept out the workshop, dumped a heap of sawdust and scraps of wood into a trash can and sat down to sharpen his wood chisels. From the small transistor radio on a shelf overhead came the sound of Anne Murray singing. *Spread your tiny wings and fly away.* It was one more song about broken love that brought Cullen Mosley tumbling into his thoughts. He wouldn't admit it to anyone, but the worktable under Buddy's hands also roused memories of a certain kind of love, hot nights and urgent whispers when the sound of buckles and zippers undone preceded the hurried clinch of undercover love. Or more rightly, lust.

He hadn't thought of Cullen in months, hadn't seen him in at least a year, but it would be untrue to say he didn't on occasion experience a remembered flash of the things they once did together. There had been something, something foreign, almost alien about Cullen's ability to ignite Buddy's urges. But it hadn't lasted. From the beginning, neither had expected permanence of any sort, and as they both knew would happen, they gradually drifted apart. It had always been a connection based on feverish sexual grappling, lacking the depth to be anything more substantial and so with no hard feelings, their times together grew fewer. Part of it had been that each time they were together, Larry's shadow loomed over them both. And so, they broke it off with an easy absence of resentment. The last time he had seen Cullen was during intermission of a play at the Little Theatre. He, Larry, Cullen and Freddy rubbed shoulders among a crowd of a hundred others. The walls of the theatre lobby hung with a dozen or more paintings by Freddy, one of which, purchased later, now hung in the back bedroom of the apartment.

****

Like Buddy with his alone time in his workshop, Larry also had what had become a long-running routine. With Damien in California, for the past eighteen months he had been driving over to Damien's house every week or so to check the mail and make sure everything was okay in the house. Utility bills and such, he forwarded on to Damien.

Letting himself in the front door, he went straight to the back door, opening it and letting Raine out to play in the backyard, a bowl of water by the steps. He unlocked the garage and turned the key in the pink Elvis Cadillac, pleased to hear the engine turn over without complaint. He let it idle for a few minutes before backing out and driving it around the neighborhood streets for a few turns. The engine sounded fine and he put it back in the garage and locked the doors.

Ten months after Larry opened his car restoration business, Damien's doctoral thesis was published by LSU Press. Not two months later, he got an offer to teach at the University of Chicago but chose instead to take a job as editor-in-chief of *Blue Note* magazine, a jazz monthly published in San Francisco. He kept the house in Goodwood, Larry agreeing to check on things every couple of weeks.

Looking around at the empty record shelves made Larry a little sad and he missed Damien's quiet soliloquies about one or another of his favorite records or musicians. Together they had packed more than twenty boxes of records, all shipped off to San Francisco. He and Buddy got a letter at least once a month, full of stories about hippies and flower children, a wild and colorful Castro district, and fog that on most mornings shrouded the city, making a milky picture of the bay and its famous bridge.

The last letter included a long paragraph about Damien's assistant at the magazine, a farm boy poet from Kansas named Zechariah who in some ways reminded him a little of Larry. Not long after he started working at the magazine, Buddy and Larry began receiving each issue of *Blue Note*, always with something of Damien's in it, an interview or review of a new jazz album. Sunk in the cushions of the music room sofa, now empty of music, Larry reflected on his past with Damien, and saw again the ugly road he might have stumbled onto had Damien not been there to save him from the crummy fate of a junkie overdose. It was only half of all that Damien had done for him, and a part of Larry would always love him.

As the months rolled along and became years, usually when sitting on the front steps, Raine at his side, at some point Larry's thoughts turned to Earl. It would always be a fresh wound when he thought of Earl dying seventeen months earlier in a gas station robbery gone bad, shot in the heart by a fresh out of prison ex-con looking for quick cash. The irony of that death hadn't been lost on Larry, and he often wondered if somebody in a beard and white robes had gotten a good laugh out of Earl's fate. Two hours before the ex-con had shown up, Larry had been sitting with Earl in the Billups office shooting the breeze. They had talked about Maurice, who was then divorced and back in town looking for work. Earl had talked about his little girl who was in first grade and gooey eyed over a boy at the next desk everyone called Piggy, whose real name was Aloysius Arceneaux. Rose and her little brother, Earl Jr., had never fully understood what really happened to their daddy, they were too young, too sensitive for such things.

Larry was not privy to where Earl's death had left his wife and children financially. Eileen had sold the gas station and he knew she was renting out the garage apartment in back. And because Earl had put money into helping Larry get his business off the ground, he continued to pay a small monthly dividend to Eileen and the children. Thanks in large part to Earl, Larry's business was on solid ground and he could afford to help the family. In the dark minutes of such thoughts, a smile crept in with the thought he would sure like the treat of another breakfast at old lady Clemens' table.

****

One Sunday morning, winter barely hanging on, they were up early, Buddy taking Raine for a run on the levee while Larry made coffee and sat at the kitchen table with a book, one by Charles Bukowski called *Post Office*. After reading the first chapter, he laid it down, distracted, feeling the pull of a yearly ritual he never minded repeating even though it was one that always left him in an introspective mood.

Buddy and the dog had been back for a while, Raine eating a bowl of scrambled eggs and Spam, Buddy in the shower. When Buddy came from the bedroom wearing Larry's gray sweater and smelling like soap, without thinking about it, Larry turned from the sink. "After your daddy and I finish in the garden later, you wanna take a drive with me?"

Buddy grinned. "I'm always game for an adventure."

"That's my sweater," Larry said, pulling Buddy against him.

"I know."

Later that day, after a drive of a little over an hour, they passed under a wrought iron arch and followed a cracked macadam road that took them to an enclosed plot within sight of a winding bayou. All around them stood numbers of carved angels, obelisks, pillars and mausoleums, the stone lingua franca of cemeteries. In the center of the plot was a ledger stone, a slab of black marble flush with the ground and chiseled with words.

JULIAN RAINE BENTLEY
1947-1968
SLEEP ON NOW, AND TAKE YOUR REST
—MATTHEW 26:45

Set in a large square of manicured ground that would one day include Juli's mother and father, Larry had always felt it was a lonely spot, and the chill on that afternoon sent a shiver down his arms and legs. He knelt beside the marker and placed a palm on the cold stone. "Still in my heart, brother," he whispered.

Buddy stood back several feet, his eyes studying the ground.

Larry took a quarter from his shirt pocket and placed it just above Juli's name, and rising, backed a couple of paces to stand close against Buddy. A pair of pelicans lifted from the surface of the bayou, disappearing around a bend, their wings beating in tandem.

Larry reached for Buddy's hand, his eyes still on Juli's marker. "Thank you, Buddy, for coming with me this time." Turning finally to look at Buddy, he continued. "I understand it was hard for you, that my feelings for Juli damaged for a while what we've always had together. I probably said it before, but Juli and me? It was a different time and place, and conditions that broke all the rules. Broke me, too. But you were there to put me back together. You've always been there."

Acknowledgments

To the publisher and editors at Flashpoint, my thanks for giving this book a chance. Another very big thank you to longtime friend and writer, Raymond Cothern, who encouraged and helped shape this book from its earliest days. His suggestions and encouragement can hardly be calculated. Appreciation also goes to a quartet of readers who waded through the early pages, patient to the end. A big thanks to Shelby Leverington whose impressions helped focus the story. I am grateful as well to Peter Harvey for reading all too many early pages and offering valued feedback. To Katherine Nelson also I give credit for sharing her thoughts during the book's early days. I know that my longtime sounding board, Karen Hall Grantier won't mind being the last mentioned. Whether in reading, listening, or talking about it, she was tireless in helping this book find the light.

About the Author

William Leet lived for many years in Japan. Leaving there, he moved to the east coast of Florida and spent the months sifting through a box of journals detailing his days among the Japanese. At the end of it he published his first story. He lived for a while in Texas before returning to Louisiana, the place he had run from at the age of nineteen. During his time in Japan, he published three English textbooks for use in Japanese schools. He has written and translated for the *UCLA Journal of Asian Studies*, and his stories have appeared in *Blue Lake Review*, *Shadows Express*, *The Rusty Nail*, *Literary Orphans*, and *The Fat City* Review. His essays have appeared in *American Athenaeum*. *Outside the Wire* is his first novel.

www.ingramcontent.com/pod-product-compliance
Lightning Source LLC
Chambersburg PA
CBHW070631100726
47907CB00007B/1944